SUMMER OF THE DOVES

Note for Librarians: A cataloguing record for this book is available from Library and Archives
Canada at www.collectionscanada.ca/amicus/index-e.html
ISBN 1-4120-8344-3

Printed in Victoria, BC, Canada. Printed on paper with minimum 30% recycled fibre.
Trafford's print shop runs on "green energy" from solar, wind and other environmentally-friendly power sources.

TRAFFORD
PUBLISHING

Offices in Canada, USA, Ireland and UK

Book sales for North America and international:
Trafford Publishing, 6E–2333 Government St.,
Victoria, BC V8T 4P4 CANADA
phone 250 383 6864 (toll-free 1 888 232 4444)
fax 250 383 6804; email to orders@trafford.com
Book sales in Europe:
Trafford Publishing (UK) Limited, 9 Park End Street, 2nd Floor
Oxford, UK OX1 1HH UNITED KINGDOM
phone 44 (0)1865 722 113 (local rate 0845 230 9601)
facsimile 44 (0)1865 722 868; info.uk@trafford.com
Order online at:
trafford.com/06-0099
10 9 8 7 6 5 4 3 2 1

SUMMER

OF THE

DOVES

A NOVEL BY

JEANNE C. ANDEREGG

A gentle note of caution: This is a work of fiction. The little town of Campbell's Point and the surrounding countryside exist only in the author's imagination. Sara Harvey, her friends, her enemies and her adventures are also imaginary though they seemed to come to life as the story unfolded.

ACKNOWLEDGEMENTS

My thanks go to both my harshest critics and my kindest friends. Each comment was taken to heart and I hope, improved the final story.

Heartfelt thanks also to my several diligent readers who over time kept me believing in my characters, their lives and their adventures.

SUMMER OF THE DOVES

In the shadowy world of espionage,

names are everything and names are nothing

SUMMER OF THE DOVES

CHAPTER ONE

I was born a Campbell. Even though I was born and raised in the Midwest, I'd always felt a deep connection with my ancestors who settled in Pennsylvania before the Revolution. Now after a lifetime of wandering, I wanted to return to ancestral ground. I had plans for this special place.

Some property advertised on the Internet looked promising so I went to check it out. First stop was in Pittsburgh to see my professional collaborator, Dave Finch. His assistant was giving me a tour around when he came striding through the door. His giant paw of a hand grasped mine as he greeted me. "How are you, Dr. Harvey?"

"Great, thanks. I'd like to stay and visit for a few days, but I'm on another mission. Listen, are you still driving your Honda?"

Dave's look was thoughtful. "Going in disguise?"

I nodded yes. "I'd like to swap for a few days. How about my rental Lexus for your Honda, straight across? It should pique people's curiosity."

Dave grinned. "You rascal, what are you up to now? No, don't tell me yet. You're itching to get on with it and I have a lab to teach next hour. I'll do it, but only if you'll promise to tell us all about it when you get back."

We shook on it and went out to swap cars. "Will the permit keep me legal until tonight? I need to spend a while in the library. We have a first draft of our paper due soon. My appointment in Campbell's Point is at nine o'clock in the morning. What's the best way over east?"

Dave thought a minute. "Until about three o'clock, Rt. 22 shouldn't be bad since most people are going the other way. Good luck."

About the middle of the afternoon I headed out of town to find a place to stay. Early next morning rumbles of thunder wakened me. I opened the big patio door on my balcony as a real storm moved fast across the valley.

"What a nice way to welcome me," I whispered. "I hope it's a real toad-strangler."

I opened my arms and let the storm engulf me. Wave after wave of huge raindrops sliced through the air. Sizzling bolts of lightning coursed across the sky, and huge thunderclaps rattled the doors. In minutes it was over. The wind shifted the storm on northeast and beyond. Slipping back inside, I snuggled into bed for a few more hours.

I took off for Campbell's Point about six o'clock, leaving time to check out the town, find R & J Realty and track down the best place for breakfast. The usual clue for me is the number of cars and trucks parked out front.

Campbell's Point is a small town straddling a county road. It has a bank with the town lawyer upstairs, R & J Realty next, a 24-hour grocery, and at the end of the block, Gary's Grill.

People were gathering from every direction and I'd found my breakfast. My mouth watered for an old fashioned flat cinnamon palmier like the ones I remembered from my childhood, bacon from pigs fattened on corn instead of sawdust and garbage, and eggs from chickens living their lives in freedom. That's the kind I was going to have too, with a rooster to keep them in line and give wake-up calls better than any alarm clock.

I swung around to pull into the last parking spot in the block. A big sigh escaped. This was it. Would it work? Had they found a contractor? Was the place right? At least I would know soon.

Gary's Grill was bright and cheerful. Sunshine streamed into the big front windows. Red, pink and white geraniums in dark green boxes decorated the low windowsills and delicate European lace curtains hung from the windows. A comfortable smell of coffee, sweet rolls and bacon, and the low hum of compatible voices greeted me as I stepped into the room.

2

A middle-aged couple motioned to me, as the man got up from his place and spoke. "Dr. Harvey? Please join us. It's pretty crowded and we'd enjoy your company."

I wasn't surprised. The town was small enough that people might have heard about the person who was coming from Washington State to look at a piece of land and a house. The man was well dressed, and looked like one of the town's professionals. He introduced his wife Millie, and said he was Hank Greer, the town's lawyer. "Welcome to Campbell's Point. We've been expecting you. I don't know how you 'do' breakfast, but everything in here is great."

A young waitress trotted up, eyes big and bright. "Ma'am, are you really from Washington? I've heard it's very beautiful."

I smiled. "Yes, and sometime soon let's get together and I'll show you pictures of where I live and tell you about it."

"Yes Ma'am. Would you like a little more time or are you ready to order?"

I glanced at her little nametag. "Well Tricia, this is probably the first of many nice breakfasts in here, how does this sound? I'd like a pot of tea and a glass of pineapple juice, a cinnamon palmier, 2 eggs scrambled and a side of bacon."

She left with my order and I glanced around the room, not surprised at the number of folks having breakfast so early. They looked like business people on their way to work in town or maybe commuters to Pittsburgh. There were a few farmers in their clean denims and well-worn boots, with their caps that said Deere and Bt and Frank's Feeds.

I could hear the men talking about feed and fertilizer prices and about the energy crisis in the West that was hurting the whole country. They knew when people paid those outrageous prices; they didn't spend money on prime beef and pork tenderloin.

Millie looked across at me. "I expect you're pretty tired. Let's see, by your time it's not four o'clock yet. When I jump time zones I always need a while to get adjusted."

I laughed. "It's in my favor then because I'm such a lark and really have trouble staying up late. When I come east to visit it's great since it helps me stay awake longer in the evening. It's a nice time to play Scrabble."

"Oh, I'm so glad you play. Hank and I spend a lot of evenings relaxing with it."

Tricia came out from the back with our breakfast plates and I sighed with delight. "We can't get bacon like this where I live. It's all the lovely yellow corn and whey you feed the pigs and the special cure you use. Artificial maple flavor can't cover up poor quality pork. One of my first projects is to find someone to raise a pig for me."

"Ah," Hank piped up. "You need Abe Forester. He's an odd duck, but he raises the best pork around, bar none. He looks so much like Abe Lincoln even did as a kid; he got the nickname real early. He's tall, gangly, with a gaunt face and a beard. That nice waitress, Tricia, is one of his kids. They live a mile or so from the place you're interested in. I know, because R & J asked me to help them pick out the contractor." Hank returned to his hot cakes while Millie and I talked about flower gardens and the weather.

I smiled. "The flowers here are so lovely. I can hardly wait to have summer rain again after all those years in the desert. When I was a kid in Illinois, I used to scare my mother by standing out in the rain until I was drenched. Once I got swept away and plastered onto a culvert grill. A neighbor named Vaughan rescued me. I think about him even now, when I'm in big trouble. I'll find myself saying, 'OK, Mr. V. how do I get out of this one?' He usually has a good idea."

We were laughing about the story as breakfast came to a pleasant close. Hank glanced at his watch. "You have about 45 minutes before they're expecting you. Looks like you came ready to walk and I expect you want to check out the town. I'm sure we'll be seeing you again soon. If the property suits you, I'll be drawing up the papers."

Millie took my hand and smiled. "I hope you like the place."

They stood and nodded goodbye as they left the table. There were people waiting for my place, so I started for the register. "'See you again soon, Tricia. Do you work just mornings?"

She shook her head. "I work when they need me and with summer coming, I may move to town to be on call. I like people and the job is fun." She went to clean up the table as I stepped out into the fresh, sparkling morning. Droplets glittered on every leaf and flower.

The car was down the street in front of R & J's so I took off down the other side to make the circle. The main street was lined with wonderful planters and window boxes filled with spring flowers. A few brave souls had taken a chance and planted their summer boxes with a wonderful mix of pink, purple and red flowers.

Gary's was on the corner. Across the street was an old building, with a place where the brick had been filled in square inside a huge arch. Surely carriages were welcomed there long ago. The windows had wonderful golden-yellow and white striped awnings on the front side facing west. The town hardware store and a small medical building finished the block.

Beyond the center of town, private homes were set back from the street behind white picket fences. The perennials were growing fast in the warmth of late spring, poppies, daylilies, and columbine flourished in the beds, waiting to burst into bloom. Several homes appeared to be competing to have the largest, most elegant rose garden, with Victorian fountains and statues. The houses with big hedges and wrought iron fences covered several blocks and the rest diminished to the less appealing at the edge of town.

I was running a bit late and hurried to make it back to R & J's in time to get a breather before we started out to the farm. When I went in, the receptionist looked up at me with a quizzical frown. "Do you have an appointment?"

I smiled and nodded yes, as she squirmed in her fancy 5-wheeler. "Oh, you must be S. Harvey. I'll let Mr. Renquist know you're here." As she rose to go to the back, the bell on the front door rang and someone entered. The receptionist turned a sweet shade of blush as she cooed, "Oh, hello Mr. Campbell. I'll show you in."

He followed her down the hall to the back. The first thing I noticed was the odd cut of his shirt. It was rather loose, with no collar or buttons, and the cuffs were gently gathered. It reminded me of a book cover illustration for an eighteenth century novel. The material was luscious, the color of clotted cream. I usually study a persons' footwear to learn about them. His boots were well-worn, pull-on engineer's boots with just enough dirt around the heels to show they'd been worn to work.

In a few minutes, I was led down the hall to the office. When I entered, the two men were standing behind the desk facing the door. I realized there was no way they were interested in shaking hands.

Randy Renquist snarled, "I hate women who don't sign their name so you can tell they're *women*."

I smiled. "It's exactly because of the prejudice of people like you that we must continue to do it. Now, I'd like to get to work."

Mr. Campbell grinned and his wink let me know that he was on my side. Renquist's jaw dropped as Mr. Campbell moved from behind the desk. Instead of shaking my hand, he gave me an aristocratic bow as he said, "My name's JW Campbell. I've been chosen to be your consulting contractor. After reading between the lines, I made a quick call to Pittsburgh, to a friend who specializes in alternative energy retrofits. She said if you like the place and need her, she could come for a few hours this afternoon to talk to you about the things you want to do."

"Thanks JW. Now tell me about the place."

Renquist started to make a pitch for other properties he wanted to show me. I raised my hand to stop him as I stepped back from the desk. "Mr. Renquist, I'm aware that we need to deal with each other, since you have exclusive rights of sale. However, things will go much better if you could hold your peace and listen. I intend to go see this specific property first.

"If after consulting with JW and his engineer we are unable to do the major design changes, then and only then, I'll decide whether

Jeanne Anderegg

I wish to look at other property. Will we need 4-wheel drive or is it reasonably accessible?"

I felt the shift in Renquist's attitude as he backed off from his pushy stance. "The last mile is pretty rough. I think we should take the R & J truck up there."

I glanced over at Mr. Campbell and saw him nod assent. The day was beginning to heat up and the extra humidity was making me a bit breathless. As I climbed in the back of the crew cab I asked, "Do you carry water in the truck?"

Renquist shrugged and waved toward the back. "There's a can back there somewhere. Besides, there's plenty of water on the place."

"Sure, along with Giardia, cholera and typhoid."

The highway out of town was on the flat for several miles, fields of alfalfa alternated with newly planted corn and woodlots tucked in the steeper places. The farmhouses were well-kept and tidy, with evidence that the women had both the time and money to plant flowers as well as vegetables. It was too early to be planting much, but here and there tiny green rows marched to the sound of birds and machinery.

About two miles out, Renquist swung off onto another county road. The climb was gradual at first. Then we lost the paved road to gravel. The wildness began to cover the road as the trees became larger and the ground steeper. Renquist leaned over to JW and pointed out a tiny cabin tucked back into the woods. "That's my huntin' cabin. My boy Marvin and his pals come here every year for deer and turkeys."

After the first switchback we lost the gravel road to dirt and started up what I hoped was the last stretch. It was probably the unknown causing the increasing size of the knot in my stomach but I was thankful when we climbed up onto a gentle plateau and caught the first sight of the house tucked into the hillside.

Someone who understood and appreciated passive solar ideas had sited it facing south. The roof overhang would shade the front in summer but allow the sun to do its warming work in winter. I slid to the truck door. "Stop! Let me out. I want to walk the rest."

I opened the door and swung down to the ground. There wasn't much driveway still intact. The years of rains and melting snow had washed away the lines where trucks had pulled up to park. I stood poised, taking it all in. Then I headed off around the left side. Would it be there?

I could hear it before I saw it; the faint splashing of the creek I'd found on the old topographic map. On each bank, ferns were pushing up fiddleheads and the trees were beginning to leaf out. The green hill rose behind the house, dressed in pink and white polka dots of redbud and dogwood. Looking up, I saw two magnificent tulip poplar trees. They were guarding the house in the back and offering shelter to a myriad of birds, all singing their hearts out. I couldn't help it; I stood there sobbing, as the men came around the corner.

Renquist looked more concerned than JW as he called out, "What in 'tarnation's wrong with you, Woman? I can't stand a woman who cries."

JW came and offered his handkerchief as he said, "I understand. I loved this place too."

I wasn't sure what he meant, but was comforted. As I walked to the back of the house, I noticed that even after all the years of abandonment, the perennials were springing to life, healthy for all the fallen leaves and forest mulch. I turned to Renquist. "I'm anxious to see the inside. Let's start from the back."

JW said, "I need to prepare you. Nothing's been touched since they left. They locked the door and walked away with their grief. They never returned."

As we walked to the door, the sadness in his eyes warned me not to ask more. "It's OK if you'd rather not go in, JW. Mr. Renquist can show me around."

Randy came up and got out some keys. "Go ahead, kid. Get the info about the repairs you'll need to do. You can kick the foundation and peer down the chimney. We won't take long inside." JW slipped away and began his checklist while we went in.

A house abandoned in the forest for so many years is a frightening sight, especially if everything has been left behind. Over time, the forest critters take up residence and eat everything they can get into, food, clothing, quilts and blankets. It would take some real doing to get the smell out. Though what really clutched at my heart was the nursery with a tiny cradle and all the trappings of a baby's life, now in shreds and powder.

It was time for a reality check. This would be a huge project. Was I physically able to follow through? Whether I could finish it or not somehow seemed unimportant now. I needed this place and this time to make my peace.

Renquist and I stepped out on the front porch to find JW sitting on the top step. I was all business. "Mr. Renquist, what is the asking price for the property?"

He got out the info sheet and quoted it to me.

"Do you think the owner would accept cash to close the deal?"

He sputtered a little and looked over at JW, who nodded yes.

"Then consider it a deal contingent on a consultation with the Pittsburgh engineer. JW, can you get hold of her in time so she could come out today?"

He pulled out his tiny phone, punched in a number and waited for a ring. As he walked away from the porch, I heard him say,

"Jenny? This is Jamie. Can you make it this afternoon? Thanks. I'll meet you at my place. See you later."

I was exhausted. The heat, humidity, the run-in with Renquist and the stress of finally seeing the place, had worn me out. I needed to find a place to stay and maybe get a nap for an hour or so before Jenny got there. I headed back to the truck with the men at my heels. The afternoon trip back would be tough and hot but things needed to get started right away.

On the way back, JW sat in the back with me as we went over the stuff on his clipboard. He'd checked out the foundation, the chimney, the wood framing, the porch and the roof. There didn't seem to be any leaks or broken windows. No question about the isolation of the place, but I pushed my vague concerns away for the time being.

The trip back to town was a lot easier, since I knew the route. As we pulled in at the back of R & J and stepped out, I said to Renquist, "Thanks for the chance to see the place. I think we can do business. Let's make an appointment for tomorrow morning at eight thirty. I'll let Mr. Greer know if we'll be ready for him then."

Renquist mumbled, "I do like a woman who knows her mind. None of this willy-won'ty stuff." He nodded and continued to mumble as he took off for the back door of his office.

Mr. Campbell smiled as he leaned up against the truck, his hands in his pockets. "You don't have him eating out of your hand yet but he's pretty close. That's the most civil I've seen him in a long time. I don't know how he can be so successful at his business, as gruff and difficult as he is.

"Now, what can I do for you? You'd probably like to find a place to stay and catch a nap before we go out again. The humidity and heat are tough when you aren't used to them."

"Thanks JW. Are there any places near by with a B & B type room for a few days?"

"Best find Millie. She knows everybody in town. She's the secretary in the law office that's upstairs above the bank. Let me know when you find a nest and we'll be by for you, probably about three o'clock; Jenny had a meeting until two. It was nice to meet you Dr. Harvey. Maybe you'll let me join your show-and-tell for Tricia. I'd like to hear about Washington too."

"How did you hear about that so fast?"

"There's nothing better than Gary's to find out any and everything going on in this town."

He gave his gracious bow and started down the street.

"Do you want a ride?" I called after him.

"No thanks, I need the exercise. See you about three."

I could hear a whistled tune drifting back. What was it? Frère *Jacques*, for heaven's sake! What an interesting young man. Then, I realized what had been bothering me about him all morning. His right hand, which he'd kept hidden while he was with us, was obviously the reason for not shaking hands. When he took it out of his pocket as he walked away I saw a badly mangled hand, with fingers of odd lengths sticking out in several directions or curled, useless toward his twisted wrist.

I needed to get to a phone to find Millie. Then I remembered the law office was just next-door, and hurried around to the street side to catch her before she left for lunch. She was just finishing up at the computer when I slipped in the door.

She looked up with a welcoming smile. "Are you ready for some lunch, Dr. Harvey? Then we can talk about where you might stay."

I sighed. "This town's like one large animal with communicating parts. How did you know what I needed?"

Her voice was like a gentle bell as she laughed. "Cell phones, unfortunately, but in earlier times we just passed it on. Jamie just called to let me know how it went. Let me find Hank and we'll try to get a place at Gary's. They usually save one for us about noon."

She stepped to his office door. "We're on our way to lunch, Hank. Come if you have time."

Lunchtime at Gary's wasn't nearly as crowded. The group was entirely different without the commuters and farmers. Now it was mostly local business people and groups of ladies.

"Definitely the aorta of news," I said to Millie as we slipped into a booth. "I'm ready for a giant pitcher of iced tea and a BLT made with toasted bread and lots of bacon." Tricia had seen us come in and was right behind, writing the order down as we settled in.

Millie smiled. "I'm glad the morning went well. I checked with Hank and we'd like to offer you the use of our cottage while you're here. It's separate from the house and very private. Here's the key. We'll go by there after lunch and get you settled."

Hank and Millie's generosity and kindness were tempting. I decided to accept and to be taken care of. Things were going so well that I wondered what could go wrong now. It might happen this afternoon when the engineer told me if she could follow my design. But I knew I wanted the acreage and the beautiful trees even if the retrofit wouldn't work.

According to my family records and the early maps, it was very close to my ancestor's first farmstead near Campbell's Point. Besides, my work with Dave Finch was in forest pathology and here was a perfect place to start a new project. I thought he'd be pleased. In fact the whole research project was designing itself in my head.

We were finishing up lunch when I realized I was bone-weary. The heat and excitement of the morning had conspired to cause a temporary crash. I turned to Millie. "I need to get some rest. Could we go now and take my things to the cottage?"

She looked at me with a worried expression and asked for my keys. She took off down the street to get the Honda, and then drove by for me. While we were on the way, she looked over with a puzzled glance. "How come you're driving a twelve-yr-old car with Pennsylvania plates, my mysterious new friend?"

I laughed. "A friend and colleague in Pittsburgh swapped cars before I came over. I have a Honda like it at home and I thought it might be better to be unobtrusive. Rental cars can draw a lot of attention in a small community."

The cottage was tucked in at the back of the Greer property, one of the older Victorian houses I'd seen earlier on my walk. We gathered up my suitcase and backpack and stepped into a lovely room, done in very elegant French provincial. Especially in the heat of the day, the colors seemed cool and inviting.

Millie smiled. "Sweet dreams. We'll call when Jamie gets here."

I headed for the shower and stood under the tepid water, then went into the bedroom and collapsed. In what seemed like moments, my mind was treated to whispers of soothing, gentle music. Looking around, I spotted a small speaker by my bed.

Millie's voice came next. "It's time to rise and shine, Dr. Harvey. Jamie and Jenny are here to take you out to the farm."

I dressed, grabbed my backpack with all my tools and equipment, and met them at the door. My first look at the engineer, Jenny, was from the side. She was breathtakingly beautiful, with gorgeous red hair held at the nape of her neck with a wooden clip.

I stepped toward her. "Thank you for coming on such short notice, Jenny. Did JW call in some chips on this one?"

She glanced at him with a gentle smile. "No, he already owes me several. Let's go. We have only a few hours and I have a date with my favorite and only uncle tonight for dinner in town He came over for a conference this week and promised me at least one evening out of his schedule. Jamie gave me the bare bones of your ideas. I think they sound possible and most we can get permission for."

She had driven from Pittsburgh in a large, well-used, white truck. Trucks are second only to boots for telling something about people's personalities. The truck was no nonsense, but with a snatch of class. She seemed comfortable with herself and what she did and she had a right to be a bit proud of her accomplishments in an area pretty much reserved for men.

The cab was large enough for three in front. I slipped into the center out of habit, since my legs were shorter. JW swung up into

10

the outside place and closed the door. I continued to be amazed at how well he got along with only one functioning hand.

JW pulled down his seatbelt and buckled it. "Tim will be sorry to miss this outing. He's smitten with your red hair, Jenny. Good thing he has Tricia to keep him in line or I might have to fight for your attention."

The easy, good-natured banter suggested a long-term relationship. The trip out seemed shorter since I knew where we were going. Jenny knew the way without directions so I figured she'd been there before. We pulled up onto the flat. The house seemed like a long-widowed lady, abandoned in her prime and alone, waiting for someone to care about her again.

When we got ready to work, Jenny showed some surprise at my equipment. I explained how I used them in my own work all the time. We began to take data to answer the main question of whether there would be enough head and volume of water in the creek to use hydropower for the electric generation instead of solar. We worked our way to the top at the fence line and did a quick calculation.

"Looks OK," Jenny said. "I'll have to fill out reports and send them to the State and EPA; then we get to sit back and wait."

JW started a thorough check along the fence line while Jenny and I went up to the stone bench behind the house to sit and do paperwork. Jenny waited until he was gone and leaned toward me as she said, "I'll do the best job I can for you. Maybe we can help Jamie too."

I folded my papers and tucked them into my clipboard. "Have you known him a long time?"

There was a little misting in her deep gray eyes. "We grew up together in Campbell's Point. The winter Jamie and I were twelve, my parents were killed in a traffic accident during a snowstorm. That same weekend, Jamie and his family lost their baby girl.

"When my folks died, there wasn't any family who could take me in. My only uncle was in Europe and they were going to send me to the County Orphan's Home. My father worked for Jamie's grandfather and their family took me in, the same time they took in Jamie and his family. We grew up together.

"That winter, Jamie kept telling me bits and pieces of what had happened when his baby sister died. The boys were home with their mother when the snowstorm began. She went into labor and Jamie went to the neighbor's for help but they weren't home. By the time he struggled back up the road in the deepening snow, his mother was in devastating pain. He and his brothers had to listen to her tortured screams.

"When his father came up the hill on foot some time later, he delivered the dead child and buried her here by the stone bench.

Then his father gathered up the family, locked the house and threw the key into the snow. He never spoke again.

"After it happened; Jamie became so quiet and guarded that they thought he'd lost his mind too. He said many times he knew it was his fault his baby sister had died, because he wasn't able to get help in time. His mother, his grandparents, everyone tried to explain in their own way that it wasn't his fault; that the baby was dead before she was born. He was only twelve and didn't understand.

"I lived with them until I finished school and went off to college. We pretty much lost track of each other until this last year when he came back to Campbell's Point to live."

We both looked up to find JW walking the last fourth of the fence line. He looked like a handsome laird striding out o' the moors. I had to shake my head to get the notion out and remind myself that it was 2001 not 1501 and we had work to do. Jenny needed to be back in Pittsburgh by seven o'clock, so we joined at the truck and headed back to town.

When we dropped JW off at his place, Jenny said, "I want to bring my uncle over Friday afternoon. I want him to see what I do up close and I think he'll enjoy seeing the farm before and after. Will you be around Jamie? Let's meet here around two o'clock."

She delivered me to the Greer's. Stepping to her truck window, I thanked her for her work and the reassurances about my design. "See you Friday, then."

When I got to the door there was a note tucked under the doorknocker.

We hope you had a good afternoon of work. If you'd like, please join us for supper. We're being totally indolent on the back patio and would love to hear about your day. Just slip through the rose garden and come up the path to the east.

Regards, Hank and Millie.

I needed to weigh my preference for privacy against the open hospitality and kindness of my new friends. I chose the latter, and after a quick cleanup found my way to the patio.

Hank and Millie continued to be a delightful surprise. Their garden was a true hideaway, with a combination of stone hardscape and artfully planted shrubs and trees that made a fairyland of late spring. In the shelter of the walls, it was like the Secret Garden of Frances Burnett. I expected to see Dickon's fox, Captain, trot across the grass and curl up at my feet.

I was exhausted but ravenous and everything looked wonderful. I joined them at the table. "I'd better start with a couple of glasses of water. Drinking water will be a continuing problem out there until we get the test report back on the well."

I wondered how Millie managed to look so fit when she sat at a desk all day. When I mentioned it, she laughed and said, "Genes, and Yoga classes two nights a week. When I have time, I teach one of them. Someone's covering for me this evening. I wanted to be with you."

Hank got up and began to serve supper. The table was laid with linen and silver and the centerpiece was a bowl of golden Lamium and deep purple Dutch iris.

Millie smiled. "Hank's the gardener. The kitchen garden is beyond the clipped hedge. It's good for the soul and the body. We enjoy sharing, and since the French cook is down at Gary's, we've learned new ways to garden and new vegetables to grow. We're even raising some herbs and greens for her."

Supper was a bowl of mixed greens with a delicate dressing of oil, lemon juice and chopped herbs, served with fresh rolls and cheese. When we finished, Millie turned to me and switched from social talk to serious business. "Dr. Harvey, we need to talk to you about Jamie before tomorrow. There are some things you should know."

"Oh?" I acknowledged, "What I have figured out so far is that the place belonged to his family, but was abandoned a long time ago. He seems to know the contracting business and is probably competent, but I think he was something entirely different before his accident."

The evening was turning cool and we moved inside. We settled in the library as Hank began. "After Jamie finished high school, he felt driven to be a doctor. He did well and earned his success with the help of his mentor. Then, his mentor died, leaving a widow with three young sons. Jamie had been so wrapped up in his career that he was terribly naïve about people, especially women. The widow seduced him and in a fit of guilt and remorse, he married her.

"The marriage was a disaster. He worked his heart out for her, and gave her more and more possessions. She sucked them up and demanded more. She acquired a collection of oriental rugs, 25 or 30 of them, some worth hundreds of thousands of dollars. He built her a big house on the lake, and only one room was truly his own, a big circular one, all glass, that looked out on the lake and had his grand piano facing the water."

Millie continued the story. "Jamie's mother developed cancer last year and his father was exhausted trying to care for her. We called Jamie to come home. The men were in the workshop trying to finish a carpentry job when Jamie's dad had a fatal heart attack and fell into a piece of equipment. I was the one who found them, crumpled at the end of the planer, covered with blood. His hand was destroyed when he tried to get his father's body away from the blade. Jamie nearly died of blood loss.

"His mother died in a rest home just a few days later. The older brothers had the funerals together, while Jamie was still in the hospital."

Hank got up from his place and stood looking out the French doors into the garden. "Everyone was so horrified by the things that had happened to the Campbell family, and it never seemed to end."

It was after nine o'clock, and I was totally exhausted. Millie glanced at me. "What will you do after the morning meeting?"

I took it as a stopping point for the tale. "After we settle up at R & J, I need to find a 4-wheel drive vehicle for the next few days. Then I'm going to find some tools and things to start the cleanup. The biggest thing tomorrow is to find out what JW wants done with the things left in the house and the sheds. What do you think he'll do?"

Millie replied. "I don't know. You'll just have to ask."

"Thank you for the pleasant evening and elegant supper. I'll try to get back late in the afternoon. After a nap, perhaps we can finish the story."

The things already revealed were devastating, and apparently there was more to come. It would not be an easy evening. Millie finished our visit with a real gift as she said, "Oh, by the way, I thought you might appreciate a little extra time for yourself in the morning so I put some breakfast fixings in your refrigerator, and some things for making lunch if you want to carry one to the farm. I'll waken you at 7:30 when we leave for work. Hank will see you at R & J at 8:30. Good night. We hope that you will sleep well."

As I turned to leave, the scent of spring flowers wafted into the room on the cool night air. Memories of my own childhood welled up, along with tears barely held in check.

It was a hot shower I sought now, as a deep chill brought on a shivering fit. The warmth crept into my body and the water washed away some of my intense weariness. As I slipped under the covers, I whispered to Michael, asking that he would somehow be with me tonight.

CHAPTER TWO

My window faced northeast and I wakened early to the sun rising. It was a strange mottled orange-red, blotched with darker spots where clouds blocked part of it from sight. Perhaps a storm would come through today.

I arrived at the R & J office as Hank and Millie came over from their office next door and JW came from the other direction on foot. We entered together, led by the secretary, Tamara, who fawned over JW as if she knew some secret we didn't.

Renquist began the proceedings. "Good Morning, Dr. Harvey. Everything is in order. Shall we proceed? The asking price is 180,000 dollars, which you have agreed to. We have a reasonable percentage loan to offer you with a modest down payment." He glanced at Hank and then at me.

I answered. "Mr. Renquist, I plan to pay cash, if the owner agrees. Would you accept a personal check? I'll pay the other fees in cash also." I leaned over and gave him the check. Next, I mentioned the question of the disposal of the contents of the house and sheds since it hadn't been part of the sale description.

JW shifted in his seat. "Sorry, I should have dealt with those decisions before now. Do as you like."

We finished signing papers, the keys were transferred, and I turned to Mr. Campbell.

"JW, do you know where I can get a four-wheel drive vehicle without going into Pittsburgh?"

He nodded. "Yes, Tim and I need to go into town in the big truck to pick up lumber. You can use my Subaru today."

So I took JW to his place and switched cars, packed a lunch and headed out to the farm. I could hardly wait to get started. It felt good to be back in work clothes, and the trip to the farm was easier each time. I kept track of the mileage to see where JW had walked in the snow that day so long ago. When I got to about the right place, there was a mailbox with Forester printed on it, probably the Abe Forester who raised pigs. The farm must be tucked back in the draw on the side where my creek ran down. A little farther up was Renquist's hunting cabin.

I slipped up over the ridge and stopped to take it all in. The new leaves on the trees were chartreuse and pea green and the sycamores were still stark in their nakedness. The Liriodendron trees were leafed out and I remembered the glorious flowers to come; big, sturdy, yellow petals with orange at the base. I began my watch for the doves.

The outdoor project would need to be balanced with clearing out the house. As much as I disliked mice, the inside was going to be a big job. Working among them, you begin to take on the odor yourself, until your skin and hair and clothes won't let you forget.

The newly cut key Renquist had given me lay bright in my hand. I slipped it in and turned it to begin a new life. The stench seemed far worse than yesterday. I went around the house opening windows, trying not to look at what was in each room. My empathic soul felt the long ago grief and pain still present in the house. I went out onto the porch to regroup.

On the back porch, I found a bucket with petrified mice in the bottom. I dumped them and began the first of many trips to the creek for scrub water. I added more things to the shopping list; a large garbage can, new broom and mop, Clorox, soap. It helped to get started and I worked steadily.

When my stomach said it was way past lunchtime, I remembered the lunch I'd packed earlier. I carried it up to the stone bench. The wonderful whole wheat bread, cheese and fresh fruit tasted like the food of the gods.

It warmed up steadily during the afternoon. Without a plan, I'd be too discouraged to keep at it. I decided the kitchen should be first. Starting from the top down, I emptied cupboards, lifting the dishes and storage containers and pots down onto the table. I saw hours of washing and scrubbing before the place would be safe to use.

Mrs. Campbell had been a neat housekeeper and her things were nice but not expensive. There was no silver, crystal or china. They had lived a simple life. Staples not stored in metal containers had been eaten or had crumbled to dust.

The shadows were getting longer and it was time to close up the house. I decided I wouldn't speak to anyone about the dismantling of JW's home. I thought about the house and its tragedies, and asked Michael to protect me.

I hated to shut the windows, but the day's work could be undone in a twinkling if a skunk decided to come inside. I added adjustable window screens to the shopping list and closed things up. After all these years and no vandalism, I didn't want trouble now. I wondered if the house was unmolested out of respect for the owners, or because people believed the house was haunted.

Going past Forester's, I made a mental note to meet him soon, to deal for a pig.

When I got to the Greers' cottage, I didn't know what sounded better, a hot shower, a nap or supper, but took them in order. I washed my hair and scrubbed and scrubbed to get the lurking aroma of mouse off my body. I even washed my hair and the inside of my nose a second time, to help get rid of it. I settled down for a nap. About 7:30, I went down the rose garden path and through the hedge to supper.

Hank was dressed in a shirt of elegant linen much like JW's, with light, loose trousers tucked into soft leather boots. He was reading poetry as I approached and looked up with a smile. "It's Byron night at the Greer's. Please join us. How was the day?"

"Encounters with a thousand mice, mostly petrified. It's going to take a long time to clean up. They weren't the most thoughtful tenants."

We settled down to a comfortable supper of soup and bread. I recognized the kale and white bean soup. It's a regional favorite in Italy and one I remembered from my years in France. A chill wind picked up during supper and we decided to move inside to finish the evening. As we went in, I saw the shadow of a servant coming out to clear the table. It answered my question about how they did it all.

Hank settled in to continue Dr. Campbell's story. "Since JW was in the hospital, Millie and I took turns answering the phone and mail and notifying family about the double funeral for Thomas Campbell and his wife. One message, of course, went to Mrs. JW Campbell. A terse message came, offering condolences but saying they would not be available to attend. A strange line at the end said that a representative for the family would be present. We didn't think much about it until a middle-aged, well-dressed gentleman appeared just in time for the service.

"Jenny was with us and on a hunch I suggested she keep an eye on him. We've teased her for years; saying she was really CIA and the engineering was just a cover. Anyone who speaks so many languages without accent carry-over is a bit suspicious. She laughs and claims it's only a hobby.

"At the reception following the funeral, the stranger seemed puzzled and finally asked me where James Campbell was. I told him James was in the hospital. He asked if he might use the phone, and very soon after, he offered condolences and disappeared.

"After the service, Jenny said the stranger's English carried a hint of Italian and his clothes were Italian. He was wearing an unusual wedding ring and on the other hand, a large signet ring. When he left money for the phone calls she thanked him in Italian. He answered in Italian and then seemed annoyed because he'd slipped into what was probably his native tongue.

"We spent the next few days taking care of details of the wills and estate and then started in on JW's bills. I used the computer to access his credit card account. The account was gone. When I called the company they said there was no account in his name; quite interesting, since his last monthly statement showed a credit balance of 15,000 dollars and debits of 1,200 dollars. When I tried to use the second one, the answer was the same. Then I tried his bank accounts, checking accounts, and investment accounts. There were no debts, no assets, and no evidence his accounts had ever existed.

"Then Millie and I thought of his possessions in Chicago; the house and vehicles. Everything had disappeared. No car registrations, no mortgage. Someone had come in the night and cleared out the mansion, including the millions of dollars of oriental rugs and JW's grand piano. The house now belongs to a company in Salerno. It was as though he'd never existed.

"Then we thought of his medical practice, his office, and staff. Someone had sent letters to everyone involved, informing them that Dr. Campbell would not be returning and firing them with a month's salary. They cancelled his office space and informed the hospital he was no longer a staff member. Of course everyone in Chicago was torn between anger and grief. His accident was never mentioned in the letters.

Jamie's wife annihilated him and his career through an intricate plan, devised to implement at a moment's notice. I'd never heard of anything like it, but my big city lawyer friends said JW was lucky to get away with his life.

"When they removed the bandage from his hand, JW was devastated, furious with us, with the incompetent doctors, with God. He said if he'd known the extent of the injury, perhaps he could have saved it. He'd lost the use of his hand and his livelihood as a surgeon. And then, we had to tell him about the rest, his wife's betrayal, her filing for divorce, and his financial situation.

"The anger was healthier than the depression which followed. A few weeks later, in the middle of the night, we got a call from the State Police, asking us to come get him. He'd tried to throw himself in front of an 18-wheeler.

"It was weeks more, before he apparently decided he wanted to live instead of die. One morning we heard a gentle whistle out in the garden. He was talking to himself and the birds and flowers. The anger and hopelessness had finally burned out. There were bills to pay and he had only one other skill left, so he started to pick up work from his father's carpentry business."

As we finished the evening I got very serious. "We haven't known each other long, but I already treasure you both very much. Please, don't allow your curiosity or anger to tempt you to pursue what happened to JW in Chicago. I've lived there and I know how very dangerous those people are. She could have had him killed, as she most likely did her first husband. Right now, JW must let the past go. Will you promise?"

Hank twisted in his chair. "Well, we were planning a trip to the Bahamas to try to find her hideout, but it sounds like it might be unhealthy too. Yes, I think you're wise and we promise."

I got up and stretched. "I think another scrubbing might help the 'Hint of Mouse' cologne so I'm off to bed. Thanks for the information. You know, I think he'll be OK and I hope Jenny will be an important part of it. I like her. I'd be proud to have a daughter like Jenny."

I was anxious to get out to the farm early since the day promised to be hot. It was hard to leave the luxury of the cottage with fresh flower bouquets everywhere, and it was so clean and cool. I slipped out of my parking space about seven o'clock. JW had promised me the Subaru for the rest of the week so I loaded the screens and other stuff from the hardware store into it and headed out of town.

It was surprising how quickly the trees and flowers were developing day to day. I needed to take a quick look around for morels or I would miss them.

When I reached the farm, something up along the fence line behind the house caught my eye. There was a woman with a basket. She moved carefully, glancing down, stooping to pick. She was lovely, her thinness softened by a long jumper of green and brown plaid. Very long braids hung down her back. She looked up, and then continued on with her work while I parked the car and began unloading.

After the screens were in place, I slung a small basket over my arm, got my clipboard and started up to meet her. There were some morels in the moist spots along the creek bank where it was shadier. It worked well to take note of plants in flower and to collect specimens at the same time and I reached the corner about the same time as the Mystery Lady.

I thought she was probably Abe Forester's wife. Millie had mentioned that Kylie Lou supplemented the family income by gathering herbs and plants to sell at the local market. Many folks still used the older remedies for aches and pains and for spring tonics. One of the pleasures of my job included getting to know the local gatherers and trading information about where to find certain plants.

A simple smile was all we needed to be friends. I reached over the fence. "I'm happy to meet you, Kylie Lou, I'm Sara."

Her grasp was firm but her hands were icy cold, even in the growing warmth of the day and her recent physical effort. I searched her face. "Are you all right, Friend? You don't look well."

Her color was ashen. She swayed toward me and then turned away to vomit violently onto the ground. In the instant it took me to get over the fence, she had collapsed.

"Kylie Lou, what's wrong?"

Her eyes were dilated and her pulse was almost too fast to count. How could I possibly get her down the hill by myself?

She reached out to me and whispered, "Help me please, tansy." She lay on the ground, trembling and heaving as I tried frantically to understand. Could she mean tansy poisoning?

"Have you been poisoned?" She nodded weakly.

Kylie Lou needed help right away. There wasn't anything at my farm to use. We needed to get her home. I hurried down to get the car and brought it up the hill to the corner in time to meet her.

"Do you have something at home to help?"

"Burnt toast."

"OK," I whispered to myself, "Charcoal for absorption, with milk, then throwing it all up."

I didn't look forward to this. At least it was a weekday and her kids would be in school. "Is Abe home?"

"He's in town."

That made sense if she were trying to do what I thought she was. No woman would attempt an abortion, with her husband at home. I felt so sorry for her and had to keep a tight grip not to lose my breakfast in sympathy. As we got closer to their place, the un-mistakable smell of hogs came down the draw to greet us. Three farm dogs rushed out from under an ancient tractor to bark and snarl at the strange car. Kylie Lou whispered instructions about how to calm them and I got out and gave the commands. The dogs sat in watchful silence as I helped her out.

"Abe must be good at dog training as well as hog raising," I murmured, as we went up the porch steps. She shook down the fire in the woodstove and pointed to the bread on the table. We cut thin slices and began to toast them, burnt to charcoal. She made a wry face and began to eat them, washing them down with milk. We quit at six pieces. Then she took a basin and went to the back porch. When she came back we went through the process again. After the third time, we stopped to rest. Her color was better and her trembling had stopped.

Spent from her effort and still weak from the poison, she wept as she said, "I was never troubled like this before and it's the fifth time I've needed to use it."

I sat down beside her and held her in my arms. "I think we caught it in time. Rest now, while you tell me what's going on here."

Kylie Lou was crying. "The doctor warned us not to have any more babies. Every time we make love, we know I could die. But Father says it's a sin to keep away from each other and it's a sin to keep from having babies. We don't know what to do."

"Kylie Lou, are you and Abe Roman Catholic?" She nodded yes.

I continued, "Hasn't anyone taught you natural family planning? It's a way you can know when it's safe to share your love and not get pregnant." Kylie Lou's eyes widened with surprise.

"If you want me to, I can teach you and Abe about it. Now, let's finish up. Would you like for me to take your morels to town?"

"You've been so kind. Thank you, but Abe will take them later. They're a nice addition to our income when things are slow. I hope we meet next in happier times."

"You're always welcome to gather what you want or need from my place. We'll talk again soon. Sure you're all right?"

Her gentle smile was reassuring as I turned to leave. "Take care, new friend."

We waved as I headed down the notch to the road.

What a morning! There was no easy way to get cleaned up myself. I spent some time wading in a deeper part of the creek, splashing water on everything I could reach, including my hair. Then, after walking to the top to retrieve my notebook and basket, I drifted down to the stone bench to finish my plant notes. When my clothes were dry, my tummy was growling so I went to get my lunch from the porch swing. Coming around the house, I nearly jumped out of my skin. JW was sitting in the swing, looking out across the hills.

"Good thing you got here now. Lunch was looking mighty good."

"However did you slip in here? I didn't hear you come up and where's your truck?"

"I came with Tim and a load of boards. There's early practice today before the first big game tonight. The Legion team is the major entertainment around here in the summer and he plays first base. I knew you'd be back: the house was open and you left your lunch."

I grinned at him and shrugged my shoulders as I reached for the lunch sack. "All right, Sherlock, you came while I was with Kylie Lou. Well, let's eat and you can fill me in on Tim's baseball talents. He seems like a nice kid. Are you two related?"

"You know all Campbells are related, not too far back, and we take care of our kin. Tim was in a bit of trouble in town and I bailed him out. Now he bails me out everyday. I couldn't do this work without him. He's a good kid, dropped out of school several years ago out of boredom and went to work for the local mechanic. During good times it worked fine but the latest economic slowdown hurt a lot of the little people, including Martin the Mechanic. He had to let Tim go and went into Pittsburgh to find work.

"Without a high school diploma, Tim's in bad shape. He's a real sharp kid and I'm trying to get him through his GED. He's doing pretty well so far and even shows a glimmer of interest in some of the stuff that went right by the first time. And of course, there's Tricia Forester. He wants to do right by her, so he needs a good job before he asks her to marry him. Small town stuff but important to me. I was away too long. Maybe I can make it up to them somehow."

I folded up the lunch sack. "Well, we ate lunch and supper. If we finish our work early, maybe we can get home in time to see if Kylie Lou's morels made it to Gary's for the dinner menu. Is it a date?"

JW stood up and stretched. "Let's see how it goes. Will I be in the way if I keep working in the living room?"

"No, of course not, this needs to be a co-op project or I'll not be in until Christmas."

I worked in the kitchen, stopping occasionally when he asked for help. We'd gotten a lot done and the heat was slowing both of us down. About the same time we agreed to call it a day.

"JW, if you could round up some more boxes for me, I'd like to start sorting and packing for you. I found some lovely things in the kitchen that I hope you'll want some day."

A shadow crossed his face and the haunted look I'd seen the first day, returned. Then he relaxed. "Thanks, I might have someone who would like to have them. We can store stuff in the carpenter's shop at my place."

We loaded boxes into the trunk and back seat, decided we were willing to take a chance and leave the windows open since the screens were in, and headed for town. As we unloaded stuff at the workshop, JW begged off on dinner, claiming paperwork overload.

"Will you be out tomorrow?" I asked.

"Yes, I'd like to give you a hand with the cleanup. Tim will bring me out again and I'll ride home with you, if it's OK?"

"That's fine. I want to work in the garden early before it gets too hot. Did your mother have a Pulaski? I need to take some trees out."

"I'll look around tonight and see, or there might be one up in a shed at the farm. I haven't been in those buildings for a long time. There are probably a lot of old rusty treasures ready for the antique store."

"Sometimes the old, used ones are much better than new ones. They fit in the hand better and already know their job. Thanks, I'll see you tomorrow."

The heat and hard work combined to make me think I might skip dinner too. Only three days ago I'd taken on this job and now I was right in the middle of it, with more than I could possibly do. I was exhausted. I scrubbed my hair and myself, and settled down for a short nap. It turned out to be all night, and I wakened to morning birdsongs.

CHAPTER THREE

I was thankful for Millie's hospitality and made a generous break-fast, then packed lunch and supper, including a beautiful blueberry pie. With people coming and going at will, it would be handy to have something for company.

It was about five o'clock when I left for the farm. I swung by the grocery store and loaded up as many empty boxes as the trunk and back seat would hold. With more Clorox and soap and another package of gloves, I was set for the day's work.

Early morning is one of my favorite times to be out. The bird songs were echoing across the draw. The flow of water in the creek seemed to be slowing daily and I accepted that the waterpower pro-ject might not pass the bureaucrats in the courthouse. People were talking about drought, but for now, the trees still seemed fine. The leaves were coming out more each day and the tulip poplars were in large bud.

The Subaru had already made its own little parking space by the porch and I headed off to look for the Pulaski. Several well-designed outbuildings clustered at the side of the house. An animal shed with two stalls stood on higher ground above a garden shed with a small lean-to greenhouse. All the glass was gone; shards of it lay inside with the broken branches that had made them. A small chicken house was closest to the house, the wire rusted now and falling apart. The Pulaski was leaning up against the wall in the machine shed.

The outline of Mrs. Campbell's garden was still visible, and there were perennial vegetables still holding on tenaciously. The berries, a few grape vines and the fruit trees were ready to burst into bloom. Her garden space was a good bit larger than I wanted or could man-age so I chose to use the space nearest the creek and started to clear out the young trees I could handle.

It was definitely not a one-day job and after clearing a spot twelve feet square, I seeded in the early vegetables. Some ponies of cabbages and broccoli went in, with a roll of chicken wire to protect the baby plants from the small critters. It was a little late to be planting but the warmer weather should get them growing quicker.

About the time I finished, the truck swung in below the house. Tim and JW unloaded boxes and tools. I wasn't quite sure what JW was working on inside but knew they needed to wait for some permits before they could do much remodeling. Tim tooted as he left and I didn't see JW for several hours. I took my clipboard and continued my survey of the property, noting the microclimates of the trees and flowering plants. Next time into town I needed to find a survey map with the soil names and descriptions.

I got back to the house just as a strange truck drove onto the last rise. The driver got out and started toward me. He was very tall and lanky, dark bearded, and moved like a cat. I gasped as I saw the shotgun he was waving in the air as he came toward the porch.

I whispered under my breath. "OK Mr. Vaughan, what do I do now?"

In his usual terse fashion I heard him say, "Jump for his knees."

"If he doesn't shoot me first!" I grabbed the broom from beside the door.

The man was really worked up, shouting about sin and hell and witches, or bitches, I wasn't sure which. He swung the shotgun up level with his waist as he ranted, "You fillin' Kylie Lou's head with stuff about love and se..." he stumbled over the word "sex". "I'll git ..."

He was moving fast and about ten feet away. There was no time to decide whether he was planning to shoot. Just as he raised the gun to aim, I crouched down with the broom handle in front at arms' length and leapt at him from the top step of the porch. Only the complete surprise saved me. The gun went off as it flipped up out of his hands. I rolled to the side and grabbed it.

JW swung around the corner of the house with a handgun pointed straight at the guy as he yelled, "For God's sake Abe, what's got into you? You're in one heap of trouble."

Tears welled up in the man's eyes and he was moaning as JW bent down to help him up.

"Good sign." I muttered, as I walked away from the men and up the steps. I'd let them do a little talking before I joined them again. I watched from the porch as Abe stood, shaking his head while JW talked. The only line I heard was something to the effect that if Abe had hurt even one hair on my head, JW would've shot him dead on the spot.

I felt like a good faint but there wasn't time now. I went inside, got the thermos of coffee and put on an apron. Things quieted down after a few minutes and I stepped back onto the porch to invite the men in. "Mr. Forester, Millie thought you might be up today so she sent a blueberry pie. Come on in and we'll try to work this out. I'm sure JW could use a break too."

Turning on my heel, I led them back to the kitchen table, got the paper cups and cut slabs of pie. The men sat down and went through the coffee ritual, sugar, milk, blowing on it. Then they tucked into the pie. It was mighty quiet in the kitchen, but the birds were making a territorial racket outside.

Suddenly I heard them. "Oh, JW, the doves are here. Excuse me a moment." I slipped out the back door in time to see the pair head for the tulip trees behind the house.

I whispered to them, "My little ones please bring peace to us now."

After a few moments I returned to the house and remained standing at the table. "Mr. Forester, do you know what your wife did yesterday?"

He looked up from his pie and nodded. "I think so, but that's womenfolk stuff."

My hands went white-knuckle on the edge of the table. "She nearly died, Abe, trying to abort her baby. For God's sake! Whose 'stuff' is that? You're responsible for getting her with child, even knowing that she could die. The only sin is not using everything you can to protect her. I can teach you how to know when it's safe. There's a book I can send home for you and Kylie Lou to read and work with."

Abe looked so upset that I feared another angry outburst from him. It was a real surprise when he began to cry instead.

"Ma'am, I don't want nuthin to happen to Kylie Lou. We have so much love; it hurts and hurts. But a book won't help us much. We had to leave school early and didn't get to learn to read much or do numbers."

He started to get up from the table. I stepped around and gently pushed him back into his chair. An idea was coming. "Abe, do you and Kylie Lou want to learn to read?"

He looked up, puzzled. "Tricia's tried to help but she's too busy now in town. Yes, we need to learn real bad." He pulled an envelope out of his overalls and handed it to me. "It came this morning from the city lawyer fellah building on the piece above us. Would you read it to me?"

I took it from the envelope, unfolding it for JW to read to us. It was full of the gobbledy-gook that lawyers think up to scare you. But this was bad. It sounded like the guy was going to shut down Abe's hog operation for obnoxious odors and for polluting the stream.

Abe was wringing his hands. "I don't know how to do anything but raise pigs. What'll I do if I lose my farm and I can't get a job in town 'cause I didn't get through high school?"

"Abe, some of your friends in town say you raise the finest pigs in the county. Would you be willing to swap? Help with your studies, for a pig at Thanksgiving?"

He straightened up in his chair, some of his dignity returning. "Yes Ma'am, that sounds fair. I'll tell Kylie Lou when I git home." He cocked his head to the side and whispered, "Would you teach Kylie Lou too?"

I put my hands on his shoulders. "I'd be pleased to help you both, Abe Forester."

We'd all had about enough, and he got up to leave. He was rubbing the back of his neck as he started to grin. "Where'd you learn a move like that, Ma'am?"

"A guy named Vaughan. I'll tell you about him another time. Nice to meet you, Mr. Forester, give Kylie Lou a hug for me."

As he climbed into his truck and headed down the drive, I turned away on the porch and fainted dead away. You know how, when you're doing a faint, it sounds like a million crickets, all doing their thing at once? Well, there they were; plus the feeling you wanted to say you were OK and just get up but nothing moves?

I came to, a little, just as JW was kneeling beside me doing doctor-like probes. He started to unbutton my shirt. I could feel him hesitate as he gazed down at my radiation tattoo. He said, "Take it easy now, no hurry to get up yet. You've already done a day's work and its only noon. Man, you could charm a snake, Sara Harvey. Sorry I missed the most exciting part. I heard the angry voice but didn't figure there was real trouble until I heard the shot. You stay there and I'll get you a drink."

As he went into the house I struggled up to a sitting position, drawing in big gulps of air, and went down again. He hurried back with a water bottle, scolding me for trying to get up. Then a fit of trembling came. I couldn't stop. JW sat beside me on the floor of the porch and held me.

There was no awkwardness between us. His arms were strong and gentle and protective. "It's time for you to sit and do nothing for a while. I'll walk you up to the stone bench to finish your Dove-Greeting Day. I have a bit more to do on the back porch and then we're going home."

"But Jenny's coming this afternoon with her uncle, isn't she?" I tried to remember what was said when she left on Tuesday.

He shook his head. "With all the excitement I forgot to tell you. She called last night to say it would be Sunday morning early. I guess he got voted in as President of his professional society for the next three years and had to stay in town for committee meetings the rest of today and tomorrow. So we'll go home early today. I'll ask Margot to keep an eye on you until Millie gets home."

I was too weak to argue. I walked slowly to the bench to wait for him to finish. The male dove was staking out his territory and the female was strutting on the ground acting very pleased with herself.

27

They were so beautiful. Their iridescent feathers glittered in the dappled light.

I wanted to just sit and enjoy the peace. When I closed my eyes I could hear the water cascading over the rocks. My mind began to make lists and plans. "No" I whispered to myself, "Just be, for a little."

The warmth of the late spring sun soothed me. By the time JW came up to get me, I was ready. I looked forward to a long afternoon's rest at the cottage. Perhaps I could slip into the Secret Garden for a time before the Greers got home.

When I got to the cottage, a young woman was waiting for me and I was glad for the help. After a wonderful hot bath, I decided a little nap might be a treat. I was already beginning to feel the sore muscles from swinging the Pulaski and from my antics on the porch. The hum of the air conditioner in the cottage was a gentle and effective lullaby and it was several hours before music wakened me to the evening. The woman was sitting by the window, a piece of exquisite needlework shimmering in her lap. JW must have requested that I not be left alone.

Thinking back to the morning and how close I'd come to dying, my heart trembled into panic mode again. I tried not to moan as I rolled upright on the edge of the bed. "Are you Margot? Thank you for looking after me."

"Merci, Madam." She handed me a note from the Greers.

Dear Sara,

> *We hope you will allow us to join you for supper at the cottage. It is much too warm to enjoy the patio tonight and everything is prepared. Margot will do the final arrangements and let us know when you are ready. There will be one guest; actually, he insisted on being included. Better bone up on what day it is, the date, who the President is, and where the Ohio goes. He is very concerned about you and will probably do his doctor duties during supper.*

> *Hank and Millie*

I smiled, realizing that I was more concerned about what to wear than where the Ohio went. The one dress-up outfit I'd packed should be perfect. The dove-gray color would seem cool tonight. I practiced moving slowly and tried not to wince as I finished dressing. I heard Margot's quiet voice as she phoned to let them know I was up and that supper could begin.

A gentle chime announced company and it began a perfect evening. Another young girl assisted Margot with supper and the conversation went to many topics but not to the incident at the farm. Supper was memorable, with an omelet as airy as a cloud. The precious morels I'd brought down from the farm and fresh herbs from Hank's garden were tucked into the filling. I was going to have a glass of wine but declined when JW said no.

His verbal probing to check on me was very adept and kind. When supper was over and we moved to the living room, he said, "Well, Dr. Harvey, I think you'll live to fight another day."

"I'm getting a bit old for such shenanigans. Maybe I'll hang up my belt and be a doddery old lady instead."

His smile back was admiring. "I think not for many years yet."

Still standing, I asked if he'd told Hank and Millie about the Foresters' plight.

"Yes, and he has no real hope that we can block it. All we can do is drag it out in court long enough to help Abe and Kylie Lou find something else to do or another place to live."

I'd been thinking about what I might do to help the Foresters. "I'll get to work Monday to find out what kind of reading programs are already in place here. You said you were helping Tim with GED prep. I'm not sure how much reading skill the Foresters need to make up but they'll need the GED too. I really like the Foresters, I hope we can help."

It was going on towards ten and I wanted to get out to the farm early, to work in the garden.

"May I borrow the Subaru again tomorrow, JW? Remember I'm having company on Sunday. We want it to look nice for Jenny."

"How early?" he asked, and I knew he would be coming too.

"Whatever you can manage is fine."

"Is six o'clock OK?"

"Yes." I thanked the Greers for the dinner and their kindness, and thanked JW for his help at the farm.

I stepped to the window as they went down the garden path. I wondered about their conversation, but exhaustion drove me to my bed. My last thoughts were for the Foresters, for JW and the Greers; and that Michael would be with me this night as I was with him. The cottage door opened as Margot came to spend the night in the living room while I slept.

CHAPTER FOUR

The alarm went off at 5:30 a.m. and I was surprised to see Margot coming in the back door of the cottage. She smiled as she pointed to the work jacket hanging by the back door. "Madam thought you might need this today."

"Thank you Margot, I appreciate your help. Everyone has been so thoughtful and kind. What is your connection with the Greers?"

"I have lived with them for many years. I took care of their handicapped daughter, Elizabeth. She died several years ago in a very sad accident."

"Oh, I'm so sorry, I didn't know." This wasn't the time to ask about it, so I hugged her and slipped out to the car.

It was a luscious morning. The sky was milky-blue and a gentle breeze brought the scent of herbs across the hedge from the knot garden. I went through my mental shopping list on my way across town. When JW came out of the house with a big armload of news-papers I knew he was committed to working in the house too. We stopped at the grocery store for some plants and jugs of water. I hadn't packed lunch so we got some things to eat and more empty boxes.

The newly worked up ground in the garden spot looked good. I decided to take a chance on some peppers and a few tomato plants, though a late frost might nip them. I'd be willing to cover them for a few days to get them in while I had help. We unrolled the chicken wire and made a fence with branches and rocks. The perennials got an hour's care and looked wonderful after so many years of benign neglect. JW worked beside me and seemed to understand my re-quests and instructions.

"I enjoy doing this," he explained. "My mother and I worked in the garden together. My brothers did the animal stuff. She loved her flowers and vegetable garden. She really liked 'putting things by' for winter. Her family survived the depression on a farm and she always felt safer when the garden did well." It was the first mention of his family and I was glad that he seemed comfortable doing it.

As we finished up and headed for the house, I asked him, "How long do we have, JW, so we can plan our work inside?" He stopped on the step. "My day is yours, Dr. Harvey. I can stay as long as you need me. I appreciate your being here to help me begin to clear away the ghosts of my childhood."

The few days airing out had helped some, and the house didn't smell quite so bad, but we would sit on the porch tomorrow for lunch. The kitchen was nearly finished and we started to pack dishes and pots to take to town for a real scrubbing and sterilizing in the dishwasher. Everything needed to be out of the kitchen before the next Lysol and soap scrub.

It was long past lunchtime when we decided to eat. As we finished off with a box of cookies, JW leaned back on the porch rail and crossed his arms, his mangled hand resting on his chest. I was glad he felt comfortable enough with me to allow his handicap to be seen.

"Well, Dr. Harvey, you've certainly impacted lives in our little hamlet. You've tamed tigers, charmed snakes and brought tears to the eyes of little Margot as well as JW Campbell. When will we learn something about you, Mysterious Lady?"

I turned to get up from my perch on the step. He touched my shoulder and spoke quietly. "No, you stay here. Let's have another mug of tea and then, I think we need to talk."

I felt a chill in my heart and I began to shiver. JW came back with two mugs and Millie's jacket. He motioned to the swing and we sat side-by-side, drinking tea. I felt a little better and managed a wan smile. "Thanks. May I call you Jamie?"

His eyes widened in surprise as he nodded. "I would be honored if you would. Now, what can I do to help?"

"Just listen, I guess. If you'd asked me two days ago, or even yesterday, I wouldn't have been ready. Before today, I would have said I'd tell the story to only one person, Michael, before anyone else learned of it. Now, something has happened. I think I've given up hope.

"Today, I feel that I'll never find him. He's probably happily married with six kids, or joined the priesthood or died in a car accident. Somehow I've lost him after all these years and no one will know what happened. I feel safe telling you, Jamie, because I think we're related. I believe that our great-grandfathers were brothers here in Campbell's Point. My birth name was Rebecca Jane Campbell."

He reached over to take my hand. "I'm glad we're kin."

My hands were like ice and I began to shiver again, almost as though something or someone were trying to frighten me into silence. Jamie moved his hand away as I began.

"Michael and I were high school sweethearts. In our 15th summer, we decided to run away and get married. We went across the state line to a town where the justice of the peace took one look at us, ushered us into a tiny room and locked the door. It was very late by the time our parents got there. They were furious and we were terrified. We thought it would blow over; maybe they'd just ground us. Instead, I never saw Michael again.

"The nightmare began that night and didn't end until a few months ago. I was sent to a boarding school in France. At Christmastime I was sent away again. Not to another boarding school but to a place of punishment and misery. We spent hours on our knees in prayer. We were not allowed to speak. The only sounds in the place were the chanting of the nuns during the liturgy and very faintly, the sounds of screaming from the birthing rooms. When my time came, I shared the agony of my sisters. Jamie, I don't even know how it happened.

"I couldn't believe my beautiful baby girl was born of such travail. I saw her just once for a few moments before they took her away. I wanted to give her something so she would know her heritage. I still had the precious locket Michael had given me. I used a tiny piece of paper to slip behind his picture. It said, 'My name is Dove Cameron.' When the little novice came to get my precious Dove, I pleaded with her to give the locket to the new mother.

"And then, Jamie, I wept. I wept for months. I wept as I scrubbed floors on my knees for hours every day. I hoed in the gardens and wept. For a few minutes each day I was allowed to sit on a bench in the inner garden of the convent. One day in summer, a dove came into the enclosure, and flew into my lap. Somehow she brought a message of peace. I gave Dove, my beautiful baby, into God's care.

"A few weeks later I was sent to another school, the exact opposite of the first. Here young girls were expected to work hard and learn difficult subjects. We were required to speak only French and to work tirelessly to develop it with no trace of accent because we were to be wives of diplomats, or crown princes or business dignitaries. Those years were the happiest of my life. I chose my college, area of study, and earned my PhD when I was twenty-six. I was planning to teach science in an elite boarding school in the South of France.

"The noon of graduation, I was kidnapped, taken to a church, where in minutes, it was over. I was married to someone I'd never met. He frightened me, and his friends carried guns.

"He told me, 'I have owned you for ten years. Your father gave you to me in exchange for a gambling debt he owed me. I invested in your education and now you will repay me by being my wife and following the rules which I will set down.'

"I couldn't believe my father would do such a thing. I'd thought they somehow decided to disown me, but still paid for my schooling. My identity was changed when I went to the second school, but I thought it was part of their cruelty to me. Instead, it was this man's doing. The person who married me was French, a college professor, and he wanted to be a college president of an American university. My role was to be the perfect faculty wife.

"The nightmare continued the first night of our marriage. He walked me to my bedroom, and said, 'Here is your room. Mine is next door. I will never touch you, I prefer men.'

"In each job and each place we lived, as he climbed from Professor to Dean, to President, he destroyed young men. They worshipped him and then disappeared, didn't return to classes or went home and hanged themselves.

"He got what he wanted and I became known as the 'Ice Queen'. A year and a half ago, he suffered a stroke. He lingered several months and finally died of a second one. As his final act of cruelty, I was required to dress in full mourning for one year. Then his estate would be mine. Jamie, it has been a living hell."

Jamie got up from the swing to face me "What a terrifying story, Sara. Why didn't you leave him?"

"The first time I tried to disobey him, he said he would hurt my daughter if I tried to leave or get help."

I rose from the swing and began to pace the porch. Jamie didn't touch me, but he stood to block my way as he said, "Sara, do you trust me?"

I wasn't sure what he meant, but I nodded yes.

He continued. "In the story you told me, you never used the word husband. What was your husband's name?"

I looked up, surprised. "I don't know. I can't remember."

Jamie looked so concerned I returned to my place on the swing. He continued to lean against the porch rail as he said, "Would you try something for me? I want you to say some phrases for me. Just repeat what I say. 'He cannot harm me now'. Say it."

I struggled to speak but nothing would come out. I felt an icy fear deep in my gut.

"Sara, say one word at a time, 'He cannot harm me now'."

Ten minutes later I was able to say the phrase in a normal voice instead of a whisper.

Jamie continued. "Good. Now I want you to add something more. 'My husband is dead. He cannot harm me now'. Say it, one word at a time."

We struggled; his will against mine. "I can't, Jamie, Please don't make me say it."

He started in again, quietly, and gently. "My husband is dead. He cannot harm me now."

Finally, I whispered, "He is dead, he can't harm me now."

Jamie kept at it. "'My husband is dead; he cannot harm me now'."

Something deep inside wanted to help. I cried out in anguish. "Help me, please help me." Finally after a deep struggle, I was able to whisper the words, then to say them out loud.

"Now Sara, What was your husband's name?"

I shook my head frantically. My hands were trembling as I whispered in agony, "I don't know, I don't remember."

I began to scream, little whimpering screams, like a tiny trapped and wounded animal. I stumbled headlong down the porch steps, ran to the creek, plunged face down into the cold water and collapsed on the rocks.

Jamie had followed me. "Sara, what was your husband's name?"

I was gasping for breath now, crying, my eyes covered by my dripping wet hands. "No, no, I can't, he will hurt Dove. Please stop."

"Say it. 'My husband is dead. He cannot harm me now. He cannot harm Dove'."

I was sobbing now, twisting away from his words as though they were blows to my body. I struggled to barely whisper it.

He persisted. "Now, Sara. What was your husband's name?"

Everything in the woods became silent. No birds sang, no squirrels barked, the breeze stopped and the hush was more terrifying than the noise. It came back then, something inside opened with a tearing, crushing blow that threw me forward on my knees.

I whispered it once, then twice, and louder. "His name was Henri Lambert. He was my husband and he is dead. He cannot harm me now. He cannot harm my precious Dove now."

Jamie came closer. "Good Sara, close your eyes and say it again, and again. Open your eyes and say it. Get up out of the water and say it. It must become your mantra. It will set you free."

I turned away, hating him for what he'd made me go through. Then, dripping wet and weeping in relief, I collapsed into his arms, looked into his eyes and could smile.

We went to the stone bench and dried off in the warm sun. The doves were busy gathering twigs and grass for their nest, cooing and fluffing at each other in perfect contentment. Jamie looked at me and smiled. "Are you all right, Sara Harvey? Or do you want to be called Becky Campbell? How will people know?"

"From what I've learned, just tell someone at Gary's and the whole valley will know by tomorrow night."

We laughed comfortably. Then Jamie took my hands in his. "It's the first time I've heard your laugh. It's wonderful, like a wind chime tuned to G. I hope to hear many more."

"It's time for a last walk through before Jenny brings her favorite uncle over tomorrow. I wonder how long he's going to stay. I can't imagine it could be interesting for very long. Are you coming up with them or do you want a ride?"

He grinned. "Tomorrow, I'm going to sleep in. You've worn me out this week, Woman. I'll come up with Jenny and you can come get the Subaru tomorrow on your way out. Don't bother about food. I think Jenny has something planned. Let's go so we can get those boxes unloaded before supper."

I could feel Jamie watching me when he thought I wasn't aware of it, a mixture of worry and something else. Since I was the driver, conversation lagged a bit. I was bone-tired and my mind was swirling with the events of the day.

Tim helped unload the boxes; then he dashed off to his truck. "I'm going over to Thad's tonight to watch the game on TV and chart plays. See you guys later."

I turned to Jamie. "I think I'll go home to early bed. See you tomorrow."

All I could think about was a hot shower and sleep; I wasn't even hungry. The phone was chiming as I entered the cottage. Margot answered it, so I took off to a hot shower. I was so exhausted I fell into bed, to waken later in the same position. Margot was sitting by the window with her embroidery.

I stretched like a sleepy cat wakening and glanced at the clock. Then I looked at Margot and grinned. "Let's go dancing. I want to go and learn country line dancing. I'm hungry for a huge greasy hamburger and curly fries and a milkshake. Let's go out to the Roadhouse and dance."

She clutched her embroidery and whispered, "Oh, no Ma'am, we can't do that; not without our men. That's no place for nice ladies."

"I don't feel nice tonight. I want to dance and be someone else for one night. I'm tired of being watched over and guarded all the time. Come on, nothing will happen if we're together."

"Oh, no Ma'am, please don't."

She watched as I got out my work boots and slipped them on. They weren't quite right but they'd have to do. I dressed in Levis and a turquoise silk shirt and then opened a small box. Margot gasped when she saw what was inside. Lifting it and putting it on, I turned to her with a smile. "Let's go Margot, the night is waiting." The wig of glorious, long red hair, made the transformation complete.

Margot was trembling, but turned to go. "I need to change clothes, I'll be right back."

I was putting on make-up when she returned.

"Ma'am, please don't do this. The Greers and Jamie will kill me if anything happens to you, and it will, with you looking like that."

"Oh, come on Margot, I want to dance."

It was about nine when we got to the Roadhouse. It was Saturday night and the place was packed. There were dozens of trucks in the parking lot. They were the biggest, flashiest ones I'd ever seen, with chrome, extra lights, roll bars and winches. They all had running boards, since they were so big you couldn't even get in without them. I tried to find a spot near something I could find later. There was one tiny space next to the dumpster and I cruised into it.

I'd never been in a place like this. I expected it to be like the program on TV but quickly found out TV didn't have a haze of smoke thick enough to choke a chimney and music so loud that you had to yell to be heard. The crowd carried us along into the middle of the room as people milled around getting ready to dance.

The only empty table was back against the wall and we headed for it. A tough-looking blond came to take our order. She was chewing gum and her bright red fingernails were at least three inches long. She was wearing bright red cowboy boots and not much else.

"What'cha want, ladies?"

Margot shook her head no. I was starving. "I'd like a giant hamburger with everything, curly fries and a chocolate milkshake. Oh, and are they giving beginner lessons tonight?"

She smirked. "I'll see what I kin do."

I was watching the dancers, trying to figure out the simplest steps, when a shadow fell on the table. It was a huge shadow. I looked up with alarm. He was big but well built, with massive shoulders. His tight jeans showed off his slim hips and thighs. His black boots were gorgeous, well polished and well worn. He reached for my hand. "Well, little lady, I hear you want a dancin' lesson. Let's take a spin 'til your burger comes." He nodded to Margot "'Scuse us, Ma'am."

He guided me out onto the floor, dodging sweaty bodies and speaking to his friends. The minute he touched me I knew I was in Big Trouble. Every time we turned, his knee rubbed against my crotch.

He leered down at me. "Like that Honey?"

I was breathless from the heat in the place and his legs were so long that I had trouble keeping up. After a few minutes, I yelled to get his attention. "I need a break."

As we got back to the table I tried desperately to think of some way to distract him.

"I've been thinking about buying a truck. Tell me what I should look for."

His eyes got huge. "You are? Well, you need to see mine first. Come on, yur grub's not here yet. I'll take you out t'see it."

He started to lead me out. "Ma'am, yur the prettiest filly I ever seen. You new around here?"

I decided I might as well keep up the game. "I'm here visiting."

"Oh yeah?"

We were about half way across the room headed toward the door. His grip on my elbow was so tight my arm was going to sleep. "Mr.?" I yelled, trying to get his attention.

"Marvin Renquist", he answered, "At your service, Ma'am." His laugh was not encouraging.

"Well, Marvin, you can let go, I won't run away."

He did let go, and I looked up, just in time to see Tim, Jamie and someone else, probably Thad, the catcher, walk into the room. Now, how could I tell them to let us by without causing a scene? I looked at Thad, and put my arm straight out like I'd seen catchers do on TV, to tell him to let us pass. He nodded OK. As soon as we were out the door, I was glad the loud music covered Marvin's yelp as I took him down. He was bigger and stronger than I figured, but he was up again fast for someone so large.

"You're a real kick Ma'am; this'll be fun."

As he lunged for me, I dodged away and ran toward the car. They hadn't picked up the trash yet and I remembered seeing some old pipe stacked in a pile. I grabbed one and turned to fight. There wasn't enough room to swing, so I moved farther out into the parking lot. I could see Tim and Thad coming out the front at a dead run, and Jamie coming around from the back. Just as I prepared to make a lethal swing at Marvin's ribs, Thad yelled "slide", and Tim took Marvin down.

Then, Thad grabbed me, and my pipe. I was struggling and madder than a hornet. He whispered, "Keep at it, Sweetheart, you're Jamie's crazy aunt." Then he laughed. "Man, you have a major league swing, maybe we should recruit you."

Jamie barked out orders. "Tim get her out of here. Thad, you go get Margot."

Jamie turned and reached out to help Marvin up.

"Man, she almost kilt me with that pipe," he whined, "She belong to you?"

Jamie seemed to be enjoying the whole thing now, and I could hear him telling Marvin thank you, hoped he was OK, and then explained that they'd been looking for me since supper. I'd slipped away from them. Then he made the universal sign for crazy and shrugged his shoulders. "Thank goodness she's going home tomorrow. Thanks again."

Marvin rubbed his chin. "Guess I'll jus' tell the guys she didn't like my truck. See ya."

He turned to go back as a couple of real cute girls surrounded him and they went back inside, arm-in-arm.

Thad came around the corner from the bar with a weeping Margot in tow. About then, I realized what a mess I'd created.

Jeanne Anderegg

Jamie said, "You guys can come back for the Honda later. Let's get out of here."

When we got back into town, Jamie got out at Gary's Grill. I could tell he was still very angry. "I'm going to finish my supper, if they saved it. Then I'm coming home to give you the thrashing you deserve, Ma'am. Take her to our place Tim, and don't let her out of your sight."

He disappeared into Gary's as we went down the street to Jamie's house. It had cooled off since the evening started and Tim went around opening all the windows. A blessed breeze moved through the house.

Then he returned to the living room. "Ma'am, where'd you learn to fight like that? I've never seen a woman do that. If you'd had a claymore instead of a lead pipe I'd be expecting the pipes to be playing *The Campbells are coming.*"

I didn't smile. "It was a young Italian gardener named Andretti who made a trade."

Tim's eyes got big. I could imagine what he was thinking.

"No, it wasn't like that. He jumped ship in Charleston after unloading a thousand cases of sherry. My husband fished him out of the bay and brought him home. He was the best gardener we ever had. The grounds were so gorgeous people would sneak in and try to steal him. Anyway, he wanted the American dream, to find a wife and settle down to life in America. His problem was that he knew no English. We traded lessons, English for Italian street fighting."

Tim grinned, "Well, you sure surprised ol' Marvin, especially since apparently you said you wanted to see his truck." Then he chuckled, "In Roadhouse talk it means you want to have a little ...well...help out his funny walk."

I was puzzled. Then realized what I must have done. We both began to laugh, just as Jamie came in the door.

"What's so funny?" he growled

Tim headed for the door. "I'll fill you in later."

Jamie asked for my Honda keys and tossed them to Tim. "Please round up Thad and the two of you go pick up the car before some stud squashes it under his fender. Tell Margot I'll be over in a few minutes with Sara."

Jamie turned to me and held up a sack. "I brought you some supper. I tried to find what you ordered at the Roadhouse." He leaned against the doorjamb. "Now, Sara, do you have anything to say in your defense?"

I got three gulps of milkshake down before I whispered, "No".

I could tell Jamie was still very angry. "Do you realize you could've killed Marvin? Or maimed him for life? Whatever were you thinking?"

38

I looked at him, planted my feet, and took a big breath. "I just wanted to go dancing."

He was beginning to smile. "You picked a helluva place to go." His hand reached up to touch my hair. "What's this, Sara?"

I turned away as I answered. "When I found out chemotherapy was going to make my hair fall out, I had my hairdresser shave it off and they made it into a wig. Later, when my hair came in silver, I wore it at evening meals after Henri had his stroke. He seemed to know me better."

I stood quietly, waiting for his reply but Jamie was off on another train of thought. His voice was filled with frustration. "Jenny and I had a fight tonight. It was about tomorrow's visitor. She wanted it to be a surprise; like a happy-ending movie. I told her I wouldn't let it happen to you that way, with no warning."

"What do you mean, Jamie?"

"She thought she recognized you that first afternoon. When she got home and looked in the family photo album, she found pictures of a beach party up on the lake, with her Uncle Mike and you together as kids. Sara, she's found your childhood sweetheart and the father of your child. Her Uncle Mike is your Michael Cameron."

My hands were trembling as I put down the milkshake. "Is that the way it happens? You're doing some mundane thing like eating or brushing your teeth when the phone rings to tell you someone has died, or has returned from the dead." I turned away for a moment. "I don't know whether to laugh or cry but thank you for telling me.

"Jenny's last name wasn't mentioned while we were together Monday afternoon. I had no idea who she was. Does Michael know?"

"Jenny promised she would tell him."

Jamie moved toward me. "We need to get you back to the cottage and I need to see Margot. Sara, I have a request."

I looked up, puzzled, my mind swirling with the news he had already given me. "What do you want Jamie?"

"May I touch you?" I nodded yes.

"May I kiss you goodbye?"

The poignancy in his voice made me realize what he was doing. Apparently the growing attraction I had felt for him during the week past had been mutual.

"Yes, Jamie, I think it needs doing."

The first kiss was gentle, filled with need and longing. The second was so passionate my knees buckled. He held me closer as he whispered, "Why has fate been so cruel to me, to us? Dearest one, my soul mate, I waited so long for you. Now I must release you to him with grief in my heart. Goodbye my precious Sara."

We clung to each other until his arms gently released me. I would not call him Jamie again. It was too intimate.

He shifted to practical mode. "We'd better go, so Margot can get some sleep, and you too. Tomorrow's almost here."

We decided to walk, and hurried down the street. Margot was waiting by the window as we slipped in the cottage door. JW whispered a few words to her and she left for the big house.

"Goodnight, Sara. We'll be there about eleven o'clock. You'll need to come by for the Subaru in the morning. Take the keys now. I have a feeling you'll be going up early."

As I readied for bed, I wondered what Michael was thinking tonight.

CHAPTER FIVE

It was a beautiful late spring morning. I hadn't slept in for a whole week and it felt good to linger in bed a few minutes longer, savoring the flower scents wafting in. The mental list of things needing to be done grew as I dressed for the farm.

Suddenly, I realized I'd gone on with my life as though the news about Michael weren't true; that he wouldn't come, and I was still alone. I slipped into my borrowed jacket and went off to get the other car. The only other person up was the papergirl, riding her bike, the "splat" "splat", of the tossed papers marking her progress down the street. I stopped to pick up extra water and headed out of town.

As I reached the clearing in front of the house, a doe and twin fawns looked up from their early breakfast. The sun had been up a while and I was at peace. I grabbed the Pulaski from the doorway of the shed and headed out to work in the garden. Most of the easy places were done. The rest would be more difficult to get into shape.

I was working in the part of the garden nearest the creek. You didn't hear road noise, only birds and crickets and the barking of far away neighbors' dogs. I moved down the gentle slope so the sun wouldn't be in my eyes, stopping to grub out the smaller trees and to work up the sod. My hands reminded me of my forgotten gloves and I stopped to go back for them.

When I turned around towards the shed, someone was standing very close behind me. The sun was in my eyes and I went into a complete panic. My mistake was turning away from him to run. In a split second, he covered the distance between us and grabbed me around the waist. I kicked and scratched at his arms. He tossed me into the air and grabbed lower so my feet couldn't touch the ground. I growled in anger and fright.

"Now is that any way to greet a visitor, Becky Campbell? If you'll stop struggling, I'll let you go." He was so strong I should have given up but I kept fighting. After a fruitless struggle, I realized only a trick could get him to put me down. I relaxed in his arms and felt him loosen his grip. As soon as my feet touched the ground, I whirled away from him and took off, grabbing the Pulaski as I headed uphill toward the fence. I'd see what kind of condition he was in.

41

I was the one who wasn't in prime fighting shape and the Pulaski was heavy. I watched for a pole, as I moved uphill. Finally, a deadfall was close enough to reach from the path. I grabbed it and snapped it in half. I hated to leave the Pulaski for him and hurled it off into the brush. The thud echoed in my gut as I turned to fight. The forest was empty, so quiet my heart pounding in my head was deafening.

Where was he? Where did he go? I stood absolutely still, listening. Nothing. I was up along the top fence line; about the same place I'd met Kylie Lou. When I glanced down toward the house, I saw him standing in the garden. I watched him a long time. He was in no hurry, just waiting. He was a big man, well over six feet tall, dressed in Levis and a plaid shirt with the sleeves rolled up. I glanced at my watch. It was only eight o'clock. Had he come early? Where were Jenny and JW?

Still carrying my pole, I made my way back down the slope. He didn't turn as I came up behind him. He was completely defenseless. I whispered to him, "Michael? Please forgive me, you frightened me."

As he turned to speak, his hands were open and turned up toward me. "No Becky, please forgive me. I'm so sorry. Tim Campbell warned me not to surprise you and I didn't listen. He brought me out early, before you got here."

This time he didn't try to come closer and his next words were a complete surprise. "If he weren't already dead, I would kill him for what he did to you."

I took several steps closer. "Michael is it really you?"

His voice was filled with gentleness. "Yes, and I'm not married with six kids, nor did I become a priest, though I thought about it, and obviously, the highway hasn't gotten me yet."

Then I knew that JW had told my story. I was glad we wouldn't need to go over it again right now.

I smiled and reached for his hand. "Come help me find the Pulaski. They're terribly expensive and I'd be embarrassed to tell anyone why I threw it into the underbrush."

It took some searching. We stopped to catch our breath when we finally found it. Territorial songs filled the woods. The doe and her twins slipped past us on the way to the creek and the sun was warm on our backs.

"It's a magical place, Becky. I hope it will give you much pleasure. I don't like the idea of you being out here all alone though."

"Well, I won't be here alone when everything is in place. It's been my dream to set up a hospice."

We discussed the plans as we returned to the bench under the tulip popular trees.

"JW's mother used to sit here watching for her family to come home from town. I wish I could have known her. She was part of my Campbell kin too. All I have now are the remnants of her garden and the things in her house. Her leave-taking must have been so sad. Each of us seems to have lived through a private hell."

Michael took my hands. "Mine was losing you. I tried for months to find out where they had sent you. I even tried to seduce the little maid. She almost told me, because she was so angry when my parents fired her sweetheart who drove the car for us. One night, she disappeared too.

"Then the next summer in August there was a small note in the local paper saying that Rebecca Jane Campbell had been killed in an auto accident while traveling in France."

He reached into his billfold and took out a yellowed, tattered piece of newsprint and showed it to me. My blood ran cold as I realized that one of the stipulations of Lambert's receiving me must have been destroying my American identity. He annihilated one and crafted another to suit his own purposes.

Michael went on doggedly. "I was in naval ROTC and after college they put me through medical school. I'm an orthopedic surgeon. Now, thanks to Jenny, perhaps at last, the next path in my life may include you again."

I stood up from the bench. Every muscle in my body ached and I needed to move around. He joined me on the path as we walked toward the house.

"Has Jenny told JW the other reason she brought you here, the real and most important reason for her?"

He sounded frustrated as he answered. "We have a difficult task ahead. I don't think Jenny realizes how poor our chances are for 100% success. Even though she believes her Uncle Mike walks on water, I'm only human, with human skills. I fear she's counting on this to transform JW back into the person he was a long time ago. It's not possible, nor is it wise. When he allowed me to do a first exam late last night, I was appalled at the poor care he's been given. He's an orthopedic surgeon too and knows full well the extent of his injuries. If we can get him involved in the planning, maybe our chances will be better. It's been over a year. We'll just have to see."

As we reached the steps, I touched his cheek. "You have become a very interesting man, Michael Cameron, I hope I'll be worthy of your trust."

We heard the low rumble of an approaching storm. The forest was hushed. The creatures were taking cover and we should too. Switching gears, I took off with the tools while he went to close the car windows and bring back the quilts from the back seat.

I still couldn't believe that my Michael was with me now, and tears were streaming down my face when he returned, a little breathless from his run to escape the first drops. "Oh, Michael, let's sit in the big chair and watch the storm, like we used to when we were kids."

We dragged the chair into the sheltered corner and made a cocoon of the covers. The rain pelted on the tin roof of the porch as we snuggled down to enjoy the storm. It whirled away up over the mountain, too quickly to do much good for the drought-stricken forest. He kissed my tears away, counting softly under his breath. He was at seventeen.

I was smiling as I burrowed into his warm chest. "Whatever are you doing?"

He grinned. "We have until eternity and I'm counting the places I want to kiss you."

I murmured with a sigh, "Round it up to 20, Michael, then I'm ready for a nap."

We wakened to the sound of Jenny's truck coming over the last rise to the house. I touched his lips. "How do you feel about the kids seeing us like this?"

He smiled, his eyes still closed.

"Good, because they're here and so is lunch."

The light, elegant lunch from Gary's was perfect. The conversation was about the house and the mountain on which it nestled. There was no wine. Michael thanked Jenny and said he had surgery at seven o'clock the next morning.

He took his niece's hand as he rose from the porch swing. "Well My Dear, I came to have you show me what kind of an engineer you've become. I'm ready for the tour."

She began a very professional discussion of the elements we were trying to achieve. Jenny was good. I knew it because of the way she interpreted my requests and did the proper research and calculations to determine their merits or problems.

She turned to me. "I'm still working on the waterpower, Dr. Harvey, since you have your heart set on it. This may be a bad year to get any concessions out of the conservation people. I'll do my best though and I've been working on a compromise I think they'll accept. And Jamie, I think Tim and I can keep the work going until you get back from St. Louis."

Jamie's back straightened as he asked, "And why am I going away?"

Jenny's fighting stance took me by surprise. "You're going away because you have to know if anything can be done. The finest hand surgeon in the country is going to work on you. Besides, I want it for you because I care about you."

His face showed no emotion in response to her declaration, nor did he reply with anything but a shrug. After a few moments, Michael had us all at the kitchen table. It was a bit past three and his plane left at eight o'clock from Pittsburgh. Driving back into town would take twice as long on a Sunday night so we couldn't dawdle with our discussion.

In a few terse sentences he told us what he planned to try. As he looked straight at JW, he asked, "Are you willing to take a chance? Are you willing to help plan the surgery and especially, are you willing to take the pain so we can communicate during the surgery?"

Jenny and I were both holding our breath until JW said, "Yes", and we sighed in relief.

Michael began explaining what needed to be done. "I'll schedule surgery for Saturday morning at seven o'clock. I want you, Doctor, to be in St. Louis on Tuesday evening so we can begin making preparations the next morning. I assume both you ladies plan to be present during the surgery. I'll arrange a place where you can watch the whole procedure but not be seen, and where Sara can do her work. I estimate two shifts and have two crews lined up. Now, I really must go or I'll have to take a private plane home."

Jenny rose quickly, and said her goodbyes as she turned to JW. "I'll call when I get home. I'll probably be in St. Louis Friday late. I have appointments all week." She and Michael hurried down the clearing to the truck. Now that it was going to happen, I wondered if Jenny realized how many ways something could go wrong. Because of my part in it, I was terrified.

JW and I returned to the porch swing as I asked, "Where are you going to stay while you're there?"

He turned to me and said, "What?" He was off on his own thought track and wasn't listening.

"Never mind. Could we stay just a little longer? I love to hear the last bird songs and see the light fade until there are only dark patterns."

We sat on the swing as the evening swallowed up the sun. He turned to me, and asked in a puzzled tone, "He's counting on you Saturday. How did he know that you were an empath?"

I rose from the swing to begin closing up the house. "He knew when we were kids or at least he guessed. Then this morning, he asked. Over the years I've used it for people I cared about very much. I'll do my best for you. I hope you won't be offended, praying is part of it."

He touched my hand. "Will you pray with me now, Sara, before we go into the ordeal? This is probably the last quiet time we'll have."

We traveled the window trap line of the house and closed it up for the night. Then, settling on the top step of the porch, I held his mangled hand as we prayed together.

There were deer out feeding as we headed home, their glistening eyes reflecting from the headlights. We drove back past the notch of Forester's place. It would be my first visit tomorrow. I was anxious to get started with an assessment of their skills. I needed a better idea about what Abe and Kylie Lou's hoped to do, before I picked up reading material for them. There I was, off on my own track too and the rest of the trip was done in silence.

JW was ready to get out at his place, when he leaned over to me. "I almost forgot. I've got a really big favor for you to consider. It will probably be several weeks until I can come home and even though I'm sure Tim can take care of our four building projects in progress right now, I wondered if you might consider staying at the house and keeping an eye on things while I'm gone. Since you'll be going up to the farm every day and he's busy with the jobs and baseball, you won't be together too much. Besides, the Greers said last night they were leaving on a trip. This is the time when Margot goes home for a month, so there won't be anyone to take care of you at the cottage."

After just a week, the cycle of being nurtured and looked after must be abandoned. I was dismayed by my disappointment. "What does Tim think about having me baby-sit?"

JW grinned, "Actually, it was his idea. He's fascinated by your stories. You can help him keep after his studying and he says you can keep him on the straight and narrow with Tricia. He does love her a lot. I hope they can stay out of bed for a while longer."

"That's a tall order, but I think I'm up to it. The answer is yes, thank you. I'll move over on Wednesday morning after you're on your way. Could we mesh trips Tuesday? I need to take Dave's Honda back and I need to do some shopping. I expect you have business stuff to finish up tomorrow."

"Let's have breakfast tomorrow at Gary's and we'll make plans. Bring your lists; there are a couple of things you could get for me. Is eight o'clock all right? The early crowd should be gone and it will be quieter."

I nodded, "Sure, I'll pick you up. I need to get home to a hot bath. Every muscle I knew I had, hurts; and some I hadn't known about before. I'm getting too old for this."

"Pipe-swinging muscles? Or something that happened this morning?"

"If Michael doesn't tell, I won't. See you, Friend."

My sleep that night was troubled with nightmares of shadowy frightening figures and gray nothingness. I finally got up about two o'clock to find something to eat. Perhaps my skipped supper had come back to haunt me. As I stumbled out of the bedroom, I found Margot asleep on the couch. She looked so frail and weary.

I'd been an added burden for her. I was puzzled by her sudden allegiance and caring for me and chalked it up to Hank and Millie's concern for me after what had happened the last few days. My own foolish antics didn't help either. She would probably smell the burned toast so I made enough for both of us, laid the pieces in deep bowls and poured hot milk over them. I needed comfort food right now.

She smiled wistfully as she joined me at the table. "My mama used to fix this for us when we were children and didn't feel well. I'm sure there's some equivalent food in every home in the universe."

Her gentle look brought tears to my eyes as she whispered, "Is there something I can do to help?"

I put down my spoon. "'I'm so frightened, Margot. As much as I want his hand to be fixed, my heart says, that for some reason I don't understand, JW doesn't want it to happen. Michael has asked me to be involved in a way so intimate that I must suffer with JW. I fear for his soul, and for mine."

After we finished our snack, we went around opening up the cottage windows. The burned smell from the toast would take some time to leave. Then we went to the front porch swing.

After a few minutes, I began again. "Do you know what soul mates are?"

She nodded yes. "They're probably the same the universe over too; like milk toast."

"Well," I hesitated, "From the first moment I saw JW, I knew that he and I were soul mates, and he knew it too. We've known each other since the beginning of time and are destined to meet, live, hate and love many times until eternity. But this time, we are not meant to have each other. I think there are several claims on him this time around, some good, and some bad, and they are fighting to possess him. I'm frightened for him because he may not have the will or the strength to resist. Time is short and I'll fight for him but I don't like our chances."

She was weeping now. "All of us; Hank, Millie, Jenny, Tim, Thad and I, have tried to help him. We've rescued him time after time. Do you know how many times he's attempted suicide? Five, six that we know of and probably others we don't know about. He was so different when you came, as if his soul were beginning to fill his body again. We hoped he was better. I fear for him too."

"Pray for us, Margot. We're going to need it."

We went back into the quiet house for a few more hours of sleep.

Margot was gone when I wakened to the gentle chimes of seven o'clock. So much had happened in the past week. It was exhausting trying to sort it out. What puzzled me most were my feelings toward Michael, almost as though he'd been put on hold while the other more immediate crises worked themselves out. I was the outsider in this drama. I felt as if I'd been put into a game without being told the rules. All I had were my gut instincts and a passion for life that would drive me to sacrifice everything to save one soul; especially when that soul was JW's.

I sat down at the kitchen table to make my lists, shocked at the mundaneness of bolts for the hinge on the shed door and paper towels for the farm kitchen, when we were talking so recently about souls and fights with the hounds of hell. It was close to eight o'clock when I pulled in JW's driveway and switched cars.

He closed the house and locked it, climbed into the Subaru and buckled up. "In the old days we never locked our doors. Now, with so many strangers and drifters we have to be more careful. 'Course I have so little to steal I worry more about vandalism when they find nothing to take. Sleep well last night after all the excitement?"

"No, I didn't. I had a night of bad dreams. Finally Margot and I had milk toast in the middle of the night. She's looking so tired and distraught and I feel partly responsible. At least she'll be going home for a visit soon. Maybe she can get some rest."

"Not much chance. She's going home to France to find out if the man she has waited for all these years is going to marry her. It's a terrible mess. He came over here once to visit and none of us liked the way he treated her. Thad is waiting for her. I hope she'll be free soon so he can ask her to marry him."

"I didn't know guys were matchmakers. What an interesting switch."

Tricia saw us come in and trotted over to get us settled in a booth. She was so sweet and innocent. I hoped life wouldn't have to spoil it too soon. She took out the order book, but she wasn't ready to write.

She leaned over to JW. "I hear you're going away to St Louis to get your hand fixed, that some bigwig surgeon came all the way over here looking for you. Is it true?"

He smiled and nodded yes. "Tricia, you might as well have the whole story so it will start out right. The bigwig surgeon happens to be my friend's uncle, Michael Cameron, and yes, he did come looking for me. Jenny wants me to at least try to see what can be done."

"Is it what you want, Dr. Campbell," Tricia blurted out, "to go back to being a surgeon again? We'd sure miss you around here. Who would fix all the stuff that needs fixing? I know it doesn't pay much but we need you, and you're family. You're a Campbell and you're part of us."

JW hesitated before he answered. "I'll think about it Tricia. Maybe I'll do that, win, lose or draw."

Her pen poised, Tricia began to write. "Now, what would you two like for breakfast?"

I looked up from my menu and smiled. "Tricia, are you working all day today?"

"No, I worked early shift so I'll be off at one o'clock."

"Tim and JW are coming out at one o'clock and bringing lunch. I'd like for you to come with them and have lunch at the farm with us. Tim has practice later and he can drop you at home or take you back into town."

She smiled. "Thank you. I'd like to."

She tilted her head and gazed at me. "You look more like a Becky Campbell than a Sara Harvey. People are a little confused but we'll get it right. What would you like to be called?"

I considered my answer. "Well, perhaps it will soon be Mrs. Michael Cameron, but for now, I'd still like to be called Sara Harvey. I've had the name a long time, and Rebecca Jane Campbell is officially dead."

"OK. We'll do it. Are you going to let the guys order lunch?"

"Sure, I like surprises, and make breakfast light. If we don't quit visiting it'll be lunchtime before you know it.

I took a moment to glance around the room. The breakfast crowd had cleared out and a few early coffee-break people were drifting in. One little covey of older ladies in the corner booth were taking it all in, so the word would be around soon. I wondered what it would be like, to be a normal woman with lady friends. During my marriage, I wasn't allowed to have friends. Henri feared they would find out something to spoil his game. There were so many things I had missed. Tears welled up in my eyes just as Tricia returned with breakfast.

"Ma'am, are you all right?"

I smiled. "I'm getting more all right each day because of you all. Thanks."

We ate breakfast in companionable silence, exchanged lists for Tuesday and added a few more things.

"I'd like very much for you to meet Dave and Dodie Finch tomorrow, JW. When does your plane leave?"

"About six in the evening."

"Let's leave here early in the morning so we can have breakfast at their place before I switch cars. I'm going to need a four-wheel drive vehicle and I hoped you and Tim would help me pick something out. You can't be loaning me your Subaru forever. I think a truck would be useful. I'll call Dodie and see if we can arrange something. OK?"

He seemed a little uncomfortable with the invitation. I was more than a little annoyed.

"Dave has been my friend and colleague for many years. I promise you'll like them." He shrugged noncommittally.

"Michael said he was going to try to get tickets to a concert Thursday night, so Jenny and I won't be coming over together. I'm so hungry for good music; I'm looking forward to it. I think he promised Copeland's *Appalachian Spring*."

I waved as we left Gary's. "See you in a bit, Tricia."

JW wanted to walk home so I swung by the cottage for some more water bottles and took off for Abe and Kylie Lou's place. It was a gorgeous day. The sky was bright, pure blue and the trees were almost all leafed out. I wondered if the tulip poplar flowers would be out today, their jaunty yellow and orange flowers perched on all the branches. The sycamores were taking their time, testing the weather before trusting their tender new leaves to the spring days.

When I got to the Forester's I remembered Kyle Lou's instructions to quiet the dogs, and walked to the house under the watchful eyes but silence of the dog trio in the yard. Abe stepped out on the porch, nodding approval. "You learn fast, Ma'am. Welcome."

Our visit went well and we talked about their plans. I couldn't tell whether they were reconciled to leaving the farm to find another place, or whether he'd thought about alternative things he could do on his land. In the back of my mind, I was thinking about the possibility of letting them use my place, but hog farms smell the same everywhere and I might not want to be a close neighbor either.

We moved to the topic of family planning and I explained how it worked. "It'll work," I assured them. "It takes patience and commitment, but it works. If it's done carefully, it's as safe as the artificial methods you've chosen not to use."

Kylie Lou looked up and murmured, "It has to."

"I'm going to St Louis to help JW during his operation. I don't know when I'll be back but you just do as we practiced and write everything down."

Their reading level was better than I feared and we talked about books they might like to read. "There are some books we can read first. Do you have a babe in the eighth grade? My favorite book of all is *The Secret Garden* and it's about that level. Every one will be here after school is out and it will be even more fun."

It was almost twelve o'clock when I got to the farm and I really needed to get some last minute data for Dave before tomorrow. I unloaded stuff and headed for the lower left corner of the plot, taking notes as I went. I was lost in my work until the truck drove past on

the way up the hill. Tricia was in the middle and loving every moment of it. The kitchen was clean enough to eat in but the porch
swing beckoned and we decided to eat outside. It was a generous
meal. JW said the extra was in case we wanted to work until dark.

"Don't you have packing you need to do?"

"Not much. I don't have many clothes; remember? I have hardly
more than the ones on my back. Millie did a kind job making things
I can put on myself, treasures really. I'll almost miss them. Maybe
sometimes I'll wear them anyway, to keep me humble."

The kids needed to leave so Tim wouldn't miss baseball practice.
The Legion season began soon and everyone was fired up to start.
Luckily, Tuesday was a day off so he could drive one vehicle to Pittsburgh and help take JW to the plane while I returned the Lexus to
the airport.

When I worked backwards through Tuesday, I knew everything
wouldn't get done. It was curious how much it mattered to me that
JW and Dave should meet. I decided it was more important than
some of the shopping, and hoped that Dave would have time for us
and didn't have an early lab or something.

JW and I got to work on the last room, sorting, cleaning and
packing. We wiped down the walls and floor with strong soap and
Lysol and called it done.

I slipped out to the front porch. "Want a bite to eat before we go
home?"

"Sounds good. I could use a bottle of water too. I hope the well
test reports come soon so we can use the water in back. I think
we've done well on the cleaning for only one week's work."

I reached out to touch his shoulder. "I couldn't have done it
without your help. I hope you've saved what you might want later."

"It's good to get this part done so you can feel it's your house.
Then, how about helping me with the house in town? All my folks'
stuff needs going through. I didn't feel like it until now. You're a
breath of fresh air, Sara Harvey, and a bucket of soapy water."

We were both laughing as we carried the last boxes to the car. "I
like to hear you laugh, JW, do you sing? I expect you have a lovely
baritone voice."

"Some nights during med school, music was the only thing that
kept me sane."

As we went back to the house to close up, I motioned to him to
sit. "Could we stay just a few minutes more, to put the world to
bed?"

He smiled as he nodded assent. "I know you love the twilight. I
do too. It covers up a multitude of sins and lets you see only the essence of form."

"Do you know any lullabies? I usually sing one for my lost daughter, Dove, in the evening. Do you know a Scottish one I could learn?

After a quiet moment, he began to sing an old lament in Gaelic. When he translated it for me, I knew it wasn't for Dove.

"What was your baby sister's name?"

"Melanie Jane" he whispered. "That was for her."

"May I sing one for her too?" As he nodded yes, I began my favorite French lullaby, the one I sang for Dove the day she was taken away and for most nights since. When I finished, we were both crying.

"Do you know the children's duet from *Hansel and Gretel*, the one about guardian angels? Let's sing that."

We were standing on the porch. The sound was incredibly beautiful. When we finished, I whispered, "Let's have Christmas here and invite everyone we care about. We'll sing carols and fill our hearts with love."

He bowed his head and put his lips to my hands. "How much more love can we bear?"

As we made the night rounds to close up the house, JW touched the walls and doorframes, almost in benediction. I hoped he was saying goodbye to his childhood memories of Melanie Jane's death, and was laying them to rest.

We pulled in the driveway just as Tim wheeled in from baseball practice. I stuck my head out the window. "How soon can you roll out in the morning? We're going to buy a truck tomorrow and run all over town, two trips to the airport and first thing, breakfast with some special people.

I turned to JW. "May I use your phone? I'd rather owe you than the Greers since there may be more calls while you're gone."

I found Dave and Dodie at home and we made arrangements for an early breakfast at their place. I took the Honda to fill it up with gas and give it a washing. The car was covered with dust and looked pretty forlorn after its time in the country. Had it been only a week?

It was a lovely evening and the Greers were sitting in their Secret Garden when I got to the cottage. They were leaving on Thursday to be gone several weeks and Margot was traveling with them as far as NY to catch her plane to France. They agreed the arrangement to house sit for JW was perfect and I promised to do my moving out of the cottage Wednesday morning. I thanked them again for their hospitality and said goodbye.

I fell asleep trying to figure out how I could get some clothes shopping in before Thursday night. Better let tomorrow develop as it could. The most important thing was getting JW to his plane on time. I knew that Michael would be very angry if JW didn't get there Wednesday morning to start work.

It was another night of bad dreams. Margot came in several times to waken me from them. The second time she was crying. "Ma'am, you mustn't cry out Jamie's name. What will happen to you if you do it in Michael's bed?"

I clung to her, terrified. "Something needs to happen soon or I'll be in real trouble and so will JW. Margot, sing to me; sing a lullaby, a love song, a happy song. I know; I'll sing one for you first." The jaunty drinking song from my college days popped into my head and I began to sing. After several verses I could breathe again and began to relax.

It was Margot's turn next and she began with one of my favorites of the *Songs of the Auvergne*. Her voice was lovely and grew stronger as she offered her gift to me. When she finished we hugged each other and I asked, "Do you think that I shouldn't go to St. Louis to help with the operation?"

She considered carefully. "No, I think you must go, because you haven't made up your mind about Michael Cameron and you will have a chance to see him in his own setting, the one in which you will need to fit. I hope that he will see you, as you really are, and not as the person you think he wants to see. I wish I weren't going away right now. I would have gone with you."

It was a few hours until dawn and we both fell into exhausted sleep.

CHAPTER SIX

Tim and JW were waiting when I went by to give them the map to Dave's place in NE Pittsburgh. We were aiming for seven o'clock. I thought maybe they would hang out on the corner until I got there but Tim was pulling in the drive as I rounded the corner of Dave's street. I still hadn't figured out why JW didn't want to meet Dave. Maybe I'd have a clue soon. Maybe it was his handicap, but I didn't think so. There was something else bothering him.

Breakfast was delightful; tiny dollar-sized pancakes with fruit and syrup and eggs and bacon. It was surprising how comfortable Tim was with strangers. His conversation was intuitive and interesting. He admired the bungalow restoration Dave and Dodie were doing and asked knowledgeable questions about millwork and fixtures. JW was so quiet that I had to give him the benefit of the doubt against his apparent surly mood. He was really hurting and I didn't know how to help.

Dave didn't need to leave for campus for several hours yet. Dear Mr. Vaughan whispered to me, "Persuade JW to stay and visit while you and Tim go to trade in the car and start scouting for the truck."

I never argue. I just do what he says, and was surprised when JW agreed. Tim and I took off with both vehicles, dropped off the Lexus and started the truck search, used ones first. We looked at several showrooms on the way back and ended up a little late. Dave was just heading out the door to class.

Tim went around the house to the patio. As I paused on the steps, Dave gave my hand a squeeze. "I think he's OK now, Sara. I told him a little bit about what you do for a living and he told me about his big dream to become a Music Therapist. He doesn't want to go back to being a surgeon and he was afraid to tell any one.

"I didn't know he knew Jenny Cameron. It's worrisome he thinks Jenny's not what she appears to be. I couldn't tell him the truth just now. Take care."

He set off toward campus with books under both arms. I stood on the top step, puzzled by his parting comment. What did he mean about Jenny?

JW and Tim were visiting with Dodie on the back patio when I went around the house to get them. "I wish we had time to stay and visit but everyone has work to do. Thanks for the nice breakfast. I may be flying low through here tomorrow morning on the way to the airport. I think I'll go over a couple of days early to do some shopping. After a year in black, I'm ready for lavender and apricot and pale blue."

We took off to start an earnest truck search. Dave had set my mind at ease about some of my concerns and JW did seem different, as though his mind were made up about something and he was committed to it. We went to several truck places and couldn't find what I wanted anywhere. Finally, I started dealing for a new one. Tim was more helpful than JW, maybe because he knew he'd probably get to drive it. Well, we got down to color and I asked how long to get the forest green. The salesman shrugged his shoulders. "No one has ever asked for it, it'll take a while."

I left JW's phone number and told him to leave a message and a price for the package.

"That's it," I mumbled, "No more truck stuff today." I was exhausted and discouraged. How could I possibly shop for clothes now?

It was several hours until JW needed to be at the airport so I asked Tim "Was there anything you wanted to do today? With only the Subaru we'll need to stay together."

"Tricia said if I got to the right place she would really like a new sweater, like the one you have. She thinks the colors you wear are so cool."

"I'm afraid it won't be easy. I made the sweater from hand-dyed wool. We'll find something nice for her though. What's on your list, JW?"

"I need a couple of shirts and a pair of Dockers and some kind of light sweater."

So we headed out to the nearest shopping mall and spent some time finding clothes. I was careful to let Tim help JW and after we paid for the stuff, they went back to the dressing room so JW could put on a new shirt. We found a lovely sage green sweater for Tricia. It would be perfect with her auburn hair and hazel eyes.

When we finished, JW said, "Now it's your turn Sara. We'll be brave and follow you into the mystery of ladies' wear."

I was very fortunate. I found not only the dress but also the color I wanted. Carrying it to the dressing room, I made the men promise to be honest about how it looked. When I stepped out to model the dress, Tim was the first to comment. "Wow, Ma'am, you're beautiful!"

I wasn't sure what they were expecting; a bare back, 10" above the knee, low in front? Instead, I had chosen a high neck with lace, a solid bodice and gossamer silk sleeves. Tiny indigo buntings embroidered in clusters cascaded down the sleeves and slim calf length skirt. The dress was pale apricot color.

As I glanced at JW, my heart turned over. He was looking at me as though I'd climbed up out of the secret places in the earth. He whispered, "My wood sprite. Every man at the concert will be fighting for your attention and every woman will be jealous of your beauty and strength."

When we headed for the airport, JW wanted to be dropped off, but I wouldn't do it. "No, I refuse to throw you out the door to go sit alone for hours. We're coming with you. Besides, the chintzy airline probably isn't going to give you supper and it's been a long time since breakfast. Let's park and see what we can find to graze on."

JW repacked his bag to include the rest of his new clothes while we locked my things up, hiding the packages in the trunk. I certainly didn't want to have my precious dress stolen.

I was more than ready to head out for Greers when JW went down the ramp to board. I took the Subaru back to the cottage for the last time. Hank and Millie were still in the garden. The fragrances of lily of the valley, lilac and herbs had settled with the night air into an enveloping shawl. The stars glistened and winked and a shooting star sailed past us on its way to earth. I made a wish and then greeted my friends. "Too long a day for this lady, I'm exhausted. Tell me about your trip coming up. No sleuthing, I hope?"

Hank got up to pour some lemonade for us. "My ancestors were Scandinavian, and we're going to meet some cousins, uncles and aunts in Norway. We've been sending letters back and forth for years and finally decided to go in person."

I was a bit envious of their upcoming adventures. "How exciting. Perhaps next year I can make a trip to Scotland and England to trace my ancestors."

I turned to Millie. "I wanted you to know how much it's meant to me to be taken into your community. I've met so many wonderful people and they'll be good neighbors, I'm sure. The progress on the farm is heartening. I can't believe how much we've accomplished in so short a time. You'll be surprised when you get back. Maybe I'll even be moved in by then."

I caught the glance that passed between Hank and Millie. Again, I'd neglected to include Michael in my life plans. I had to admit then; my problem wasn't going to go away. I said a few words of thanks to Margot for her kindness and wished her a good visit too.

"I've decided to spend tomorrow at the farm, after I get moved over to JW's. If I don't see you in the morning, have a good visit and thanks again."

I slipped away to the cottage, making mental lists of all the things I needed to do before I left for St. Louis. Since my dress was no longer an issue, Thursday was soon enough to leave. If it weren't for the bribe of the concert I would have waited until Friday night. My feelings about the upcoming surgery were mixed. Somehow we would all be very different afterwards.

I took a few minutes to pack my things for a quick leave-taking in the morning, put all my possessions in the back seat of the Subaru, and then returned to the cottage for the last time.

I decided not to wake Tim early. I left my things in the Subaru and headed out of town about seven o'clock. The weather was supposed to be cooler but there hadn't been the right kind of soaking rains. The fields were beginning to look parched and some of the newly seeded corn didn't have enough water to germinate. The forest floor was tinder dry. In the heat of the day, the new leaves were limp and pale. At least the tulip poplars were in full bloom and the dogwood and redbud still glistened in the understory.

I hoped to get a start on the watering system and the garden needed hand watering before I left. One more round of observations and the data for Dave would be ready to go. Maybe there would even be time to just sit for a while later in the day. I was becoming very attached to the serenity of my place.

With all my times at the farm, only Abe's truck had appeared uninvited on my stretch of road. You can imagine the feeling in the pit of my stomach when I reached the last rise and found a car parked in my space in front of the porch; a mixture of territoriality and terror. Who could be up so early and have business with me?

I pulled in next to the dark blue Subaru rental car, leaned down and loosened the catches on my boots. I hadn't used the knives for several months, but this might be the reason for my many hours of practice with them. No one was visible on the porch or in the yard or around the buildings. I felt more resigned than anything else as I stepped around the side of the house.

From there, I could see a man sitting on the stone bench. He would have known of my arrival from the dust cloud on the road. When I drew closer he rose and started to move down the path. He was tall, and moved with the lithe and supple motion of a well-trained body.

His clothing was simple and fit well. I took my eyes off his to glance down at his feet.He was wearing moccasins! I searched his face. The high cheekbones, dark hair and stunning complexion suggested I was in the presence of an extremely attractive American Indian.

He stopped at a polite distance. "I search for Madam Henri Lambert." He was speaking impeccable French and seemed comfortable doing it.

"I am she." As I answered in French, he handed me a small bouquet of tulip poplar flowers, freshly picked from the woods.

I murmured thanks. "How did you know these are my favorite flowers?" I hadn't spoken French in more than a year, except to Margot and it felt a bit awkward.

He smiled. "Dr. Campbell told me of your feelings for these flowers."

I stepped back, considering his face. "May I ask why you are here?"

"Ah," he spoke with admiration, "Two questions in proper order, there are only three more and all will be revealed. I was told you have a mind like a steel trap."

"Well, answer the second question so we can get on with it." I retorted. Actually the parrying with words was a delight, and he had disarmed me.

He stepped closer. "I am here because I have been asked to lend you a hand today with whatever chores you may desire and then to escort you to St. Louis as quickly as possible."

I turned partially away from him, wondering how I could reach my weapons with the least motion. "And who told you my mind was like a steel trap?"

"Wonderful. That's three. Professor Dave Finch said it, when we were discussing you just yesterday on the phone."

Now I was really worried. This man knew far too much about me to be a stranger, and he knew one of my old friends as well as a new one. I thought frantically for the next correct question. This was ridiculous. I wondered what would happen if I failed to guess the last two.

"What's your connection with Dave?"

"Ah, you stray from the track. You're getting soft. I sometimes work for him, but you will not reach your goal now."

I shrugged my shoulders. "What is your name?"

"Jacques Grayson."

The name meant nothing to me. "Well, I admit to becoming soft, and I have perhaps lost your respect. However, if JW sent you to help, I can certainly use it. Have you had breakfast?"

He smiled. "The last question makes up for the others you missed. I'm starving. Flying after midnight has lost its fascination."

By the last statement he had lapsed into English and we walked in companionable silence to the back door of the house. If he came to help, we might as well get started.

"I planned to be here all day," I explained, "First I open all the windows to put the screens in. It's going to be a long struggle, getting the mouse smell out after all the years of neglect. You go clockwise, I'll go counter clockwise and we'll bring in the food and water from the car."

He reached in his pocket and pulled out a house key. At my quizzical look, he explained. "Dr. Campbell gave it to me in case you weren't here."

Now I was angry. "And have you already been through my things; do you know that I drink tea, not coffee, and that there is a mysterious room with no apparent entrance?"

His smile was gentle. "I was going to ask you about that."

I didn't like his familiarity or his teasing, but he was there for the day and I decided to go along with the game, whatever it might be. He was much taller than I and probably much stronger, and it looked like his job required him to be in fighting shape. If he knew Dave, there would be no element of surprise in any self-defense moves. I decided to be vigilant until I figured out what he really wanted. I was weary; it seemed like too much work to figure it out.

Then, a shiver of fear ran down my spine and cold sweat broke out on my face and hands. I'd completely forgotten about Nelson since coming to Pennsylvania, but surely she hadn't forgotten me. Remembering the blind terror of those last few weeks in Spokane caused me to stumble at the doorsill. Jacques was there so quickly I didn't fall.

He held me in his arms. "Are you all right, Madam Lambert?"

I was trembling. "No, not really, but thanks for saving my face."

My head lay for a moment cradled in his arm. The scent of his young, freshly scrubbed skin and the trace of mint on his breath brought back a forgotten memory. I looked up quickly and then turned away. The memory was nagging at my consciousness. I know this man. Where? ... Where?

He went out to bring in the food and I made some tea. We sat on the porch swing and ate powdered sugar doughnuts, brushing the fallen sugar onto the floor. I sighed. "I love this time of day, still cool enough to work hard, and filled with scents and sounds of the creatures who share my space. Let's do the data gathering first and then the digging. Watering last since it's easy. It will be so nice to have the irrigation system in before summer comes. And if you're determined to be my guard dog, we have a date to watch Tim's baseball team play tonight."

We worked smoothly together as he took notes from my dictation. He had no trouble with the Latin names and used all the proper spelling, punctuation, and abbreviations. This man was very well educated and personable. We ended up at the car and I packed the papers in my briefcase. The coded note accompanying them lay on top. I thought about adding a postscript, asking about Grayson, and then decided against it. The job wasn't done and something wasn't right about the way it was playing out.

We took a break and loaded up on water. It was dry and dusty work and my mouth felt like I'd been eating mud pies. I let my guard down a little more and was jolted to alertness as Mr. Vaughan whispered, "Honey, it's time to be vigilant. Be careful whom you trust, it's not over yet."

"Alright," I answered.

Grayson was watching me and said, "Are you feeling well, Madam?"

I smiled. "Just talking with an old friend. He shares his thoughts when I need help."

"Ah, Mr. Vaughan from your childhood?"

That did it. I felt like a frantic, trapped animal. Reaching down, I pulled the knives from their places in my boots. At least I would go down fighting. I stood half crouching, facing him on the porch. "Who are you? How do you know so much about me?"

My heart sank as I watched him move away and pull two knives from some hidden place at his belt.

He returned to speaking French as he said with politeness, "I was hoping this wouldn't happen, Madam, but since it has, let us call it a make up lesson. I need to know how much you remember. I also need to know whether you have stayed in condition. Please be kind enough to put your knives away for now and I will do the same."

Then, I recognized his calm cadence and gentle voice. We went to the area in front of the porch and as I closed my eyes, he began talking me through the stretching exercises, loosening me up for the real work. We fell into the well-remembered rhythm of numbers and instructions as he corrected with patience and firmness. By the end of the hour I was exhausted, but he kept pushing.

Finally I made a poor choice of space and he grabbed my wrist. He whirled me around and took the other. "I was right. You have become soft. To your last breath, you must be in control of your body. It is your only freedom."

At least I had worked him hard enough to make him break a sweat. The scent of his body brought back memories of nights of practice when the only thing protecting my sanity was his teaching, his touch, his whispered encouragements and insistence that I must keep in shape and keep practicing; that I never knew when it might save my life.

During the years he had been my guard and teacher, we always practiced in the dark, or I wore a silk scarf on my eyes. The fighting techniques were to be used in darkness and relied on touch alone. He spoke only French and I never saw him during the day, even when I knew that he was guarding me in my Idaho field plots in summer.

I stayed close to his exquisitely trained body, feeling his strength and power. "Dear friend, I named you Shadow Dancer. I have missed you."

He leaned over me. "Move slowly, and walk toward the house. I'll be beside you. We have uninvited company and we need to get out of here."

When we reached the porch steps, I turned to take a dry dishtowel from the railing and saw someone lurking by the sheds.

Jacques whispered, "Just one, probably a scout to watch what we're doing. You don't have very nice neighbors, Madam. He's the redneck who accosted me at the grocery store earlier this morning. We need to change our plans for tonight. We can't afford a confrontation at the baseball game. Tim and Thad will understand. We'll have to leave the chores for another time. Is there anything here you would miss if something happened to the house?"

My heart sank. "Oh, you don't think he'd do something that awful, do you?"

"Yes. I'm afraid I do. It has happened before."

So we opened the laboratory room, wrapped the microscopes in quilts and loaded them, along with my precious research material, papers and books into Jacques' car. Then we transferred my notes for Dave, my suitcase, backpack and my new dress.

"Does JW have fire insurance on his car?"

I nodded yes as I began to cry. "Jacques, I'm frightened. I don't want you to be hurt because of me."

His smile was gentle. "I would do it even if it weren't my job."

We closed up the house and locked what we could. I said a silent goodbye to it and hoped the man would only vandalize it. In my heart though, I knew what would happen. At least there were no animals to be hurt, and the doves would nest again.

Jacques stepped to the car. "I'm counting on him being a coward and arsonist at heart or we won't make it down the hill. Sorry about your garden. I'll try to make it up to you somehow."

We slipped into the car and started down the road. The first couple of hundred yards he was weaving all over. When I realized what he was doing I was really scared. The dust cloud we stirred up saved us. No one could have gotten a good look to shoot, with the dust swirling between us. We hit the gravel road and headed for town.

He reached over to take my hand. "Not the way I intended the day at the farm to end. Is there anything at Dr. Campbell's that you

61

need to take to St. Louis? Oh, I forgot in all the excitement, I brought you a note from JW. It's in my right hand shirt pocket."

I fished it out. It wasn't sealed, just folded over, so he probably expected Jacques to read it too. After I glanced at it, I told him to head for Pittsburgh. My fists were clenching and unclenching as I teetered between frustration and anger. "How could you? It would have been so much easier if you'd delivered the note first."

He slowed to the speed limit as we merged onto the highway. "There were some things I needed to know, since I haven't worked with you for several years; whether you remembered me, but most important, whether I could trust you with my life?"

I needed a dozen deep breaths to calm down. "I assume you read the note. What's going on about the next two days?"

He was silent for a long time. "I'm sorry, Madam Lambert. I can't tell you yet. All I can do is to ask for your patience and obedience."

JW had said in the note that he didn't want me to come over until just in time to appear on Saturday morning, but if I insisted on coming for the concert, please not to wear the new outfit but something unobtrusive and downright dowdy. Jacques was in charge so I took orders. We stopped at Dave's to drop off the notes, books and microscopes. We left my precious work boots and all our hardware.

Dave was home and helped us unload. He said, "I'm so sorry Sara. I had no idea this could happen here, in this day and age. We'll try to make it up to you somehow."

We made it to St. Louis by evening. As we pulled into his place, the garage door opened and closed silently and he helped me out. "Come on, we both need some food. Then we'll figure out what to do next. You're having quite a problem with names these days aren't you? What do you wish for me to call you?"

I shrugged. "I'm as confused as everyone else. I don't know. I guess Sara Harvey."

He smiled. "That was the clue you missed during our guessing game; when I used your married name. Besides, I needed to know if you had made a psychological breakthrough about Lambert, as JW suggested. The crew has been terribly worried about you this last year for lots of reasons. Dave chose not to tell you today; we just got word Nelson was murdered last night."

That did it. In very lady-like fashion, I crumpled into his arms. I heard his mumbled "Oh, shit!" as the cricket chorus began. When I came to, he helped me up and into the house.

His home had such an interesting and unusual layout. The rooms all faced a large interior patio, with trees, brick paths and stone hardscape. A waterfall cascaded from one corner and even though it was the middle of the afternoon, the lighting was soft like moonlight in the gathering dusk. I was enchanted. "What a wonderful sanctuary."

He nodded, "Sanctuary is an apt description. I do as I like; wear what I please and practice many hours at a time."

He touched a small panel on the wall and set some controls. One of the mirrored glass walls slid back to show a very large empty room lined with mirrors. It looked like a ballet practice room, except part of the floor was wood and part was stone. In an inset space below the fountain in the corner, there was rock and debris and water about 6 inches deep.

I think he was enjoying my surprise. "We'll get to work after we have some supper."

He returned the wall to its place and we took a short tour of the rooms. The guest quarters opened into the exercise room so people working out wouldn't be seen by casual outsiders. I thought there weren't many of those, since the house didn't have any of the normal family rooms. There was no living room or dining room set up for entertaining.

The kitchen was very structured and neat. Everything was behind doors or built in. Nothing sat on the stone counters or wood floor; the cupboards had no handles but were opened from hidden recesses in their base. There was no glass in the cabinet doors and the gleaming cherry wood traveled the walls and hung from the central ceiling in sinuous curves. At one end of the room a huge walk-in pantry housed shelves for food storage and a large freezer. The indirect lighting shimmered off the uneven levels of the ceiling.

"Jacques, it's lovely. Who designed this house for you?"

He hesitated a moment, perhaps not wanting to share such an intimate piece of information. "Jenny Cameron. She did it when I came to St. Louis several years ago."

He was watching me and wouldn't have missed my look of surprise.

"JW Campbell and I were in the same med school class and he recommended Jenny to me just before she decided to specialize in the work she does now. She works for Dave Finch now, and uses the Retrofit Engineering as a comfortable cover."

My heart sank. Another one of the people I cared about was involved in our dangerous business. JW had been correct in his reservations about Jenny.

"And JW?"

"No, but he'll help us keep an eye on you while you're in St. Louis."

"Does he know about Jenny's work?"

"I think he suspects, though I don't think she's talked to him about it. But now, we need some supper. Any requests?"

I stepped closer and touched his arm. "I really need some comfort food. Could I make some milk toast without smelling up the kitchen?"

He laughed. "The exhaust fans are heavy duty here; sometimes people want broiled meat or strange fish. Toast won't be a problem. Perhaps I'll join you. It hasn't been an easy day, has it?"

The cooking pans were stored in wonderful pull out shelves under the island. The dark glass surface of the range top and the down draft broiler were perfect, set into the stone counter. I stood waiting for the toast to brown. He brought butter and milk and two handsome stoneware bowls with patterns of oak leaves in the bottom. The soft swirling colors of greens and browns were incredibly beautiful. The milk heated quickly and we sat down at the island counter on stools formerly hidden in the side but now pulled out from the counter.

Jacques turned to me with a smile. "Margot told me to be prepared for your request. She's terribly worried about you. She almost didn't go to France on her trip."

"Even Margot?"

He was almost apologetic. "Well, actually Thad. He's worked for us since he came over from France many years ago. He's one of the best in the business. Also, the Greer's cottage is a safe house for us and Margot helps when she's needed."

My mind was working swiftly with this new information. Dave probably alerted the Greers to my coming and asked them to keep an eye out for me. I finished my bowl but it hadn't done much to comfort me.

I was so weary and frightened. "Jacques, I feel so inadequate. How will I ever make up for so many years of total isolation? I did my job but I didn't know how much danger we were in or how many people's lives were at stake or how many different people were helping. I'm not frightened, I'm terrified!"

He reached out and took my hand in his. "Madam Lambert, if all goes as planned, in seventeen days, the project will be over.

"What project?"

"We'll talk about it after we get to work."

As we finished the supper dishes, I remembered the mail I'd picked up yesterday. "I think there was a note forwarded from the drop mail. Would you go get my case, please? Let's see what it is."

The note brought devastation to each of us, for different reasons. The frantic and pitiful message was from Nelson, saying she could no longer protect herself and she would be dead by the time the note reached me. She said goodbye and that I was her special and precious friend.

Then the real blow came. She believed someone had persuaded one of the other operatives named Larry that she was working for Andretti and was trying to kill me. She said Larry would kill her to get her out of the way."

"My God!" whispered Jacques. "Another death laid at Andretti's door."

We clung to each other, each lost in our own thoughts. Mine, of a dear and valiant young woman, sent as my maid and helper but also as my protector. I remembered the terror of the four obvious attempts on my life in the last year. If I hadn't left for Pennsylvania on a whim, I might be dead too.

Then, I wondered if the project I was to take part in had to do with Andretti.

Jacques turned away. "I need to call Dave. I'll show you to your guest room. Please make use of anything there and let me know what else you need. I'll be back to get you for practice."

I found a neatly folded selection of workout clothes and a bath well supplied with towels and robes. In the closet I found several outfits the right size and design for what was ahead. It was still quite warm outside but the air conditioning was on in the house. I dressed and stretched out on the floor to rest and wait. Jacques found me sound asleep a few moments later.

His gentle touch wakened me. "Dave sends his deepest regrets on the loss of your friend, Nelson. He also said you might as well know now; the farmhouse and outbuildings were burned to the ground. The arsonist must have started the fire with the car. It exploded and the house went fast. The firemen tried to save the big trees behind the house, but the fire jumped the firebreak. Most of the farm is in ruins. The fire went up over the ridge and burned out a small cabin too. The fire marshal's evidence said arson and it will be in all the papers by morning."

I sighed. No tears would come now. They would have to wait until the affair was over. Then he sat beside me on the floor and began to explain what we were planning to do and how things were changed with the new information. "I tried to persuade Dave not to assign you to do this. You're too exhausted and upset to be safe. I told him I wasn't sure I could get you back into fighting shape in just two weeks. He said I had to."

Jacques got up and held out his hands to me. "So, my fighting partner, let's get started."

We slipped into the comforting warm-up. He whispered instructions in French while I began to feel my muscles stretch and work, calling out for oxygen and rest but getting neither. Each hour we rested for ten minutes. I fell asleep each time. We had done just bodywork, no weapons.

Besides protecting myself from surprises, I had one job to do alone, with a space of about twenty seconds when no one could protect me and my own skill would be all I had.

After four hours, he decided to stop. "Go soak in a hot tub and get some sleep. Let's try to get started by seven o'clock in the morning. When we take our first break you can give Angela your shopping list if you need something. You need to be dressed as a mouse Saturday morning. Do you have a rosary with you?" I nodded yes. "Well, you'll need it too. I don't want you to think we don't care about JW's surgery. We do care very much and you are an integral part of the process. Good night, Sara."

I managed to get cleaned up, set the alarm for six thirty and fell into a deep, troubled sleep. Several hours later, Jacques wakened me from a screaming nightmare. His gentle arms held me as I sobbed, "How did you know to come?"

"I have a listening device like the one at the cottage. Margot warned me about your nightmares."

I calmed down and only little hiccoughs escaped. He gave me his handkerchief as he asked, "What can I do to help?"

I reached up to touch his face. My voice dropped to a whisper. "Please, Jacques. I want you so much. Kiss me. Hold me. Make love to me." Tears streamed down my face.

Jacques stroked my hair and gave me a gentle kiss. "I love you too much to ask you to be my lover. We can't do it."

"Why not?"

"Because we're not married and are not likely to be. We mustn't break God's heart by tempting the other to sin."

I sighed with disappointment, knowing in my heart that he was right. "Is all of life like this? Having to give up so much for honor and trust? I don't even know what happiness might be like. I have always done the right thing. Must I die without knowing a man's love?"

He held me in his arms and rocked me gently. "Sara, we don't know what may be in store for either of us. You were Lambert's prisoner for almost 25 years. You have many experiences ahead of you and good years to do them in." He was smiling now. "I hope they're not as exciting as the Roadhouse caper. I hear Thad wants to recruit you for the baseball team."

I was resigned to his wisdom, at least for now. "Do you believe it's possible to love more than one man at a time?"

"Yes, I think so, especially someone as empathic and loving as you are."

"May I love you then, no matter what else may happen to us?"

He rose from my bed. "Perhaps, but not until we finish our job. It's dangerous to be distracted by personal affairs while we're working together, in fact, Dave would be furious."

"Let's not tell him then." I rose and touched his arm. "Jacques, what is your cover now?"

He took my hands and kissed them. "I'm Michael Cameron's anesthesiologist."

My God! I thought, what a tangled web we weave, or was it perhaps planned for us to be the others' keeper? The rest of the short night was dreamless.

Thursday's workouts brought waves of exhaustion, as my little-used muscles were coaxed back into working order. Fifty minutes to work, ten minutes to rest each hour, two very light meals and a nap tucked into the afternoon. We didn't stop until eight in the evening. I remembered the concert I was missing, and promised myself that I would immerse myself in an orgy of concerts and singing and dancing when this affair was finally over.

As we finished, Jacques stepped to a cupboard against the wall and brought out a box. It was designed very like the sensuous, carved cherry cabinets in the kitchen and I suspected the same artisan had made it. Inside were two of the most beautiful and unusual knives I'd ever seen. The blades were about seven inches long with handles almost flat but ending in a rounded knob. They had the characteristic patterning of Damascus steel. He lifted one of them from its cradle of soft deerskin and laid it in my hand. It was heavier than it looked and viciously sharp.

I looked up with surprise at his sigh of relief. "We feared it might not fit your hand. They belonged to another warrior woman from a long time ago. The knives are worn sideways at the belt and thrown underhand for a single strike. Your job the next two weeks is to learn how to throw them while talking and moving into position. At the moment it's thrown, other knives will also be in the air. You must learn how to get out of the way. Andretti is right-handed and carries a handgun in his right pocket. We are counting on him using his usual two-handed shooting style. On Sunday I'll give you the lines you're to say, including the ones to signal us to attack."

"Jacques," I murmured, as I returned the knives to their case, "Why couldn't you just shoot him or dispose of him in some other way?"

He shook his head. "I don't know. Maybe closure for all of us, a communal execution, an answer for all our friends and partners he has murdered or betrayed."

"And Dave decided, without asking me, that I was to be included?"

He sighed, "I follow orders. Dave said we needed to do this for you."

I turned away. "It's against my religious beliefs to murder, Dave knows that."

Jacques finished the conversation. "Yes, but this is justifiable self-defense against a proven murderer; and we can't protect you forever."

I was puzzled. "Why would Andretti agree to come to the Idaho Rendezvous? Wouldn't he suspect an ambush of some kind if he's done what we've been told is his doing?"

Jacques gave a considered answer. "I suspect he and Dave have a different relationship we don't know about, perhaps different issues. We don't know what may have happened between them."

I turned away in exhaustion. My energy tank read empty as Jacques finished the conversation. "It was a satisfactory session today. You still have spunk, Sara, but we have a long way to go before I'll be comfortable about your safety. If you're willing, we need to practice very early. I'm on duty tomorrow morning six to two. Let's do one session at four o'clock before I leave. Then you can go back to bed. Angela will be on duty here in the morning at five o'clock to keep an eye on things. Tomorrow I'll show you some of the other rooms in the house. I expect you'll want to spend some time in the sanctuary tomorrow night. Good night, Sara, sleep well."

I felt safe in my room, though a little trapped. I wasn't used to being inside with no windows or outside air, no scent of flowers or soil or rain. Sanctuary and prison swirled and exchanged places in my mind as I prepared for bed and a very short night.

The next morning the workout was going well after I loosened up. Maybe I wasn't such a wreck after all. Suddenly, I found myself flat on the floor with an angry teacher leaning over me. Jacques was furious. "You're not concentrating, Sara. You're careless. You're spoiled. You think someone will always be around to protect you. Well they won't. They can't. Only you can do it. Fight! Your survival depends on it. Put everything else out of your head; your mind must be empty except for that one thing."

He frightened me into trying harder. Quickly, he corrected me, "Don't try harder; try smarter. Who is it? What are they planning to do? Do you want to stay and fight or escape? When you're working you can't be distracted, and right now you have to work every moment to try to stay alive."

We started again. At the end of the session, he bowed to me.

"Much better. Now sleep another couple of hours. Give Angela your shopping list and she'll go out this afternoon when Tim gets here."

Now I was even more worried. Tim hadn't planned to come over for the operation. And why wasn't he staying with Michael and Jenny? But I was glad he was coming and said so. Tomorrow I would see my men doing their other jobs. I wondered how JW was and how the whole affair would work out.

I drifted off to sleep for a couple of hours and then went back to the training room. I needed extra work to strengthen my abdominal muscles, since anything hanging out could be neatly sliced off if I made a miscued move with a knife. I began wondering about a clothing design to hide the knives and yet leave safe access to them at the right time. In a few moments I designed the outfit in my head and sketched the design for the belt and buckle to hold the knives. Tim got there around noon and he took the pattern to the craftsman.

Then I thought about tomorrow's work and what outfit to wear. Angela checked in on the intercom and we got together to make a shopping list. When I told her what I wanted to do, she was surprised. "Are you sure? Your hair is so lovely."

When she got back, we put on a mousy, brownish-gray rinse, even on the eyebrows. Then I put on the ankle-length navy skirt, plain white blouse and navy cardigan sweater.

"You look like a nun." Tim said.

"That's the idea."

After a simple supper, Jacques took me to the sanctuary. It was like a monk's cell carved into a cave, with an altar, a crucifix, a priedieu, and a small cot. The ceiling of the room was a large skylight. He closed the top and the room was bathed in luminescent shimmer. "Not as nice as being outdoors by moonlight in your field plots." He took my hand. "Sara, would you include me in your prayers tonight?"

"My prayers haven't been very effective for those I love. They didn't save Nelson or Margarite or prevent any of the other operatives from being murdered. Jacques, I'm frightened."

He didn't give me any comfort. "The plans have changed for tomorrow. You need to be ready by five o'clock since we're picking up Jenny. We'll take the car Tim rented. Good night."

I decided the monk's cell could wait until tomorrow night and returned to my room. When all was ready, I fell to my knees and wept.

CHAPTER SEVEN Jacques begins his story

I wasn't looking forward to this day one bit. It certainly wasn't the usual form of the operation and I was in the tricky position of having to anticipate what would be needed. I wasn't exactly sure what Sara's job was, or how long she would be able to do it. With all the other things coming up, I worried about her health and stamina. She and Jenny would be in the tiny cubicle for a long time, watching and doing their job.

I thought I'd better pack lunches for everyone. When I went to the kitchen, Tim was already up, bless him, and he started to put them together while I went to get the women. Sara was wearing a large, beautifully-crafted Russian cross around her neck with her navy blue outfit. Her hair was its original glistening halo of silver. She had wrapped the priedieu from the sanctuary in a blanket and was carrying it under her arm. As she went by into the hall, she said, "I will do my best for you today, Jacques. God be with you in your work."

We left in good time to reach the hospital at six. As the technician came to hook up the microphones and sound system, I gave Tim last minute instructions in case there were unwanted visitors.

When I glanced up into the observation area, every seat in the operating amphitheater was full. Word had gotten out about what would be happening today. All of the students and many professors were waiting with interest for the operation to begin. The seating was arranged so that Jenny and Sara were hidden from the rest of the onlookers. I checked the microphones and sound to make sure the women could hear our conversations at the operating table as well as talk to us. There was a second private line between JW and Sara that he could operate with his left hand.

At seven o'clock, Dr. Cameron began with explanations about how they would proceed and the special techniques to be used. Although I knew about the use of empathic help for anesthesia I had never taken part in an operation using such a person. We began the unusual protocol.

Sara had settled onto her kneeler and was praying softly, first for Michael, then for JW, then for all the surgical crew on the floor. JW was sitting upright, his arm cradled on the narrow, specially designed operating table.

Everyone in the room seemed to be holding their breath as Michael Cameron made the first incision. I'd always admired his teaching skills in the surgery, and today he was at his best. Jenny was listening to him as I talked to Sara, checking to see how JWs' pain level was. The small cubicle was sited so I could see into their space, while they needed to watch the monitor to see the operation in progress. Sara had not opened her eyes since the session began.

Her most important job today, was as an empath, channeling JW's pain so that he could remain alert and conscious with the least amount of anesthesia possible. If they could maintain the connection long enough, he would be able to help the surgeons by moving his hand and fingers when asked. I passed along the information to and from Michael when it was needed.

We were three hours into the session. Michael was able to free the wrist and return it to full mobility. The other two surgeons took over to work on the thumb. Now Sara was talking to JW. The connection was private and I didn't know what was said. Then, one of the other surgeons was speaking with Sara as they worked with the insertion of a piece of bone. The attachment of one of the thumb tendons couldn't be done during this surgery. It was a real disappointment and she began to cry.

I spoke to her. "You can't do it all by yourself, Sara. Remember you're part of a team. We know you're doing the best you can. Just try to keep going as long as you're able."

We'd been working six hours, and everyone needed a break. I gave JW a measured dose of pain medication while they put him down flat. The second crew was ready to work and began preparation for the next round. Neither Jenny nor Sara could eat so I took one of the lunches out into the gallery. I saw a stranger slip out the door just as I looked up. It wasn't Andretti.

The ladies took a break and Tim walked them up and down the hall outside surgery. Sara's color was a little better and she walked most of the kinks out of her legs. After they were safely settled inside their tiny space, Michael and I took a shower, put on clean scrubs and scrubbed up for the next round. People didn't give up their seats. Everyone was fascinated with the way the operation was progressing.

The other surgeons had finished the thumb before the break and we were beginning the index finger. This was the time when we'd know how well the fingers could be managed. So much tissue and bone was missing. It would be delicate work reconstructing the damaged areas. I always try to have hope, but the rest of the job looked almost impossible.

Sara spoke to me as we began. "JW won't be able to take much more, and I may not be able to help him much longer. Be prepared to put him under."

I could see her lips moving as she spoke to him. Tears were coursing down her cheeks. At the same moment JW moaned and passed out. Michael told me to put him under and after it was done I turned over the job to my assistant and dashed upstairs to the cubicle. Sara had collapsed onto the floor. I threw a towel over her face, grabbed her in my arms and raced out of the room and down the hall to the ER. She was feverish and her breath came in tiny gasps.

I made a quick report to the technicians. "I don't know what happened. Start from the beginning for a diagnosis. I'll be back when the surgery is over. Put her on the ninth floor in the locked ward when she recovers and don't let anyone into her room. Find a guard for her."

I didn't want to leave her but I had to get back to work. I showered again, put on new scrubs and scrubbed up again. Michael looked up when I returned. I shrugged my shoulders to say I didn't know what had happened and we returned to work. Now we realized how much more difficult it would be without Sara's help. JW was still unconscious, although I hadn't given him any more anesthetic.

The index finger was rebuilt with bone and then the decision had to be made about the last three fingers. Michael spoke quietly with Jenny. She told him that JW had asked to have the inoperable fingers set in the best position so the other fingers could play the piano.

It didn't mean that we wouldn't try again or think of some other way to work on them, but everyone was exhausted. We finished up resetting the last three fingers. Michael thanked the crew for their efforts and for working on a Saturday for him. We took JW to the fifth floor recovery room. I was concerned because he hadn't regained consciousness.

The trip to the ER to find out about Sara's condition was even more puzzling. She wasn't conscious either. Her vital signs were almost normal and her fever had gone down quickly with a wet sheet wrap. They said her temperature had been 104 degrees when she was brought in. We moved her upstairs to the locked ward. I was sitting with her when Jenny and Michael got there.

"What the hell's going on?" Michael growled.

I shook my head. "I wish I knew."

Jenny began to cry as Michael took her in his arms. "Honey, we did the best we could. We'll just have to wait and see how it turns out. Do you have any idea what happened? Did she say anything that would give us a clue?"

Jenny was sobbing now. "I only heard a little bit toward the end. She kept telling Jamie not to leave us. Then she said, 'Please don't try to climb it with only one hand'. That's when she started crying so hard."

She shuddered and turned away, "Sara worked so hard and she was in so much pain I almost couldn't bear it." She turned to look at her uncle, "How could you? How could you do it to her?"

Michael looked hurt and confused as he reached out to Jenny. "She asked to do it. I didn't know what she was going to try and I've never worked with an empath before. I don't think she knew what she was getting into. Maybe it was just too much for her system.

"Two people we love are in deep trouble right now. Would you and Jacques go sit with JW while I stay here with Sara?"

It was the first time I'd ever seen Michael Cameron cry. What he was saying to Sara was so intimate that Jenny and I hurried to leave the room.

JW was still lying on his back, his breathing was even and normal and his color was good. I showed Jenny the call button for the nurses' station. "They'll be here in 30 seconds flat. I need to get down to the ER to see if the records have any clues about what happened. I think there won't be any, but we need to try. I'm terribly sorry about the whole mess, Jenny."

She'd stopped crying and her face was all puffy and red. "It was unfair of me to be so hard on you guys. I was frantic. I couldn't interfere with what you were doing but I saw something awful happening.

"I'm more worried about Tim now. You know how he worships Jamie? I don't think we should have sent him away."

Just as she finished speaking, the door swung open and Tim stuck his head inside. "OK if I come in? I got to the parking lot and just turned around and came back. I want to sit with him too."

"Sure, in fact we're glad you did. Keep an eye on Jenny until I get back."

It was a long night for everyone except Sara and JW, who lay in their beds unaware of our increasing concern for them. Jenny and Tim had dropped off into a restless sleep and I was next to the bed cradling Jamie's left hand. I got the Bible out of the side-table drawer and began to read Luke out loud. He was always my favorite because he was a doctor too. The pager in my pocket was set to vibrate and I felt it just as JW stirred and opened his eyes.

He whispered, "Where's Sara? Is she all right?"

I answered the pager. It was Michael saying that Sara was awake and asking if JW was all right.

"We don't know what passed between those two during the operation and I figured it was none of our business.

73

Another set of reports from the lab was ready and I went to get them. Michael had requested some unusual tests and they all came back negative. Michael and I switched patients. I went to check on Sara, while he went down to look in on JW.

Sara didn't know what had happened to her or how she'd gotten to her room. She insisted on seeing JW. Since I wanted to take the lab reports down, I helped her into a wheelchair and we made the trip down to the fifth floor. Jenny and Tim headed back to Michael's place to get some real sleep and Michael had stepped out for a moment. The room was empty except for JW, resting in his bed with his eyes closed.

Sara rose from her wheelchair to stand by him. "Please leave us alone, Jacques."

I nodded as she turned back to speak with him. I opened the door and let it swing shut. No way was I going to leave her alone in his room. I stepped back into the shadows and waited.

Just as she leaned down to him and began speaking, Michael returned to the dimly lit room. He took one look at the figure bending over his patient and totally lost control. In two strides he was across the room, had grabbed the person by the hair and the back of the gown and thrown her away and down onto the floor.

He jabbed the nurse's station call button. "Whoever this person is, get her out of here." He screamed, "Nurse, NURSE!"

Sara got up from the floor and turned to face him. Her voice was filled with anger. "Michael Cameron, your violence terrifies me. Your arrogance breaks my heart. If you ever touch me or speak to me again as you just did, the Cameron clan be cursed forever."

She stood rock still during all this, until the end. Then, she crouched down and rising quickly flung her arms at his face, her fingers curved into a Celtic curse.

"My God!" I muttered, "I don't know who dug the deepest pit with that exchange."

The nurse came into the room just as I grabbed a blanket from the next bed and wrapped Sara tightly with it. "You need to get back to bed. JW will be better able to talk a little later."

I glanced over in time to see JW turn away. I'm sure he knew how explosive the situation was and didn't want to make it worse. I put her in the wheelchair and took her away past the night nurse and a chagrined and confused Michael, who by now was so exhausted I didn't want to watch what happened next.

Sara was exhausted too and made no complaint when I put her back in bed. She looked up at me through bitter tears. "Oh, Jacques, how could I have said such cruel and unfair things? He'll never forgive me. He'll abandon me again and I'll be alone. Just put me out of my misery. I can't bear it any more."

74

Summary of the Doves

Summer of the Doves

I sat beside her bed and held her hands. "Listen to me, Sara. In two weeks, all this will be over, unless something terrible messes it up. Right now, I want you to try to rest while I get you checked out of the hospital. Your vital signs are normal and as far as they're concerned, you just had a fainting spell from the heat in the cubicle. We need to get you to a safe place where you can rest and practice. The success of the Idaho Rendezvous is in your hands alone."

She turned away from me and faced the wall as she whispered, "I don't care. I hate you all. Go away and leave me alone."

I called a nurse to come stay with her. I had her lock the door from the inside while I left to get the paperwork done. In a few minutes we were able to slip out by the back surgery elevator and were at my house and safely inside.

After I put her to bed, I sat down to make a plan for each day to follow and what needed to be done in what order. Then I counted backwards from two Saturdays and figured it was safe to let her sleep the clock around if she needed to.

I returned to the sanctuary and sank to my knees on the priedieu. Sara's rosary was still in the little drawer and I took it out. I hadn't prayed one in many years but the cadence returned quickly and I was comforted by the repetition. Finally I collapsed onto the cot and slept.

All of the sliding panel doors are designed to operate silently. Sara's soft weeping wakened me in the late afternoon as she said, "Oh, Jacques, I'm so frightened for us all. How did we get mixed up in this? All the people I care about are in such danger because of me. My precious Jenny, Dave and you, what will become of us? How can we go on?"

I sat up on the side of the cot and held out my hands. "Come on, let's get to work. That's how we dare to go on; knowing our cause is just and that we care about each other's safety. It's five o'clock. Would you fix us some supper while I make sure Tim is on his way home to Pennsylvania? I don't want him in danger too. Then we'll get warmed up for some strength training. We have our work laid out for the next two weeks, no question about that."

We worked until quite late. I was on duty Monday morning and needed to leave early. On my workdays, training together would have to be from three in the afternoon until ten at night.

On Tuesday, a package from Dave Finch arrived by overnight mail. Inside was a terse note telling me the enclosed letter was from the lawyer settling the Lambert estate and I was to give it to Sara. I waited until after the evening practice. When I gave it to her she

75

said, "I'm so numb with fear and grief, nothing could make any difference now."

The envelope from Spokane was addressed to her married name, Madam Henri Lambert and was written in French. It was dated January 1998 and bore no stamps.

> *My precious Sara,*
>
> *I have returned from my physical checkup with news I could not bear to share with you. The doctor says my heart is weary and there is not a great deal that can be done. None of the fancy surgeries will help and my body can only handle so much medication. Although I know that it is too late to give you more than a small understanding of what happened in our life, perhaps you will find it in your heart to forgive me when I have finished this story.*
>
> *As you know, my one ambition in life was to become a college president in the United States. My sins were ones of greed and ineptness. I made my fortune smuggling gems in and out of various countries. I used the young men students who were my lovers, to do the footwork. My terrible misfortune was in allowing Andretti to help in the organizing of the operation. In a very short time he had figured out how to combine my petty scheme with his own work, which included his wholesale florist business and a sophisticated worldwide courier service.*
>
> *By this time he had threatened your safety and blackmailed me into silence. He gave me just enough of my gains to keep us going in our lifestyle and kept the rest of the gems for himself. Only his arrogance kept you safe as you began to pass information about the courier drop points to your own people.*
>
> *I tried to leave the information for you to access so that you could protect as many of your people as possible. I always admired your ingenuity and bravery and your method of cryptography was so perfect. Only because I worked with it in the military and because Andretti was not expecting a woman to betray him, were your coded messages safe all those years.*
>
> *I did the best I could to protect you and I never told Andretti about your daughter. I hope that you will be able to find her now, and that she will be safe in your care soon. It is with great sorrow that I must tell you she became deaf as a teenager and has led a difficult*

76

life. Her adoptive parents named her Roslin Marie Parmentier. Her parents are both dead now and I believe she is working as a companion for the children of an industrialist in Nice.

I beg now for your forgiveness of my greed and treachery against you. May God forgive me for what I have done and may He grant you happiness now.

Henri Lambert

Sara looked up into my eyes. There were no tears. "Did Dave know about this?"

"I don't know." I was glad I didn't know. It would have made things impossible during those years when I was working for Lambert. Would I have killed Andretti in cold blood if I had known? I didn't know that either.

The next morning after I left for work, Sara gave a shopping list to our operative, Angela, and began an even more concentrated effort to get in shape.

The belt and buckle arrived from the craftsman late Wednesday evening and I was anxious to try it out. The wide leather belt was fastened with a metal buckle patterned with Celtic knots and symbols. On the right side, a mystical animal crouched, facing left. His eyes were the handles of the two throwing knives. The craftsman knew to meld the design and equipment so it would be balanced a little below her waist.

The next step in the process was to swing out the backstop for knife practice. Knives have always been my least-favored weapons. It's much too easy to have them turned on you or to lose one from your hand and end up defenseless except for hands and feet, fighting for a loose weapon. With such a short time, we didn't use other knives in practice but used the real ones. Sara's coordination and strength had improved immeasurably in just the few days we'd worked together, but I was still concerned about whether she would have the strength to drive the weapon underhand into a man's body from a distance of eight to ten feet.

I was relieved when she seemed to be able to hit the target with great accuracy. We practiced her follow-up move endlessly. We might not know until moments before the confrontation whether a chair would be in the way. We knew the size of the room, the shape of the table, and how many chairs would be around it. The placement of the various members of the group was crucial for Sara to be in position to throw her knife.

My practice room was large, and usually, it was empty except for a narrow bench bolted into the wall. Today I noticed an easel in the far corner with a large vertical canvas on it. It was turned to the wall. Underneath there was a box of paints and brushes.

"Doing a little art work?" I queried, as we finished our first workout.

Sara shrugged her shoulders. "I'm working on a little gift for Andretti. I'm not finished with it yet. I keep thinking of more things to put in it."

"Is it for public viewing? What's it about?" I began to move toward it.

She stood to block my path to the picture. "It's a picture of Andretti with all the dead agents and victims of his hand; all the young men killed in foreign countries, all the evil things he has done to us, including my 'accidents'. I keep thinking of more."

"That sounds pretty inflammatory."

"You can give it to him after he kills me in cold blood." She was weeping now. "I'm so weary. I can't run any more. I don't care whether he kills me or not. I just hope he's merciful and quick and stops with me. I can't bear to think all of you would get killed one by one, after he gets me. I don't even know why he hates me so."

"Good God! Sara, what's gotten into you? Everything's going to be just fine."

The minute it came out of my mouth, I regretted it. We didn't know enough to say such things and our odds weren't too great for everything being just fine.

I reached for her. "Do you want me to stay with you tonight?"

She was trembling as she turned away for a long moment; then turned toward me with her hands clasped together. "No, I'll be all right. Would you waken me when you leave tomorrow morning? I need to write some notes to the members of the team.

"Michael and my lawyer as well as Dave Finch know and understand what I was hoping to accomplish at the farm in Campbell's Point. There should be enough money in my estate to find another place and still set it up. The farm they destroyed was going to be so wonderful and sheltering, a place where doctors, nurses and patients could have a restful and renewing experience. I was going to call it Liriodendron Retreat Center.

She continued, "There was to be a wonderful laboratory, the kind I always dreamed about, with fine equipment and reference books. There was to be enough money for the doctors and nurses to do research, without having to beg for grants from questionable corporate sources." Her whole face lit up as she described how her dream would take place no matter what happened.

Then she asked me, "What do you hope to do after this is over?"

We were crossing the large space in the workout room, headed for the kitchen as I answered her. "I've already turned in my resignation at the hospital. I'll be done the end of this week. It's time for me to start out on my search for a mate. I'm going to sell this place. Someone has already asked to buy it for much more money than I paid for it. It will give me a comfortable cushion while I travel."

"Jacques, I'd like to tell you about the dream I had last night?"

"I'd like to hear it , unless it's filled with murder and mayhem."

"Oh, no, it was a lovely dream. I think I've seen the woman you're seeking."

We settled down at the kitchen counter with sandwiches and milk as she began to recount the dream. "First I saw you, dressed in a soft, fawn-colored corduroy shirt and blue jeans, with your special woodland moccasins. You were leaning on the railing of a rough wooden bridge overlooking a wonderful dancing brook. The light was dappled as it came through the leaves overhanging the water. The water was so clear and pure you could see fish swimming in the shallows. It was an enchanted place. The air was crisp but very still; no breeze ruffled the wisps of grass or the leaves because the forest was so thick with trees. The birds had settled into their noontime nap and even the brassy crows didn't announce your presence.

"In the quiet of midday, you heard laughter that sounded like the ringing of bells. Then a lovely voice began to sing. The next sounds were of small children, laughing and singing with her. You saw them first, walking down the path with simple fishing poles and a bucket. A lunch basket hung from one of the woman's arms and a tiny girl clung to the other. A young boy about five years old was marching ahead, obviously in charge of the expedition.

"She was so lovely, with long black hair bound up in braids. She was tall and lithe, and wore a long aqua blue jumper with big pockets. A small bear peeked out the top of one pocket. Jacques, she was wearing the same kind of moccasins you make for yourself, and the children had some like them in a tiny size.

"When they saw you, they were like deer startled in the forest. They stopped to look and to assess the danger. Then the woman came toward you, without fear or hesitation. She said to you, 'I see you've found our special fishing place. May we join you? Thomas, you may set up the poles while I lay out lunch. My friend, will you share our meal?' It was simple fare, much like what your mother would have packed for you if you'd been off on a childhood adventure.

79

"While the children played at the water's edge she kept a close and watchful eye for their safety. Her voice was filled with gentle sadness. 'Today is the second anniversary of my husband's death. He was killed in an industrial accident. He always loved this place and used to bring us here to play. And why are you here?'

"The rest of your conversation was so intimate I'll not share it unless you insist. I'm convinced she's very real and is waiting for you to find her."

I was fascinated by her story and asked, "Was there anything in the dream to give me a clue to help find her?"

"Yes, for some reason I think she's a physical therapist and works in a hospital. When I close my eyes I can visualize where you met, in a dark forest of conifers, and birch. The forest floor is heavy with needles and cones and ferns of many kinds. I think the fish were trout, and the stones in the brook reminded me of the gneiss specimens from my geology class. The odor of the conifers was haunting and unmistakable, and I thought I could smell the lake too. Was your home anything like what I've described?"

I took Sara's hand. "What a lovely gift you've shared. I shall miss you, Madam Lambert."

She kissed me gently. "May your quest be fruitful, Jacques."

We tidied up the kitchen and returned to the workroom. She seemed more at ease and less frightened. She reached out to me as she asked, "Would you help me to know Michael better? You have worked together for several years. I know I must have hurt him very much. How do I let him know how sorry I am that I'm afraid of him? Will he ever be able to understand what I've been through? Or more important, will he want to try?

"We aren't fastened together for eternity, just because we had a child. Perhaps we shouldn't try to marry or belong to each other. How do we make up for so many years apart, traveling on such different paths that we're strangers now?"

I took her hands in mine. "I have a great deal of respect for Michael Cameron. He's a competent, caring physician and one of the gentlest men I've ever known. He has his hard side, all men must, or we don't survive. There are things women will never understand about what men's lives are like. In many ways we're light years behind in the freedom women have fought for and won for themselves.

"As to Michael's intentions, I can tell you that the day he found you, he became intent upon being a part of your life. And Sara, he has worn your locket around his neck for thirty-five years. As far as I know, he hasn't been involved with any other woman in all those years although he was pursued without mercy by some of the women in his life. Be patient with one another and love with gentleness."

"Could I make a request for our last practice before we turn in?" I was a bit puzzled but nodded yes. "What would you like?"

Her request took me by surprise. "Since I've decided I'm going to fight to stay alive, there's a technique I really need to learn. I'm not sure why, but Dave wouldn't teach it to me. My other dream last night was not as pleasant as the first. I've practiced it from a book but I need your critique and presence to help me feel the moves."

She explained what she wanted and I decided to go along with it since it was a self-defense move of the purest kind, the kind you hope you'll never have to use. She stepped to the easel and picked up a stick about as long as the distance from the floor to her hip. It was perfectly plain and well balanced. I was not an expert but I knew what she wanted. We worked for several hours before she was satisfied with the results. When we finished, she shared a gentle kiss and whispered, "Thank you, perhaps it will save my life."

We shut things down for the night. "If you need stationery and pen tomorrow morning, Sara, there are some things in the small writing box in your room. If you need more, there's a good supply in the office next to my sleeping area. Now, let me walk you around to show you the rest of the places in the house where you might want to go."

I explained to her how all the controls were connected to the central panel with cameras and sound recorders. It was possible to see into all of the areas, including the garage.

"So Angela has been able to see all we do during practice?"

"Yes, why?"

"I don't know exactly, but for some reason I don't trust her. Call it woman's intuition. I didn't like the way she touched me, the night we worked on my hair. All we need now is a double agent to mix into the stew. I guess I'm being paranoid, but would you call sometime in the morning if you can, and speak to me, just to check on how things are going?"

"Sure. Are you going to be all right tonight?"

She managed a wan smile and a heartfelt hug and we said good night.

CHAPTER EIGHT

I knocked on Sara's open door when I was ready to leave for work. She was at the desk and had already finished some of the letters. They lay with names on the envelopes, waiting to be given out at the Idaho meeting. "I'll call about ten, if that's all right?"

She rose from the desk and came to me, tears glistening in her eyes. She looked so frightened. "Remember how much I loved you, Jacques. I pray you won't be harmed."

She trembled as I held her and saw her tear-streaked face. "I'm going to call Dave today. We can't put you through any more stress like this. We'll just do it ourselves."

She slipped away from me. "No, you mustn't. Dave would fire us all, and it wouldn't solve anything. We have an ugly mess on our hands and I must to help too."

I had many misgivings as I left her and headed to work. At ten, I called the house. Angela was supposed to be on duty and Sara had a phone in the practice room. There was no answer. I was doing paperwork in Michael's office, trying to get ready to leave my job. JW was finishing up his physical therapy. After leaving a short note for Michael, JW and I headed for the house. Instead of the usual fifteen-minute drive, we made it in ten.

What greeted us as we pulled up in front was ominous. The garage door and front door were wide open. A couple of junkyard strays were on their way in the front door and we could hear snarling inside. I held JW back. "It could be a trap. Be careful and stay with me."

We pulled the car into the garage and went around to the front. It was quiet except for the dogs. The house looked so different that at first I couldn't figure out what was wrong. Then it occurred to me; someone must have disabled the main control panel. The mirror-paneled doors were open, the gaping spaces pooling into the central patio. The skylights were open and the shutters that usually covered all the windows were swinging outward into the street, the windows gaping open behind them.

I didn't know where to go first but we started in the control room. Everything was trashed. The only thing moveable in the room was a chair; now lying on its side with several legs shattered. It must have been used to smash the equipment in the room. There were glass shards scattered over the desktop and floor.

A bloody mess greeted us as we went to the workroom. The dogs were fighting over a body sprawled on the floor. I grabbed the stick from the easel as we passed and used it to back off the dogs. I turned the head just enough to see that it was Andretti. Why was he here?

I whispered to JW, "Where are the women?"

I told him to call the police. While he was using his cell phone, I stepped over to Andretti's body to look again. My God! Apparently Sara had needed the technique I'd taught her last night. Andretti's throat had been slit. I knew she never would have done it except as a last resort. Then I was puzzled. She hadn't used the stick we'd practiced with. It was clean and still on the easel when I'd picked it up moments ago.

We started a search for Sara and Angela. The guest room door was ajar. As we looked inside, we could see heaps of clothing, broken pottery and papers strewn around the floor. It looked like blind rage had driven the destroyer. Who could have done it? What were they looking for?

We went to each of the other rooms without finding the women. Finally, we returned to the workout room. Andretti was lying face down with his arms curled in front. At the same moment, JW and I saw small slender fingers under his shoulder. Was someone curled up under him?

There was a discrete knock on the wall as a policeman stepped into the room. "I've called for a backup. Is there anything else we need to know right now?"

I motioned to the body. "Can we move him?"

He helped us lift the body just enough to slide the woman out. It was Sara.

She whispered, "The box in the kitchen is a bomb." Then she fainted.

I hated to take her to the hospital again but she was in bad shape. A lot of the blood on her was hers. I looked at JW. "Call Michael and let him know we're coming. It'll be faster than calling 911."

I gathered her up in a sheet and headed for the garage. The policeman nodded and said he'd take care of things. He was already on the phone calling for the bomb squad.

Sara was absolutely still, ghostly white and hardly breathing, almost as though her soul had left her body. The ER staff took over and we waited as they tried to stabilize her. I called Dave to tell him about the attack.

Michael paced frantically in the waiting room. "She can't die now, not after all she's been through," He grasped JW's shoulder as he pleaded, "JW, do something."

"I don't know if I can since she's unconscious," JW answered, "but I'll try."

One of Michael's associates came to tell us Sara had a badly shattered arm and they were beginning the repair. It took them a long time. She was taken to a room afterwards and JW began to talk to her; about the forest, the doves and what kind of a day it was and all about the color of the sky. He began to sing lullabies and then he went on to beautiful songs I'd never heard before, love songs with such sadness in the melodies and words that it wrenched my heart. The three of us were trying so hard to reconnect with her and bring her back. We felt helpless. JW kept talking to her and singing as though he thought she could hear him.

She was barely conscious later in the afternoon when the door to her room opened and Dave and Jenny came in. Jenny took her wonderful stubborn stance and said, "All right you four men; you all clear out. Leave us alone until I let you back in. I have some business with Sara."

I didn't know about the others but I was glad to get out of there. We walked down and got some food while we waited for Jenny to let us back in. She paged Michael, and after he answered, he had the strangest look on his face. "Jenny says we can come back, one at a time, but to be very careful about what we say. Sara is conscious but doesn't remember anything about what happened today."

Each of us went to speak to Sara and wish her well. She was pretty uncomfortable with the new, bulky cast. They had taken a long time to put her back together. The pain medication made her so groggy she finally just said good night.

Dave asked us to meet at Michael's place in a couple of hours and we scattered to take care of the rest of the day's obligations. As Jenny and I left the corridor, I glanced back to see JW and Michael greeting a priest and ushering him into Sara's room. I needed to get home to see what could be done about closing up the house. I took Jenny with me, to take a look at how we could do the repairs in the control room.

The police were still there. There was yellow tape around the place and the doors were still open. The same guy was in charge and we asked about the bomb. I hadn't even seen it. He said the bomb squad worked a long time on it. When I asked if they'd been able to save everything, he shrugged. "It looked like it might be worth big bucks until they got it down to headquarters and had someone come in to take a look. Everything was paste, except the bomb. The box will be at the station for you to pick up. I need for you to come down and sign some papers if you can tonight. We're done here for now."

He turned to me. "Did you know the dead guy?"

There wasn't any reason not to tell him, so I gave him Andretti's name.

Then the cop said, "Any idea who did it?"

"Not really. There are a lot of things that don't make sense right now. Sara doesn't remember anything about what happened so she can't help you. We've been told Andretti tried to kill her at least four times in the last year. How he ended up dead I don't know. Did you find the weapon?"

The cop shook his head no. "I can't talk about it right now. We need some more facts first."

He gathered up his crew and while they took down the tape he said, "Do you need to have someone here tonight to protect stuff? I don't know if you'll be able to close it up with all the electricity out. You'll need to call from somewhere else to get the phone rewired. It was a professional job of terror all right, there were no prints."

"We need to look around a bit more to see if we can get the place secure. We'll let you know when we get to the station."

Jenny and I got right to work on the control panel. As she wired around the damage, I replaced some dials and buttons and hooked everything up to the diesel generator in the garage. Because of proper venting, it could run all night to keep the doors and windows shut.

No way was I going to spend the night in there. I went down to the corner and called the emergency number for the electricians who did the original installation and made arrangements for them to come the next morning at eight o'clock to begin the repairs.

Jenny was pretty distraught when I got back. "What a horrible experience for Sara. I'd like to stay a few days to help you clean up the house. Maybe we can piece together what really happened. I don't have any appointments this week. I was getting ready for the Idaho meeting." We looked at each other. Now that Andretti was dead, there wouldn't be an Idaho Rendezvous.

We went next to the police station to sign forms and let them know we got the place closed up. We picked up the bomb box and went on to Michael's. Everyone else was already there.

This was the time in a case when, as district chief, Dave Finch earned his six-figure salary. We were all shocked by the turn of events and each one of us felt guilty because we hadn't seen it coming. Although some agents came and went on a project, we all felt responsible when someone got hurt or killed. Michael and JW didn't work for us and Jenny was the "new kid on the block" but all of us were hurting; partly because of our personal ties with Sara, but more, because we knew something like it could happen at any time, to any one of us.

Dave began to debrief us, filling in with stuff we hadn't known. He was the one who decided how much each person needed to know to do his job. Even with all the planning, unexpected things happened.

Dave turned to me. "I hear Andretti left a little surprise. I expect he was hoping that after he killed Sara, Michael would open it and be blown away; one more spite murder."

The bomb had been wrapped as a gift. Inside the outer wooden box was a second box made of crystal. A lovely pearl necklace lay in a nest of apricot velvet. The bomb nestled under the velvet was set to blow up when the pearls were lifted from their place. The gift card said "For Madam Henri Lambert in anticipation of her upcoming marriage." It was not signed. As rich as Andretti was, it seemed odd he would give a gift of such little value, almost an insult. And then I remembered; it was going to blow to smithereens.

Jenny gasped. "Why was he so intent upon taking Sara's life? Or whoever else might open the box?"

Dave shrugged. "She may not know, or she may have been told at the end but may not choose to tell us. For right now, I want to finish this first meeting by giving you some questions to think about before Saturday."

He handed out half page lists to each of us. "I think Sara will be present and I hope we can seek and find closure to this affair. Now to simpler problems, would anyone be willing to fix the meal for Saturday? There should be six of us."

Jenny and I said we'd do it. I'd be disposing of my food before too many days anyway, since I was leaving for the Northeast.

Michael's home was convenient for company and there were rooms for everyone who needed to stay. I took a bit of a ribbing for not wanting to go back home after what had happened there today. I wanted to stay with the others, as we would have in Idaho.

Michael had surgery at seven o'clock tomorrow and JW had physical therapy in the morning. Jenny and I were going to do a concentrated cleanup at the house in preparation for turning it over to the buyer, and she offered to help me begin packing my stuff to put in storage. Dave said he wanted to spend a day at the Missouri Botanic Garden research library. We made a date to meet at Michael's and to eat out in the evening.

As we scattered to find our rooms, I noticed Dave and Jenny heading toward Michael's office. Jenny didn't even say good night to JW, nor did he attempt to speak to her. It seemed a bit strange since everyone thought they were closer than mere friends. I chalked it up to the stress of the day's events and headed off to bed.

Jenny's room was next to mine and I heard her later, talking on her cell phone. No words, but I could sense the tightness in her voice and the urgency in the flow of her conversation.

Something continued to nag at the back of my mind. How did Sara know that the box was a bomb? Where was the murder weapon? And who shot Sara? Was someone else in my house that morning when Andretti was killed? I mulled over the implications of those questions as I drifted off into exhausted sleep.

Next morning we got up at different times, foraged for breakfast, and then Jenny and I headed to my place. We needed to be there in time to let the contractors in at eight o'clock and to see what else they might need from us. The most important thing was to get electricity back on the grid so we could turn off the generator. Jenny dropped me off while she headed out to get some work clothes. The electricians got there just as I did and we went in together.

I asked them to get the general electricity going first so I could get the recordings and visual surveillance tapes out of the machines and stored in a safe place. The system blocked access to the tapes in the machines even as they kept running on batteries if anything unusual occurred to the electrical system in the house. Then they could be opened when the electricity came back on line. I dreaded looking at them but it needed doing before I went to Sara's.

I made a tour around to assess how much cleaning would need to be done professionally. At the same time, I was making a first search for any clues about what had happened after I left for work. When I returned to the control room, Jenny was back and talking to the men about wiring diagrams. I reached up to remove the tapes. They were gone. That was really strange. I wondered if Angela had taken them out the day before. That was possible since she was involved in surveillance too. And as for that, where was Angela? She had disappeared.

Then I realized with all the excitement and confusion, I'd forgotten about the special set of performance recorders I'd installed recently. They were just for the workroom, to analyze moves during practice. Actually, I'd just put in a new tape a few days ago. These recorders came on automatically when workroom doors were opened, and were controlled from a different place. Most important to us now, they weren't part of the main surveillance system.

Who was that guy of Sara's? Mr. Vaughan? I could swear he was talking to me now. He was saying "Don't go to it or say anything. Don't trust anyone." It made the hair stand up on the back of my neck. Sara said she never questioned Mr. V. but always obeyed him; I did the same.

First, Jenny and I tried to clean up the glass in the control room so we wouldn't track it all over the house. It was too late. No one would be going barefooted in there for a long time. I wrote it on the list for the cleaners. We changed our minds several times about the menu for Saturday's lunch. Somehow, I figured people wouldn't have much appetite anyway.

We went to the guest room. I still couldn't get over the total disarray. Everything was pulled out and thrown in a heap. Why would anyone smash pottery, and who could have done it? It looked like an act of tremendous violence. We didn't know how long Angela was at the house; only that she must have been there long enough to let Andretti in. If only we had those tapes.

Jenny and I started to search through the debris, sifting and shaking each handful to find a clue of some kind. I assumed the police had already done a thorough search. About half way through the pile, though, I looked down into the depths of the pale green carpet and saw the flash of an earring. I knew Sara never wore them and I couldn't remember a recent complaint from anyone about losing one. The kind of women who worked with me didn't wear jewelry. I reached down and picked it up, curling it under my hand as I lifted it up, while my other hand did something else at a distance in the pile.

The most important thing missing in the room was the one thing I wanted to retrieve. Where was the set of personal notes Sara had been writing for each of the people who would be at the meeting in Idaho? We didn't find her purse or personal papers either. After working another hour we switched to packing. Jenny offered to go pick up some packing boxes. I gave her some money and went off to my personal office to begin sorting and packing books and papers.

We needed to have the telephone reinstalled, so I left the house to go to the pay phone on the corner. I returned and went on with my sorting. A couple of hours later, Jenny wasn't back. She had my car and I couldn't get anywhere anyway. I figured she'd stopped to do errands of her own. When the third hour passed, I had a nagging feeling we had a problem. I went back down to the corner and phoned Michael's place. JW answered.

I didn't waste time in pleasantries. "This is Jacques, have you heard from Jenny today?"

"No, what's up?"

"Well, she went on an errand that should've taken an hour at the most and it's been about three and a half hours since she left. Is Dave there?"

"Yes, he just came in the door. Wait and I'll get him."

I started right in. "We have a problem. Jenny's missing and I don't like what's been going on here today. Could you come over?"

"I'll be right there. Anything I should bring?"

"No, and definitely don't bring JW or Michael. They're too mixed up in this already, and remember, they don't even work for us."

"Understood. I already know what you're going to tell me. I made a bargain with Jenny last night in exchange for information. Her time is almost up. I'll be right there to get you. She told me where to find your car. I hate like hell to have to tell Cameron and Campbell about what she did, but at least she promised to leave them out of it. I'll be there in about twenty minutes.

"If Jenny comes back, against her promise to me; kill her!"

I decided to remove the tape from the practice room recorder and slipped it into my pocket. I counted every minute by seconds and prayed that Jenny wouldn't come back. I couldn't believe what was apparently true and I didn't want to think about what a mess we were in. I told the repairmen to lock up on their way out and waited on the doorstep for Dave to come.

As I climbed in the car, I held out my hand and opened it to show the earring. Dave didn't hesitate. "It's Jenny's. I expect that's why she offered to help you clean this morning, even though she had so few hours before the time she bargained for was up. I'm sure she was desperate to find it so she wouldn't be connected to the murder. Did she know you'd found it?"

"I really don't know."

Dave started down the street. "You people just assumed she came over from Pittsburgh with me. I couldn't find her anywhere there, but got her on her cell phone. I checked her cell phone use numbers after you two left to go back to the house yesterday. She was already in St. Louis yesterday morning.

"Let's go get your car before the neighborhood kids strip it, and we can get a look at the layout of Sara's daughter's place. I don't know how Jenny found out about her, but she used the government computer system to track everyone down. She figured out Roslin was in St. Louis and came here to find her. She told me last night about a guy named Tom. He's protected Roslin and looked after her since the night the French family she worked for abandoned her in south St. Louis. I think you men need to meet him as soon as possible.

"When Jenny found out last night that I knew she'd murdered Andretti, she bargained for time to escape before I sent the Feds after her. I gave her twenty-four hours in exchange for information about Roslin's whereabouts. Then I made her promise she wouldn't harm Sara, Michael, JW or you, and that she would leave the country and never return. She has until eight o'clock tonight. She really played it close when she took the time trying to find her earring. I just got a call from the airport. She boarded a plane for the Bahamas a few minutes ago.

"When I confronted her last night, she had Sara's notes, purse, and personal papers as well as the set of surveillance tapes and sound tapes.

"I think I know what she's going to try to do next and we need to keep a close eye on the Bermuda papers."

I was trying to sort things out and something just didn't compute. We were planning to kill Andretti in Idaho. Why did it matter that it was done in a different place and time or who did it?

I looked at Dave. "How did you know Jenny killed Andretti?"

He didn't answer at first. Then in a calm voice he said, "I looked at the tapes."

We were down in Soulard now. Most of the houses were simple and small, old and much in need of paint. We turned on the street where Roslin was supposed to be. My silver car was parked in front of a small apartment building. A couple of street kids were hanging out, eyeing the car; probably balancing the value of the parts against the chance they'd get caught. I got out of Dave's car and stepped to my own. I hoped everything was still under the hood because I sure wanted out of there. I couldn't believe it was still there, unlocked, with the keys inside.

One kid yelled at me "How you 'ford a car like that, nigger?"

"I worked like hell and became a doctor, kid. I hope you have the guts to do the same."

I climbed in the car and waited for Dave to lead me out of there. I thought fondly of the cool evergreen forest, the quiet and solitude of the mountains and was thankful that soon, I could leave St. Louis behind. I followed Dave the best I could and finally realized where he was going. He was on his way to the hospital to see Sara. I needed to see her too. I still couldn't believe what had happened.

Neither of us was prepared for what greeted us in Sara's room. She was seated in a chair, looking lovely, except for the droopy hospital-supplied gown and robe that struggled to cover her bulky cast. Her hair was freshly washed and her food tray was empty.

She smiled. "I thought you'd never get here. I waited all day for you. Can you get me out of here tonight? I need some fresh air and flowers and dirt under my fingernails."

She got up from her chair and came to greet us. "Come on guys. Did you think I'd tell Jenny that I knew anything about what happened at the house, or during the attack? Self-preservation is an instinctive talent, especially for a woman. No way was I going to tell her I remembered anything."

Dave and I looked at each other with relief. Sara didn't have amnesia. She was just fine except for a couple of broken bones, and now it was time to celebrate. We looked at our watches and found we still had time to get to Michael's place by seven o'clock.

I smiled at her. "I promise that Michael and I will spring you tomorrow morning as early as we can get here. Now, you be a good girl and get some rest before the meeting tomorrow."

She sighed. "Well, if you promise. Remember, I don't have anything to wear that will fit over my cast."

Dave said nothing about Roslin's whereabouts so he must think we might have a problem persuading her to come with us. We needed to talk with Tom.

It was Friday night and the stores were open late. We had a quick supper; then scattered to shop for Sara. It would be very interesting to see what each man thought Sara would want; and what they thought she needed.

We decided to pull rank at the hospital and go back to Sara's room for a few minutes after visiting hours, to take her gifts before we went to meet Tom. I swung by my place to pick up something I'd been working on for her. She was very glad to see us.

Dave had known her a long time. She'd told me they were unofficially engaged when they finished up their doctorates in Paris. She disappeared from his life for several years after Lambert claimed and married her. Dave returned to the States, married another woman and taught in Pittsburgh. Sara began to communicate with him again by drop mail as they started their research together.

In his gift box were blue jeans, a sturdy work shirt of Black Watch plaid, and a new pair of deerskin work gloves. In the top of the box lay an envelope. There were three recruitment letters on letterhead from different departments at his college; the first, for an adjunct professorship in Life Sciences to teach ecology, the second, for an assistant professorship in Foreign Languages to teach advanced French Conversation. The third, however, brought tears to her eyes. It was an acceptance letter of an application and transcripts from Paris to enter the English department to begin a degree in ESL, something she'd wanted to do for years. I think Dave's gifts were a subtle encouragement for her to realize she was free now and possessed plenty of competence to try anything that was in her heart.

She thanked him graciously and went to JW's box. His gifts were oriented around her love of gardening. He'd put together a basket of hand tools, to replace the ones destroyed in the fire. He found a garden smock covered with roses and carnations and a pair of clogs for muddy gardening. Tucked in the top of his box was a CD of Humperdinck's *Hansel and Gretel.*

Next, it was my turn. I'd served as Sara's guard for the six years while I worked for Lambert. I went with her when she did her extended summer research work in the Idaho forest. I helped her escape to present her papers in Portland, the year the meetings were there. One of Lambert's rules was that she could do all the research and publishing she desired but she couldn't attend a national or international meeting. I managed to disable her other bodyguards long enough to give her a half day of freedom. It turned out to be an important political coup because Dave's associates were beginning to say that Dr S. Harvey didn't exist. She did a super professional job with her presentation and quieted all her critics from then on.

My gifts for her included a suit of gray silk with gold, blue and forest green threads. In remembrance of the many nights of self-defense practice, I'd put together a small box with several long scarves like the ones we'd used to cover her eyes. In the top of the box was the special gift I had just finished for her; forest moccasins designed for the women of our tribe.

All of us were interested to find out what Michael had given her. The clothing he chose was definitely not for summer. There were two sweaters, one apricot, the other dove gray and a pair of soft dove gray wool slacks. A pair of elegant white winter boots nestled in the bottom of the box. In the top lay a soft gray leather portfolio with a silver clasp. Inside she found a note and with it, her registration and plane tickets to the next international meeting which would be in Helsinki next winter. There was another smaller note within the first. When Sara read it, she looked up at him and whispered, "Yes".

She thanked us all and then smiled. "I still don't have anything I can wear."

JW got up and handed her another smaller box. He had chosen to give her his own beloved linen shirts that Millie had made for him, along with several pairs of pull-on corduroy pants. They would help her to be independent and the shirts would fit over her cast.

As we left the room, Dave sent Michael, JW and me to meet Tom.

CHAPTER NINE Sara continues

Dave came to sit beside me. "You were magnificent, Sara. What would I do without you?"

I smiled. "Well, you seem to be having a bit of trouble choosing female operatives. What happened to Angela? Have you heard from her? You know our tangled web nearly got us this time? Do you think it's over, with Andretti's bunch at least?"

"I don't know; but I hope so. As for poor Jenny, I don't know why she was there or what happened. I'll tell you what she's probably going to try down in Bermuda. She told me she wanted to kill JW's former wife and boys for what they did to him in Chicago after his accident last year. She's in way over her head and there are other people out to get that pseudo-Campbell clan.

"The boys spent some of the money stolen from JW to buy a big yacht. They've been trying to break into the drug smuggling business with Mama in up to her ears too. Well, I hear they've tried to do it without paying the right people their cut, and both the Colombians and the Mafia are after them. Jenny is third in line to kill them and doesn't know yet about the drugs. We have a man down there that'll keep an eye on things and let us know what happens.

"Sometimes the big guys just blow up the yacht with all on board. Others come aboard first to retrieve the drugs, slaughter everyone and then blow up the yacht. Either way they've taken care of a small operator. If Jenny happens to be on board she'll be a victim too. If she acts too interested in the yacht or its owners they'll get her because they'll figure she's DEA. What a waste. She was sure a fine linguist."

I touched Dave's hand. "I don't want the others to see the tapes from Jacques' or to hear the audio. What they're going to learn tomorrow will be hard enough without the truth. I haven't had a chance to see them yet, have you?"

He hesitated before he answered. "Yes, I looked at them this afternoon."

"May I see them?"

He took me into his arms. "No, I don't want you to see them. There's no reason to bring back those memories. It's over now."

I was puzzled by his answer, but my pain had come back and I wasn't ready to argue with him. I went to get a drink of water. "Want something; I know how to raid the snack room?"

He shook his head. "No, thanks. For some reason, this whole thing has got my gut tied in knots. I guess one of your famous lines is that you are getting too old for this. Well, I think I am too. Do you think we could just let the younger ones have all the thrills and danger now?"

He took my hands in his as I whispered, "Sounds to me like a winner. Maybe it's time to be just one thing at a time. I'm not sure what yet but it's very tempting. In all the excitement I still haven't had a chance to tell you about the changes in my new project. I think it will be a perfect research study for one of your students. Can you imagine the morels popping up on the hillside next spring?"

"My one-track-mind Sara. Hush, it's very late and we need some rest. Tomorrow won't be an easy day." His hug was gentle and weary. "Sleep well."

Dave headed off to Michael's and I sat and thought about the men in my life and the troubles each one carried in his heart.

Then, I wondered how long it would be before I could sleep soundly, without nightmares. It wasn't to happen that night. I wakened about three o'clock, whimpering in the dark of a strange room, my bedclothes tangled in my new, bulky cast. Warm, sheltering arms were there and Jacques was holding me. "It's all right, Dear Heart. I'm here and I won't let anyone harm you. It's over now and you're safe." He'd come back to stay with me, perhaps for the last time.

I was sobbing now. "Jacques, it was so horrible, so terrifying. What will become of my beautiful Jenny, whose twisted mind must have driven her to murder?" I whispered, "I don't understand. All those years that Andretti had dealings with my husband and came into our home, he never gave me any reason to fear him. He was always a perfect gentleman. Did he care about my well-being all those years? Why would he have tried to kill me this past year, and then have saved my life at the end?"

Jacques answered after a few moments. "Sara, I wish I knew. Something about this whole affair just isn't making sense."

My arm hurt, my shoulder ached terribly and then I remembered I hadn't taken any medication since noon. "Would they have anything as simple as aspirin in this place without charging two dollars a pill?"

"I happen to have a couple in my pocket. I'll get you some water."

As he moved away from the bed, I had such a feeling of loss. He would be leaving on his new assignment in a few days and I would not see him again. I thought about what he and the others had meant to me. Dave was my mind mate, JW was my soul mate, and Jacques was my spirit mate. How could I possibly replace them with a stranger for whom I felt more fear than love? I wept and the hurt wouldn't go away.

Michael and Jacques arrived as promised next morning to bail me out. We swung by Jacques' place to pick up food for lunch. It would have been easier to just go there when we were ready to eat, but I couldn't bear to think about going into his home after the happenings just two days before in that beautiful place. I wondered how people sold houses where murders occurred. Was it was more difficult and did they lose money on it? I didn't go inside.

When we got to Michael's, Dave began the meeting.

"Jenny won't be with the group today. She resigned as of Friday evening." Then he said, "At this time I feel any more details would be unproductive. Would any of you like to speak?" We were surprised when Michael rose from his place.

He turned, looked at me with great compassion and said, "Please stand and state your name." The room became deathly quiet. No one knew what he was going to do, least of all, me.

I stood and answered. "My name is Sara Harvey."

"Dr. Harvey, I was visited by a policeman at six o'clock this morning. He delivered a summons for me to appear in court Monday afternoon relative to a complaint lodged by the doctors who cared for you and set your broken bones on Thursday afternoon. I need an explanation for their report which stated you have suffered a broken wrist, a broken collarbone, and many broken ribs that were not set or cared for properly. They were able to date them within six months and they believe the injuries were sustained in 1989. Would you be kind enough to explain?"

My blood turned to ice water and my voice was cold. "I am not at liberty to answer that question."

The men sat in silence as Michael continued. "These charges are grounds for criminal proceedings against the person or persons who did this to you."

I turned away from him to face the window. "It doesn't matter now." I closed my eyes and prayed for strength against his questioning.

Michael persisted, "Was it your husband, Henri Lambert?"

I turned back to him and repeated my answer. "I am not at liberty to answer that question."

Now Michael stepped toward me until we were only a few feet from each other. "Was it someone else, Sara Harvey? Whom are you trying to protect?"

I turned away from him again, struggling against my rising panic. I repeated my answer. "I am not at liberty to answer that question."

I was exhausted. My body hurt, my heart was broken. I felt as though my soul and spirit were being torn from my body. I couldn't withstand his questioning much longer.

And then he surprised me, as he said, "Why not?"

The room was so quiet that I heard the refrigerator turn on in the kitchen, and the sounds of birds making a racket in the trees outside. Cars went by in the street on their trip to take happy chattering children to Saturday activities or to the store. What would it be like to live such a normal life?

The men were not moving. They were on high alert, holding their collective breath, as they waited to find out what I would do.

Then, I answered him. "Perhaps I am trying to protect myself. I could not answer, because I am so ashamed of what was done to me."

Michael did not touch me. I know I would have screamed if he had. Instead he continued his gentle questioning. "Sara, there are four men in this room who care very much about you. Please open your heart and let us share your anguish, whatever it may be. We don't want details now or perhaps ever, but for your own sake, you must tell us who it was."

My body felt as though it had been turned to a pillar of salt, bitter, acrid, and abandoned. I whispered, "I don't know. I was blindfolded and bound. All I remember is his terrifying touch and the scent of his body. If I ever figure out who it was ... he will die!"

The room was hushed as the men realized the implications of my statement.

They kept their word and nothing more was said about my confession. Since Michael and JW were not part of the team, they were asked to go off and do something else until lunch. JW needed to do physical therapy on his hand and I watched Michael helping. The gentle strength Michael used with me earlier had been so powerful. Could I hope he had meant it when he said four men cared about my welfare? It would mean he was including himself. I thought of his love note from the evening before and allowed myself to believe it might be true.

I was daydreaming while we went through discussions about procedures and protocol; different ways we could have handled the recruiting problem we didn't know we had. I was so weary that my painkiller finally put me to asleep.

They did waken me in time to join them on the back patio for lunch. Michael was discussing the visit with Tom and what they would do next. I couldn't believe my daughter Roslin was in St. Louis and the men hadn't told me before now. I asked Michael if I could join them when they went to see her a second time. I was surprised when he said it would depend upon the afternoon meeting and when it was over, since I needed rest before we went down there so late. Her break time was 10 o'clock in the evening and Tom usually went to share supper with her. The men hadn't met with her yet.

Everyone attended the afternoon meeting. I hoped it would be over early. I was so weary I hurt everywhere; bones, flesh, psyche. Jacques handed me some more aspirin and a glass of water. When it was my turn to speak, I rose and addressed the group. "Gentlemen, this meeting has turned out to be far different from what I expected. Usually, as you remember, the afternoon session includes a set of sparring matches with weapons and hand-to-hand fighting. It is a time to vent anger and frustration and yes, sometimes, hatred.

"I feel none of these things. I am supremely thankful that we have survived and are still pledged to one another. No matter what may happen to us now or in the future, I believe our loyalty and honor have been vindicated. My dear ones, I trust you with my life." I picked up my papers, turned from the table and went to take a nap.

The men must have decided not to waken me before they went to meet Roslin. It was about one o'clock in the morning, my usual nightmare time, but I wasn't frightened. I just needed to get to the bathroom. Gentle hands helped me as I struggled to get untangled from my sheet.

"Oh, Madam, I'm so glad to see you. I'm so glad you are safe." The lovely cadence of Margot Penard's voice brought joy to my heart. Somehow, they must have managed to get her to St. Louis to help us care for Roslin. She was saying something about Roslin being so beautiful.

"Is my daughter here, Margot?" She nodded yes.

"Is she asleep?"

"No, Ma'am, she waited to see you."

I couldn't help the tears welling up in my eyes. "Give me ten seconds and I'll be ready to go to her."

"There are others with her." Margot answered with a smile. "I think you would be more comfortable if you dressed."

"Who's there?"

"They dropped Dave Finch off at the airport when they picked me up a few hours ago. He needed to get home to take care of an-other crisis. Your Michael, Jacques and Jamie are with her now. I didn't know Jacques knew sign language. It's even French. Come, let's hurry now."

The men were seated around the kitchen table. Jacques and Roslin were talking a mile a minute using signing. Michael and JW were gazing at her in awed silence. She was sitting so I could see her for a few moments before she saw me. Her hair was a glorious red, long, and done up in French braids. The tilt of her nose and the beautiful gray eyes were surely mine. Her proud carriage and air of innocent trust were surely Michael's.

When she saw me, she rose from her place, took something from her pocket and opened her hand for me to see. My locket lay glistening in her palm. I wept as I held her in my arms. "My dearest child, welcome home."

Roslin whispered, "Thank you, Mama, I love you."

Everyone was staring in disbelief, and then with joy. What miracle had restored her hearing? Jacques stayed long enough to make sure he was no longer needed. He seemed puzzled but made no comment then. I saw a hint of sorrow in his eyes as he left us.

JW stepped to Michael's side. "Sir, may I have the honor of looking after her?"

Michael took several long moments before he answered. "Yes, but only if she agrees to it. I have a feeling her life has been, in many ways, as tragic as her mother's. Love her gently."

JW kissed Roslin's hand as he wished her good night.

I asked Michael what sleeping arrangements he'd made for Margot.

"I have one guest room with two beds. I'd like for Margot to stay with Roslin for a few nights until her sleep pattern returns to more normal hours."

Then, he spoke to me, his voice filled with tenderness. "I'll be in to care for you, if I may?"

I wasn't sure what he meant but I nodded, yes. At least it was Sunday and he didn't need to get up for work. I kissed Roslin good night as she left the kitchen hand in hand with Margot. Both were speaking French with much joy.

How thoughtful of the men to think of sending for Margot. I wondered if she'd come home early because of something that happened in France. Later we would have a visit to get the news from Campbell's Point. I still hoped to return there to make my home.

I needed to call Renquist and have him get some properties lined up for me to see. He would love dealing with me again. I chuckled at the thought. My thoughts were dashing from one thing to another when there was a tap on the door. It was Michael, in his pajamas and robe.

He said, "I thought you might enjoy a chance to get cleaned up before you return to bed since you were wakened from your nap so late."

He held a large soft robe for me and turned away as I slipped out of my clothes. "Come, it will be more comfortable in the bathroom."

The robe fit over my cast and I sat on a stool as he ran the hot water into the sink. He found a bar of lavender soap in the cupboard and began to wash my face. He rinsed and then patted my face dry with a towel.

The sleeves of the robe were large enough so that he could reach my arms and wash around my cast. Then he did my legs. He moved behind me and loosened the tie on my robe, so that it fell from my shoulders but still protected me in front, as he washed my back and shoulders. He lifted the robe back onto my shoulders, prepared a fresh warm, soaped cloth and put it in my left hand. "The rest of the job is yours. I'll see if I can find some pajamas for you while you finish up."

When he returned, I was weeping.

"What's the matter, Sara? Did I hurt you?"

"No," I whispered, "you didn't. No one has ever touched me like that before. Thank you."

The pajamas were large enough to slip over my head and I didn't have to struggle to get them over my cast. Michael wiped my tears away and we returned to the bedroom. He found some extra pillows and we made a nest to prop my body at the most comfortable angle. I was so weary. What a difficult day and now I needed rest.

Michael knelt by the bed and kissed me. "If it's all right, I want to stay until I know you're sleeping well. Goodnight, My Dear."

There wasn't much night left. In fact I could hear the first sounds of the robins announcing their territory and the first sweet love sounds of a dove calling to his mate.

It was almost nine o'clock when I wakened. Michael was asleep in the big chair by the window. The house was quiet, so the others must still be sleeping too or were off about their own business. I sat on the edge of the bed for several long moments watching him in sleep. He seemed so vulnerable and so innocent. How could he want a wounded woman like me? I couldn't live in denial of those wounds and he had already acknowledged that. Could I be humble enough to accept his love? Could I allow him to share my shame and my history? I knelt by his chair, and laid my head in his lap.

He wakened and stroked my hair. "Go close the door and bring a blanket back with you. This is probably the only quiet time we'll have today. We need to make some plans."

I smiled. "If it's more than two things, I'll need pencil and paper too."

He pointed to the desk and I found what I needed. I closed the door and brought the blanket. We made a nest in the chair and it was a few moments before we settled down to work. His kiss was gentle but full of commitment and promise. My answering one was too.

He started right in. "We have the pleasure and help of Margot for only a few days. Then she must be back to serve the Greers when they return from Scandinavia. I'm hoping that you and Roslin will be able to travel by then and can go with her. Just as soon as JW's second surgery is over, he will go back too. He can arrange for physical therapy in Pittsburgh. I need to find someone to drive you back or you'll all need to fly. Depending upon what sort of pledge you and I can make, I have several options."

He was trying so hard to be open and fair but wasn't considering what Roslin or I might want or what I might be able to arrange.

"Shall I listen to your plans?" I smiled, "or tell you instead how I think it might work out?"

Michael looked puzzled, but thought about it. "I have a feeling I'd better listen to you first, and save myself a lot of foolish blather."

I snuggled closer. "Now, may I have a kiss as long as your blather would have taken?"

That signed and sealed, I made some alternative suggestions he thought sounded interesting. "I think the Greers will open their hearts and the little cottage so Roslin can stay close to Margot while she becomes settled and acquainted with our friends. JW needs to get back to his business. I think I'll accept the offer of the Foreign Language department but only if they will allow me to go to school to begin my ESL degree too."

He smiled. "Now it's my turn to ask for a kiss as long as your talk."

That taken care of, he said, "And what about me?"

"Michael, what would you like to have happen?"

There were no tears here, no weaseling around, no problem saying how he felt. "Sara Harvey, I love you; more than ever, if that's possible. I would even move to Pennsylvania to be a part of your life. In fact, I've had two job offers in Pittsburgh from scouts who were present the day of JW's surgery. Did you know they did that? They're just like baseball scouts who go to games to find talent."

I kissed his nose. "Well, if you'd asked me the same question, I would have said I love you so much I would move to St. Louis, to be a part of your life. So we have a few more options than we thought. Remember, Roslin is thirty-four years old. I haven't talked to her enough to know about her English skills. Her needs should come first, as long as she wants and needs our help. Apparently JW is interested in what happens too. Michael, I think it will work and I would like to try. It won't be easy, but nothing worth doing ever is."

I barely managed to get the last word out, before my mouth was firmly closed by his kiss. We sat in companionable silence.

"We really should be getting up. Do you know what I'd like to include in the day? Would you take me to your church? I thought we might find a service at five o'clock since we missed the morning ones. Maybe my strange clothing won't be so noticeable then."

"Good idea. I'll check the schedule. The church is only a few blocks away. We can walk. One of our biggest problems for getting people around in the next few days is going to be drivers. I'm the only one you've got now."

"How come? Where's Jacques?"

He lifted me down and rose to go to the desk. "Jacques's gone. He said good-bye to me this morning after he made sure Roslin would be all right. I think he waited until you went upstairs because he couldn't bear to see you again. He left you a note."

> *My Dear Sara,*
>
> *Please forgive me for not waiting to tell you good-bye. I was so devastated when I watched the tapes from the workroom and realized the terror you endured; I felt I couldn't bear to face you. It was my carelessness and my fault alone that you were attacked. I'm going to New York to my new assignment. Perhaps the honesty and innocence of the forest will help me to heal, as I know it has helped you over the years.*
>
> *I was unable to deal with closing up my house. Professionals will be coming in on Thursday to pack everything for storage and to get the house ready for the buyer. He still wants it and the lawyer will take care of it. I left a key with Mike so you can go there and take anything you wish. Please feel free to enjoy what you would like.*
>
> *I was filled with joy when I met your lovely daughter Roslin Marie. I know how very important it was for you to find her and to gather her into your family. I found it amazing that her hearing was restored when she reunited with her family. Love is very powerful.*

I pray that you will find it in your heart to forgive me.
Jacques Grayson

I handed the note to Michael. "Dear Jacques. I hope he finds his Indian woman. Did he explain to you about the trip to the house?" He nodded yes.

"I would like very much to accept his gifts and I know exactly what I want to search for. Perhaps JW and I can go tomorrow in the daylight and it won't be so frightening. We could take a taxi, or perhaps we could all go, after you finish the hearing.

"We'd better begin our public day. It won't take me long to get ready. I have only one choice of clothing. I'll meet you downstairs and we'll organize the rest of the day when we find out who's here and what they want to do."

It was a glorious early summer day. The sky was sapphire blue. Chubby teardrop clouds drifted across it like a group of snowy swans. It would be quite warm later in the afternoon. Much more rain in Missouri than in Pennsylvania the last few weeks had helped the flowers to flourish. I wondered if Michael might be a gardener. There was so much for us to learn about each other in the coming weeks and years.

Everyone was gathered at the outside patio table with their rolls, fruit and mugs of coffee. I smiled in contentment. "How long have you been up?"

They assured me it hadn't been long.

"Any requests for today?" I paused for a moment. "I've made mine to Michael since this will be his only day with all of us this week." I glanced at him. "Did you find the times for Mass?"

He nodded yes. "The one at five o'clock would probably suit us best."

I smiled. "Any of you who'd like to join us; we'll leave here at 4:30. Otherwise, I just want to be with you and keep reassuring myself that all this has really happened."

I turned to Roslin. "My dearest daughter, I've thought of you as Dove Cameron for all these years because I didn't know what name your family had given you. Have you thought about what you would like for us to call you?"

Her answer was logical and filled with love. "My dear family, I've been known as Roslin Marie Parmentier all my life. I would like to keep my name. I hope you won't be offended; it doesn't make me any less your daughter."

I realized at once that her English was in fact very polished, and language would not be a problem in her adjustment. I wondered how she'd managed it with her hearing handicap.

She continued, "Let me tell you about the locket that linked our lives and prepared me to know you when you found me, such a short time ago.

"The locket was in a small box of my mother's things. I didn't know that I was adopted until she was dying. She told me my own mother gave her the locket to keep for me. There was a young boy's picture in the locket. I spent many hours looking at him before I realized there might be some other clue. When I removed the tiny picture, a thin piece of paper fell into my lap. You know what it said, Mama. I read it and kept whispering it to myself, 'My name is Dove Cameron'. I didn't know what to do. I just kept the knowledge in my heart and waited. After my mother died, I was in very desperate times and took the job with the family in Nice to survive. Because I was deaf, it was very difficult. They gave me only board, room, and never any pay. I could not save any money to escape and he ..."

She began to cry as she continued. "When they brought me to the United States to do the written English at the business meeting; I saw my one chance for freedom. They did not abandon me in Soulard; I stole a few dollars from Madam's purse and got on the bus. I ran away, just as far and into as unlikely a neighborhood as I could find."

She smiled as she rose from the table. "Would someone be willing to take me for a walk? I would like to truly hear my freedom now."

We all rose together but it was Michael who nodded to JW. The rest of us would have our chance later. Just now, those two wounded souls needed each other most.

As I touched Margot's arm, we noticed her wince in pain. "Margot, please stay and tell us the news from Campbell's Point. I feel as though I've been gone for a year instead of just a few days. How's the baseball team doing?"

She knew a good bit about the game because of her friendship with Thad and Tim, and told a delightful story about the last game they'd played before she left. Of course Thad was the hero. We visited a few minutes more and then I said, "What happened in France, My Dear?"

She didn't cry but her eyes glistened as she said, "He married someone else several years ago and didn't tell me."

Margot rose from her chair. "When I reached out to touch him, he struck me so hard I think something's broken. Is it too late for you to help me?"

As I looked up at Michael, he was already on the way to the phone to alert the ER crew. I wrote a quick note to JW and Roslin to let them know where we were and we headed to the hospital. I think Margot's tears were now ones of relief and I held her as best I could, to protect her arm. I was glad Michael didn't have to do this surgery, resetting a bone must be a terrible part of his job.

It seemed like forever before Michael's working partner Rick came out. "It went fine, Doc. She can stay here or go home with you, if you can care for her."

One of the other doctors piped up, "Your house must look like costume preparations for Trick or Treat Night, Mike. What's going on over there?"

"I seem to attract trouble, guys. I'll see you tomorrow at six o'clock. I need to come back to work to rest up from the weekend."

The three young ones stayed at home while Michael and I walked to church. His home was in a pleasant neighborhood of older houses, mostly Sears and Craftsman era bungalows. The yards were well kept and had pleasant gardens and landscaping. Every porch had hanging baskets of petunias and verbena and Pelargonium. It looked like they didn't compete with their neighbors but shared a feeling of live and let live.

The streets were lined with sycamores and maples, and the cars parked at the curb on this late Sunday afternoon suggested comfortable affluence. Other couples were walking to church, some with little ones in tow. It was almost a step back in time to see people in a big city, free to walk their neighborhood without fear.

The church was of the same vintage as the houses and I was gladdened to find the statues and stained glass windows of an earlier time still in place or perhaps they had been returned from their Vatican II exile in basement storage. As we stepped inside, the familiar odor of incense, flowers, and dusty air brought me to my knees. Michael knelt beside me, and I wept.

Before the service, I remembered those who had no one to pray for them. I prayed for Andretti's soul and for Jenny. Michael's presence was balm for my pain and I was at peace.

As we left the church after Mass, the priest was greeting parishioners at the door. When I thanked him for the thoughts in the homily, he glanced at Michael. "This is the lovely Madam Lambert of whom you have spoken?" His slight Gallic accent was a delight.

Michael smiled. "It is indeed. May we come to visit with you this week? Would you save an evening appointment for us?" Father James nodded yes.

We took another route home and discovered delightful streets and a cluster of small stores including a bakery and tiny restaurant with several tables scattered about the sidewalk. Michael took my hand. "Would you like to come for supper here, after we go to see Father James?"

"That would be lovely, Michael. It would be our first date in a long time."

We picked up the pace and hurried home. When I checked to see how Margot was feeling, she said, "I do not feel well, Madam. I think the medication for my pain has made me ill." The men figured out something else for her.

Roslin and I made a survey of the food in the refrigerator and cupboards and decided we could do fine without going to the store. When I thought of what she had been eating for the last several years, I was humbled anew by her attitude and grace. We stopped often for heartfelt hugs. As I stroked her hair, I couldn't help but remember all my days of weeping and grief and the years of not knowing how she was or where she might be.

Margot and the men came into the kitchen as we finished our task. Suddenly, I was swept away in a tide of exhaustion so deep I reached for a chair. "My Dear Ones, I need to get to bed. Let's wait until tomorrow to decide how we might make our trip to Jacques' house. We have until Wednesday night to do it. I think all of you might like to see it. It's a hauntingly beautiful place and I need to make my peace with it and lay my nightmares to rest. Perhaps with all of you present, it will be possible."

Michael was standing beside me and his look of concern surprised me. "Are you sure you want to do that?"

"I may want to go in twice. Once to clean up the worst of the evidence and then I want my family to see what Jenny did at the height of her career. It sheltered Jacques for several years. Have you been there?"

"No, he didn't share his personal life. I didn't know where he lived."

I reached for his hand. "I need you tonight, Michael."

He helped me to the bedroom and I waited while he got ready for bed. Then he came to me. We went through the bath ritual of the evening before.

"You're so gentle and thoughtful. I love you, Michael Cameron."

He settled me in bed and asked, "May I stay with you, Sara?"

He opened the windows wider and left the light on by the bed. How could so much happen in just one day? I was so weary that I felt physically ill. Perhaps I should find an oncologist to consult. When the one in Spokane essentially dismissed me to go home and get my affairs in order, I decided I would rather have some quality of life than go through the alternatives. But now, I cared whether I lived or died and I was terrified of the prospect of a cancer death. I reached out to him. "I need you, Michael. I'm so frightened. Please come and hold me. Promise me I won't die a lingering, painful death."

He came to me and sat by the bed. "I wish I could, Sara, but I can't. We don't know what's going to happen to any of us. All I can

105

promise is that I won't let you go through it alone. I won't abandon you.

"The first thing we need is to get a second opinion about your condition. If you'll allow me to choose someone, I'll make appointments for a general physical and for an oncologist as soon as I can get you in. Would that help your fear?"

"I think so. It's better to know than to guess or imagine what's going on inside. I don't think I've ever been as weary as in the last few days."

Michael smiled. "Don't you think it might be because of all the stress and trauma of your training and attack?"

"I hope to God you're right, Michael, I don't want to lose you now."

We rearranged the pillows and I moved to make room for him in my bed. We lay as best we could, his arm curved over my waist as we drifted off to sleep. That night I didn't waken with a nightmare. In fact, Michael slipped away in the morning for work and I didn't feel him leave.

CHAPTER TEN

The men left early for the hospital. A note on the kitchen table said the hearing was at one p.m. and they would be home after it was over. Surely it wouldn't take very long and I hoped there would be no trouble. When the girls came late to breakfast, we ate our simple meal on the patio and sat visiting until it became too warm for comfort.

They found the note when we returned inside and were pleased the men would be home early. They didn't know anything about the hearing, and I didn't tell them it was about me.

We felt like fairy princesses. closeted and waiting for something wonderful to happen. We decided to explore. This was Michael's home and it suited what I knew about him so far. He honored the basic architecture of his bungalow, but not slavishly. The floors were original wood and the woodwork had not been painted. There were two fireplaces, one in the library and one in the living room, with lead glass windows above the bookshelves on each side. In the library, large French doors opened out into the garden.

His yard was generous in size with room for a small pond fed by a gentle water cascade. In the cascade on a shelf of shale rocks, sat a statue of a water sprite playing the flute.

It was interesting that Michael chose to turn the formal living room into a master bedroom, but it made sense. He probably didn't entertain much and when he did, the library would be the perfect place, with a fireplace in winter and entry into the garden in summer.

We noticed a paneled door in the library in between two large floor-to-ceiling shelves of books. There was no clue to its use or where it went. We all gathered, giggling, convinced it was Bluebeard's closet. The door wasn't locked. When we opened it, all three of us gasped. It was like the Greers' cottage in feel, as though someone were expected and welcome.

There were silk daffodils and tulips in a bowl on the table and several women's magazines stacked on an end table. At the small writing desk, someone had laid out stationery with envelopes and stamps. I looked down to see the denomination. They were 34-cent ones so this wasn't a museum. It was decorated to be a woman's room, with English chintz and pastel colors on the walls. A collection of orchids in pots and African violets under grow lights in a shaded corner suggested a frequent visitor. We looked at each other, puzzled, and a little scared. Perhaps we shouldn't have explored in Michael's house.

I wondered if Michael had a mistress. No, there was no scent of a woman here, no hint of cologne or powder or lavender soap. Nothing was out of place, as though someone used the room daily. I hurried to look at the titles of the books on the shelves. They were mostly about gardening, cooking and travel, but some were about English and Scottish history.

"We'd better leave." I whispered to the others, "I don't know who uses this room but I'm scared."

We were coming out the door of the secret room into the library, as Michael and JW came in. Well, at least we might get an explanation. But I was concerned that we had invaded his privacy and he might be very angry. My frightened tone must have surprised him as I pleaded, "Michael, please forgive us, we were exploring the house and playing fairy princess, when we found this exquisite secret room. Please don't be angry with us."

We stood still, waiting for his answer. He wasn't angry. In fact he smiled and apologized for not giving us a tour of the house; pleading distractions of the direst kind, like broken bones and extra company.

Then he explained, "It's my mother's room. She comes during the symphony season and for the Muni in the summer. She spends the night instead of trying to get home afterwards. In their later years, my folks moved down from the lake to be nearer to me. When my father died, mother moved to the town where her childhood friends still live. I hope she'll have a chance to meet you before the summer is over."

I hoped Michael wouldn't notice the sigh of relief from each of us as we chuckled at our busy imaginations. That's what make-believe used to be all about when we were kids, but that was a long time ago.

Michael took my hand and led me out into the garden. "Things went well but I'm glad you didn't have to appear. Now, I want to request, from the bottom of my heart, please don't ask to return to Jacques' house. If you can make a list, JW and I will go now and try to find the things."

His tone of voice concerned me. Why had he discussed it with JW?

I whispered, "Why?"

Michael took me in his arms. "Dave wouldn't let us have the tapes when he took off for Pittsburgh, so this morning JW and I watched the set Jacques left for us. I don't want you to go anywhere near that place, to be reminded of what happened, or to hear or see anything you might not have known about at the time. I won't often try to force my will on you, Sara, but this time I must try."

We stood there together as I decided what to do. The men seemed to be trying to protect me from something. I wondered what it was.

And then, I didn't care anymore. I was relieved. I hadn't wanted to return. Perhaps my demons would leave me alone more quickly if I didn't encourage them to reappear.

I reached up to touch his face. "Thank you, Michael; your request is wise and I won't argue. I'll go in right now and make the list, with instructions about where to find the things. The police may have moved some of them. I don't even wish to see the things when you find them. You can take a box and pack them for another time and place."

I sketched a map of the layout of the rooms and their names as I explained, "First you'll need the codes for getting in and out of the rooms. I hope they're still in the computers. If they aren't, here are the numbers." Then I gave the list to the men.

1. Cherry box lined with deerskin, probably in the work-room cupboard
2. The belt and special buckle that held the knives, and the knives, which should be in the buckle unless the police have taken them
3. The unfinished picture of Andretti; on the easel in the workroom. Just cut it from the frame and roll it
4. The two pottery bowls with oak leaves in the bottom from the kitchen cupboard, and
5. The priedieu from the sanctuary.

I also asked them to see if any of Jacques' shirts were left, ones I could use over my cast for a few weeks.

I made sure they had their cell phone in case they got caught in a room someplace and couldn't get out. After the men left for Jacque's place, I settled into Michael's favorite chair by the French doors and waited.

I really didn't know much about what had happened that morning of the attack, it happened so fast. Andretti and I were at the end of our conversation about the portrait I was painting of him, and I remembered how devastated he was when he saw so graphically what I believed about him. I told him what Dave had said about his being the one who had tried to kill me and he was in the middle of a passionate denial.

I was standing, facing him with my back to the entrance door, when the attack began. The searing pain of my shattered arm made me collapse into Andretti's body. I thought I recognized Jenny's voice. She said something about a bomb and then something to Andretti about me. My mind went blank except for a desire to survive. I wasn't making sense of most of what she was saying. After the first shot, Andretti gathered me into his arms and turned around with me. Before the second shot, I thought I heard another voice say, "Shoot again." With the second shot, Andretti collapsed onto me and I became as still and small as I could, curled under him.

I heard the sound of feet running away. After several long minutes of deathly quiet, someone came back. There was a slight shift in Andretti's position and I felt the warmth of his life's blood draining onto my face. Someone had slit his throat. I was sure I'd be next. Then the phone rang.

Jenny must have panicked when she couldn't get the outside door open. Jacques told me earlier that he had reprogrammed the system to lock both directions after unauthorized entry. Even Angela couldn't override it.

The only way she could get out, was to disable the control panel and the only tool she had was the chair. I heard the sound of glass and wood smashing. With the electricity off, the switches, doors and windows, and locks would open. Only she could have known it because she designed the house and its wiring.

As I waited for the men to return, I became more frantic. It was almost two hours before the front door opened and I heard their voices. Michael came carrying a box and stopped to say they were successful, but Jacques had taken all his clothes. I wondered if the men had decided I shouldn't have them to remind me of his earlier presence in my life.

Michael seemed preoccupied and weary. It must have been a difficult day for him. With the hearing, the viewing of the tape and the trip to Jacques' house, he had relived a great deal of my pain.

He came to me and suggested we sit in the garden by the pond. "Our appointment with Father James can be this evening at 6:30 p.m. or we can put it off until you're ready to go. I don't want to rush you."

I took Michael's hands in mine. "My Dearest, if you would like to go tonight, I'm ready. We need each other now more than ever and I want to make the commitment with you to start the journey." We sat quietly for a few more moments and then got ready for the evening.

The first session with Father James was magical. There was so much love in the study that I spent most of the hour crying. Michael's love, my love and the love of God were all mixed together into a gentle brew. We enjoyed the promised supper at the street café and returned home about dark. We checked to see that everyone was fine and offered our good night.

Michael's schedule would be a bit difficult to get used to, but I enjoyed starting to bed early on summer evenings, when the birds were tucking their babies in for the night. The dove was singing his good night love song to his mate and the nighthawks were just taking to the skies. The scent of lilies of the valley lay on the evening air. Not too many weeks away, the lightning bugs would begin their summer enchantment of those with a childlike heart.

That night I decided to ask Michael to allow me to do the bath ritual for him too. I had a deep need to touch him. As I worked on his body, I saw the deep abrasion scars and knife scars of a fighting man. I was frightened by them but didn't say anything.

In the middle of the night a big rainstorm blew in from the northwest. Huge bolts of lightning and wave after wave of slashing rain beat against the windows. I got up to make sure the windows were closed around the house and met everyone else doing the same. No one was afraid and we were wide-awake so we went to the kitchen for a snack. We found the cookies that Roslin and Margot had baked the afternoon before, and devoured them with glasses of milk.

On the way back to bed, I reopened the windows facing away from the storm so the lovely fresh air could come into the house. I felt so sheltered and safe and so thankful for my family around me. I came into the library to open the windows and found Michael sitting in his favorite chair in front of the French doors.

I whispered to him as I bent down to give him a kiss, "Oh, Michael, I'm so happy I want to sing. I feel so surrounded by love."

He reached out to me. "I love you, Sara. Your happiness is my delight. But come to me, My Beloved, I need you now. I'm grieving for Jenny, who will die before the week ends, and I grieve for Jacques who will do something he may regret for the rest of his life."

I went to kneel by his chair. I knew what he meant about Jenny because of Dave's recent warning. But how would Michael know? I didn't understand what he meant about Jacques and I feared for him. "Is there anything we can do?"

He sighed and shook his head. "Sometimes souls are driven beyond bearing. Jacques' demons are driving him to disaster."

We sat together with our own thoughts until I needed to go to bed to get warm. His touch was gentle. "Good night, Sara. I'll see you this evening. I'll call you if I can get those appointments arranged." Our kiss was filled with tenderness and I went upstairs alone.

Tuesday dawned with pale blue sky and air so fresh and clean that we decided it must have come straight from the Canadian prairies. Flowers were iridescent with tiny rainbows, and robins stomped the damp ground, drumming up fat worms for their breakfast.

The girls and I decided to be domestic and scrub the kitchen, clean the refrigerator and stove; scrub bathrooms and do the washing and ironing. Since two of us had only one workable hand and arm, it was an interesting morning. We rummaged around among the leftovers and made a pot of vegetable soup for supper. Roslin and I slipped outside to see if there might be some herbs tucked away in the garden. To our great delight, we found a tiny herb garden flourishing in a corner by the kitchen door.

I told Roslin about the little town of Campbell's Point and the main street with Gary's Grill. When I mentioned the French cook at Gary's, she looked up with interest. "A friend from home came over here a few years ago. Wouldn't it be fun if it turned out to be Yvette?"

We spent a few moments on the bench by the pond as she told me more about her friend. Then we picked several bouquets of flowers for the house and carried them into the kitchen to arrange them. I liked Michael's home; it was quite comfortable and welcoming. I wondered what it must have been like for him to have all those years alone. About that time he called to let me know both appointments were arranged for tomorrow.

I made a list of things to do in the next few days including a talk with Tim. I wanted him to open the package of books I ordered in Pittsburgh, with the ones for Kylie Lou and Abe. It looked now as though it would be several weeks before I could get back there and I didn't want them to think I'd abandoned them. I wanted to ask Tim if he and Tricia might be willing to help the Foresters with their reading, and more important, whether they would be willing to help with the next sections of the Family Planning. I saw no reason to keep the information from Tricia and Tim. I trusted them to use the information honorably. Maybe we could call Tim tomorrow.

We made fresh bread to go with our soup. Supper was as nice as any at the Greers' and the setting just as pleasant. We visited with the men and JW announced his acceptance into the Music Therapy program in Pittsburgh. When we left them to finish their coffee, I was thinking ahead to what Roslin might want to do. She was not having any trouble with her English. I didn't think she would need much looking after if she went to Campbell's Point with Margot and I didn't come to stay. I went to the pond bench to greet the shadows of nightfall. It was JW who came to sit with me. "May I join you for a few moments? Michael needed to finish some paperwork."

"Of course, JW. You enjoy this time of day too. I'm frightened about tomorrow but I think it's better to know than to make wild guesses. I'm glad you'll be there. May I claim you as kin so they'll allow you to be with me?"

"Which kinship would you like to claim?"

I was quiet for several long moments. Then I whispered, "Since it would be neither wise nor possible to have the one I really want, I think son-in-law would please me most."

I watched his eyes grow glistening tears as he reached over, took my hands and kissed them on the palms, then the backs.

"JW, I've enjoyed a small taste of happiness in the past few days since we found Roslin; happiness, contentment, a feeling of being wrapped in a blanket of love. Why has it come with pain and sorrow too? What happened to Jenny? And Michael said something about Jacques being in trouble. What did he mean? I have a feeling you know but I can't be told."

He didn't answer. I took his bandaged hand into my lap. "Could we sing Dove's lullaby, and then would you sing some of those beautiful songs you shared with me in the hospital? It was so difficult to hear every word and to feel every touch, but not be able to move or show you that I knew you were there."

We began with the lullaby. I closed my eyes as we sang and didn't see the girls come out into the yard. Michael opened the library doors to step out and be with us. Michael began to sing too. I recognized his deep baritone voice. Where had he learned that song?

Then Margot and Roslin shared several from their home. When JW began to sing his own songs, all of us were carried away into our own sweet places. They were about the seasons and flowers and happy times. Then he began to sing love songs. They were so haunting and beautiful I felt as though I were eavesdropping on a very personal part of his life. I glanced over to see what Roslin's response might be. She was weeping.

We went back into the house, leaving the lovers sitting on the bench, hand in hand, in obvious need of a kiss. Margot was weeping too. She must be wishing for Thad tonight. I took her hand. "When will the Greers be getting home? I don't know how we would have managed the last few days without you, but I have the feeling you need to go home now."

Margot thought a moment. "I think they'll be home this Sunday night. I don't know how they'll feel if I'm not there when they arrive or about my injury and not being able to work."

I turned to Michael. "Do you think she'll be ready to go home by the end of the week? I've gotten used to looking funny. I could take her on the plane and come right back."

He took my hand. "I've been rearranging my schedule to be free after Thursday so I can take you all. That's what I've been doing this evening. We can leave on Friday morning and be in Campbell's Point the next afternoon. Would you ladies like that?"

He got two big, one-armed hugs as we whispered, "Yes".

He went out to tell the others, while Margot and I began to make plans. We were like little children anticipating a big event. I couldn't believe how much I wanted to return to Campbell's Point. I wanted Roslin to visit the town and see whether she might like to settle there. We'd try to have a meal at Gary's with everyone Sunday at noon. We might need to work around a baseball game. I knew there were enough beds at JW's for all of us, so we would have a place to stay. It would be a tight squeeze with five in the car but I didn't care. After we got there we would have plenty of vehicles and drivers since Tim could help.

When we returned to the library, JW and Roslin were visiting with Michael. They seemed to be waiting for me. JW was explaining to her about his going back to school and how long it might take. She smiled and took his hand. "May I help by finding a job? I could teach French, or perhaps the cook at Gary's might like some authentic help. This weekend visit is coming at a perfect time for us all. Roslin smiled as she reached to touch his cheek. "Jamie, my only request is that I won't have to wait until you're through school for us to be married. I want to be the mother of your children."

We returned to the patio as I whispered, "Well, that's that. I hope they'll be very happy."

Our own kisses were gentle and comforting. We went to the bench to talk, but the mosquitoes drove us back inside. The lovers were gone and Michael returned to his paperwork.

When I got to the kitchen to make the tea, I was overtaken by a wave of exhaustion so severe that I needed to sit down. I was weeping when Michael came to find me. "Come with me, Sara. You need to get to bed. I'll get you ready first."

When I was tucked in with my pillows and settled for the night, he sat by my side and asked what I needed.

I smiled. "Do you remember just a few days ago when we were making grand plans for everyone's lives? Many things have worked themselves out without our help and many surprises have come at us. I was concerned about where I would stay when we came back. Somehow, I think it will work out too." I was so exhausted I literally fell asleep as I was talking.

We were up and out of the house by six o'clock, and I was still yawning as we entered the security area at the hospital. My first appointment was at nine o'clock and the men left me on Michael's office couch to catch a few more hours of sleep. JW walked me to my first appointment and waited as the woman doctor poked and prodded and asked a million questions. We finished up with the oncologist about the same time Michael finished his day. I was still yawning. "I'm so weary, Michael, I really need a nap. Don't forget to call Father James to reschedule our session for next week. I don't want to miss a single one and set back our plans."

He walked me upstairs and helped me settle into bed. "We'll come get you in time for supper. Sleep well, Dear Heart."

I hoped Michael didn't see my worried expression. Those were Jacques' words of endearment for me, and now I was reminded of his apparent troubles.

I was still sound asleep when Roslin brought me some supper. It was getting dark and the crickets were tuning up for the night. She stayed while I ate and we talked about my illness. She picked up my tray to leave and began to cry. "Mama, please get well. I can't lose you now." She put the tray down as we clung to each other.

I sat up in my big chair, working through a myriad of twisted thoughts. Something was very wrong; I felt it in my gut. I finally went back to bed and restless sleep. It was about one o'clock when I wakened from a terrifying, screaming nightmare. Everyone came into my room as Michael held me.

I was sobbing and twisted away from him. "Something terrible is happening to Jenny and Jacques. Everything is chaos; there's blood everywhere. My God!" I whispered, "Jenny's dead."

I closed my eyes to the horror of the scene. "There was a huge explosion. Everything flew up into the air and then fell, burning into the water. Michael, her soul is gone."

Michael took me into his arms again. "Dear God! Are you clairvoyant too, Sara?"

"Sometimes. But never have I witnessed a scene as brutal and tragic as this."

Michael didn't send the girls away. I think he knew how worried they were. They waited with me until I calmed down enough to stop crying. I whispered to them, "Thank you for staying with me. It isn't easy being so sensitive to another's terrors."

They returned to their own beds, except Michael. He went through the bath ritual again with gentleness and calm. When he finished we closed the door of the bedroom and curled up together. He held me in his arms until I slept.

When I finally wakened he was gone and I felt a crushing sadness as I remembered the night's events. Margot was sitting in the big chair by the window. She didn't seem like herself without her ever-present embroidery.

"Good morning Madam. Jamie decided to stay home today to get ready for the trip and to keep an eye on you. You frightened us all. If you're ready to get up, I'll let Roslin know. I feel so useless with my arm in a cast. I'm worried about whether I will have a job when I go home. I think the Greers may bring someone back with them to replace me, since they expected me to be leaving to be married. I don't know what will happen to me now." She was weeping as her hands twisted in her lap.

I went to her, knelt by her chair and took her hand. "Dear Margot, please don't worry. JW told me that Thad has been waiting for years to marry you. He loves you very much. Michael and I love you too, and we won't let anyone hurt you. We'll even try to buy your freedom if we can. You may stay with us and be part of our family." I hoped she understood what I was trying to say.

Packing took little time. We didn't have a suitcase full among us. I still couldn't wear any of the clothes gifted to me by my friends. How much longer would I be in my cast? I didn't know. Margot would be in hers for a month or more. JW would have a new one late next week when we returned to do his second operation.

It was shamelessly late for breakfast and we laughed about it. In fact it was so warm we closed up the house right after breakfast and turned on the air conditioning. Something was nagging at the back of my mind. When I remembered what it was, I turned to JW. "Have you talked to Tim since we found out we're coming home this weekend?"

JW chuckled. "I caught him last night in the middle of a ball game out of town. He said, 'Great! Thanks for the warning. I haven't washed dishes since you left. Maybe Tricia will help me out.' With his usual cheery 'See Ya' at the end, he admitted the game wasn't going too well, but maybe Thad would cheer up since Margot was coming home." Margot looked up from her dishwashing. Her shy smile was radiant.

About noon JW answered the phone in the library. He was gone a long time and I wondered who it was. I asked when he returned, "Was it Dave Finch?"

JW nodded. "How did you know?"

"Because I was expecting him to call today if he'd heard about Jenny and Jacques. Who did he want to speak to?"

JW answered truthfully. "You, but I told him he would need to talk to Michael first. Those were Michael's orders when he left this morning. You weren't to speak to anyone outside the family today except Father James."

"I'll bet Dave wasn't too happy about that."

JW seemed puzzled. "I thought he would be angry. Instead he said, 'Wise man, that Cameron. Tell him I'll try to catch him tonight, before you all leave for Campbell's Point.' How would he have known we were going away?"

I was puzzled, but had no answer I could share.

Michael was the next to call. Father James would see us tonight at 6:30, but if I would like other arrangements to call him back. Dear Michael. Did he know how much I treasured his quiet, steady love? I let the three young ones fend for themselves for supper and chose to sit in the silence of the library, waiting for Michael. It was probably good we were going away now, since it would be late next week before some of the tests from the hospital would be read. I was torn between wanting to know and wanting to pretend everything was fine, when I feared it wasn't.

I settled down in the library for a nap. When I wakened, I glanced out the library door to see Michael standing in the grass using his cell phone. I hadn't meant to usurp his territory and would need to apologize when he came for me. I was surprised when he came to the French doors, put his finger to his lips and motioned me out into the garden.

"JW said that Dave called and knew we were leaving for Pennsylvania. No question but what your people play hardball. We've been infested with bugs. Dave must have left them when he was here Saturday for the meeting. I've called to have someone take care of them while we're gone."

My eyes must have shown my surprise. "Whatever would he do that for?"

Michael grinned, "I hope it's just little boys playing games. A little gotcha! I'll caution JW to do their lovemaking quietly tonight. I expect Dave even did the front porch swing. Now, I'll bet our choices for supper are leftovers or leftovers. Let's sneak out and have something before we go to our meeting. There should be plenty of time."

"Give me five minutes and I'll be ready. Come up while I change."

"Can you do quiet kisses?"

I smiled, "Let's go see."

We settled in for supper at the little café. It was strictly family style and the owners did all the cooking. It was relaxing to just sit and let someone else take care of us.

A little later, when we entered Father's office for our session, I wondered how he would handle the discussion of my first marriage. I didn't know whether Michael needed to hear all the sordid details. Father asked me what I felt I could do. Then I realized that JW had probably told Michael all my story and Michael might have spoken to Father James about it already. With all the things happening in the last few weeks and the information coming forward, I wasn't sure what was true and what wasn't.

I was surprised by the evenness of my answer as I began. "I'll try to answer your questions to the best of my understanding. I really didn't know my husband at all. He was a very private and driven man and I wasn't able to help him. I wanted to love him and to honor our marriage vows but he wasn't able to share any of his life or himself with me. It was incredibly lonely and I suffered for him every day."

I was weeping, and the men sat in silence with me. They gave me time for what needed saying and they validated my pain. I felt only gratitude for their kindness. Father chose to move on to other things and we spent the rest of the hour in more gentle and comfortable territory. My love for Michael was expanding until I wondered how my heart could hold it all. We walked home in the twilight, hand in hand.

Tomorrow would be a long, hard day and Michael was our only driver. He asked, "What time would you like to get started in the morning?"

"The earlier the better. You know I'm a lark."

He asked the others what they were willing to do, and then picked six o'clock. "We'll stop when the sun gets to the worst angle and have breakfast." He went off to pack.

CHAPTER ELEVEN

As much as I liked domesticity, I was ready now for an adventure. We felt like every living thing was up and singing, including us. It was fun to point out The Arch and other landmarks to Roslin. She'd never left Soulard in all the time she lived there. The countryside was in its most lush and busy growing time.

We started our junk food binge by eating breakfast biscuits stuffed with sausage and egg. Michael needed to stretch every hour or so and we needed to unfold from the back seat to rest our aching limbs. We traded off for the front seat once around and then left JW up there since his legs were the longest. We three girls sat in the back and giggled like teenagers, stooping to knock-knock jokes. JW finally cried uncle and threatened 99-Bottles-of-Beer-on-the-Wall, if we didn't hush.

"Are we there yet?" we chorused, as we left Indiana for Ohio. Everyone was punchy tired when we stopped on the east side of Columbus for the night.

It had been a good day of togetherness and I was contented as I gazed at my family while we ate supper. Margot looked happier the closer we got to home and I knew we were doing the right thing to try to get her home before the Greers returned. Thad would take her under his wing and I needed to let him know we were ready to do what we could to help. I didn't want to interfere with the Greers' authority but I was appalled that Margot was in the same kind of bondage as Roslin's had been, with only room, board and no pay for years.

Michael reached for my hand after supper. "Could we take a walk around the block? I need to get the kinks out of my legs. Looks like a park at the end of the street, let's head for it."

I had a feeling he needed to talk. We found a bench to share our own silence as we listened to children's happy voices and watched little boys practicing with their in-line skates.

"Michael, what's wrong? I can feel your hurt in my deepest heart."

"I wasn't going to tell you until we got back to St. Louis. Dave called last night late. I told him I didn't want to talk to him until Wednesday when we were on the way home, so it wouldn't spoil our trip. He insisted that it must be told now. I should have hung up.

119

"His story was essentially the same as the one my operative Bill phoned in yesterday morning early, except Dave didn't mention Jacques. I think he didn't know Jacques was there. Bill was sitting in a patio bar where he counted them as they boarded.

"He said there were eight people on the yacht when it left the dock, two women and six men. Three of the men were young, probably JW's stepsons; two of the men were in their late 30's, probably Mafia. He said they acted like they were old friends of Mrs. Campbell, complete with fanny pats and heavy fondling.

"A sixth man swam out at the last minute and climbed aboard using the ropes off the far side. Bill said he was wearing only swimming trunks but was carrying several pieces of equipment, including rope and a military style knife. Bill said he had dark skin and a braid of long dark hair that hung down his back. The two women were of about the same age, middle 30's, most likely JW's wife and Jenny. One was a blond, the other a redhead.

"The yacht headed out to sea at midnight and anchored about two miles out. The explosion in the middle of the night rattled every window in Bermuda. There were no identifying features for any of them, except for the bits of the women's long hair caught in the debris."

Michael's voice dropped to a whisper. "There was no trace of Jacques, Sara. I hope to God he jumped in time to escape. It was just as you saw it and the time was the same as when you suffered your nightmare."

We sat and grieved together until darkness reminded us we were in a strange town. It was several blocks back to the motel and we hurried back to the lighted street. I didn't want to leave Michael when we got to the motel so we walked around the parking lot while we calmed down.

Michael stopped and held me. "I'm sorry if I've spoiled your trip, but you needed to know, and I was desperate for you to bear some of it for me. I didn't want Dave to be the one to tell you. We won't speak of it on Wednesday. We need to stop at Dave's just long enough to pick up some papers. He says a package was delivered to the police. According to him, it's similar to the one at Jacques' place, but much more beautiful. The bomb squad gave it a safety check and it's clean. And this one's legitimate. The police say it's worth millions and we need to pick it up at the police station from the safe."

I was puzzled. "How very odd. Perhaps there'll be some kind of note in it to explain. Have you told JW about Jenny and his former wife?"

"Only the bare essentials of the report. Nothing about Jacques or that he was on board. I know why Jacques boarded the yacht, but I can't tell you about it now. Let's not say anything to Roslin about any of this. JW has a chance to start fresh in his life and I wouldn't want to do anything to spoil it for him."

I took his hands in mine. "Would it be possible for us to start fresh too? I knew your life story included much more than professional outward appearances. On the night you allowed me to see you during the bath ritual, I saw a body trained to peak performance. The knife scars and especially the abrasion scars were an added clue. You're not just a doctor, Michael. I love you so much I can't bear to think of something happening to you now."

He took me in his arms again. "Sara, Dearest, I joined the Navy and then went to medical school. I doctored for the SEALs when I was alone and my life wasn't of much importance to anyone. Since I've found you, I think things will need to be different. Please use this visit to Pennsylvania to help me continue to learn about you. I want to meet your friends and see the places you've grown to love. Perhaps we will fit well enough to choose it as our home. Now, we must get back to our family and get some sleep before tomorrow."

Our kiss was gentle and comforted us both. I whispered, "I love you, Commander."

I began the night with heartfelt prayers for the souls lost on the yacht, then for Michael, Roslin, Jacques, JW and Margot. After all the years of praying for my beloved child and Michael, I still couldn't believe that they were with me now.

I lay in bed thinking about taking Michael and Roslin to walk the main street with its tiny stores, and to meet the Foresters. We needed to drive out to the farm acreage to see what could be done. Perhaps Michael would like to go visit the two hospitals that recruited him while Tim took the rest of us to shop for clothes. I wanted to make arrangements for a big dinner at Gary's on Sunday and we needed to get together with Renquist to look for property on Monday.

In a weak moment I was tempted to go back to St. Louis with Michael and just be a doctor's wife instead.

I was the last one to waken on Saturday morning but the first one ready to take on the day. We decided to stay in the area after breakfast to visit the shopping mall. I felt like an Alaska prospector's wife who had only one change of clothes and only got to town once a year. With the extra complication of my cast, shopping was not easy. We were able to take care of all our important needs though, and I was glad we wouldn't need to go into Pittsburgh on Tuesday.

As we headed east, the rolling foothills of the Alleghenies came to meet us. The beautiful tulip poplars, maples, sycamores, and oaks were now glorious in shades of green. The honey locusts were coming into bloom and the fields were lush with tiny shafts of corn and chubby soybeans marching in rows for miles. The first crop of hay was almost ready to be baled. As we crossed the Ohio River, the farms were smaller, the fields more oddly shaped and there were more animals. We got to JW's by afternoon.

Roslin was very quiet during the trip. It must have been over-whelming to realize how big our country is, many times the size of France. I didn't even know the name of the town she grew up in. We had a lot to learn about each other.

Tricia and Tim were finishing up the dishes when we got there and supper was almost ready. After the meal, Tim was headed out for a baseball game so JW, Michael and Margot decided to go along for the evening.

I turned to Roslin. "Would you like to go with them?"

She smiled. "I want to spend the evening with you, Mama. It's time to start getting acquainted."

We began with JW's Atlas and found her town in France and mine in Illinois. We talked about what our mothers and fathers had looked like and what was fun as we grew up. Neither of us had brothers or sisters.

Roslin continued, "My best friend of all was Yvette Sorley, the one who came to America. Actually, I had hoped to find her when I decided to run away into St. Louis. But I was without money and had more handicaps than I could overcome. It is amazing that you found me in this huge country."

"Jenny Cameron, Michael's niece, found you. We will be forever grateful to her for it."

"Where is she now? I would like to thank her some day soon."

I took her hand as I whispered, "It won't be possible. She died recently in a tragic accident."

We talked about gardens and flowers. Her love of nature was as deep as mine. As we got closer to her teen years, she became more reticent and sad.

I whispered to her, "It must have been so hard for you and your mother when your father died."

She rose from her place beside me on the couch and turned away so I couldn't see her eyes. I was concerned by her hesitation. She spoke in a strange, wooden tone. "My mother killed him, when she found him abusing me while she was supposed to be at work. He was drunk, as he often was at night. It was not the first time he had used me, but it was the most brutal. Mother went to jail for several years and I became deaf that night. I was never able to tell Tom about the cause of my deafness. I was so ashamed."

I took her in my arms. "My dear child, I'm so sorry." I sat with her, rocking gently. Then, I felt her begin to cry, deep sobbing cries that seemed to come from the depths of her soul. I was crying too and tears drenched our faces.

Our men found us when they returned from the game; embraced in each other's arms sound asleep, with tears still wet on our cheeks. JW wakened Roslin and helped her up.

Michael waited until they were gone. "Will she be all right, Sara?"

"God willing, yes. She has her mother's sense of survival and the resilience of youth. We were sharing growing up stories and we got to about age 15. I'm not sure I'm ready to share any more of my story with her yet. Even you haven't heard much of it. I need the present now. The past is too sad and somehow useless to help me now."

I took his hand. "Tell me about the game. No, tell me about Thad and Margot's first welcome home kiss." We went out to sit on the porch. Tim and Tricia were saying their good-nights.

"The night is pretty late, young man," Michael commented, "Tricia needs her beauty sleep before the big party tomorrow. We're going to walk around the block and I want her on her way home when we get back."

Tim grinned, probably figuring we were going to do some of the same ourselves, and he had a bit more time. He was right. We slipped around the corner and stopped for the first of several long, gentle kisses. Each one carried away another image of violence and pain and I felt Michael's love protecting me from the terrors of the night.

Then he announced the wonderful surprise. "JW and I decided to give you a gift tomorrow. We went by Gary's and made all the arrangements for the dinner. It was fun making out the guest list. We hope you'll be pleased. Gary said to leave it to him, the menu, and everything, so you can just enjoy the party." He was grinning now. "Do you know what we're celebrating? Our three week anniversary."

I gasped. "Are you sure? I can't believe it's been only that long. You're as comfortable as an old shoe, Cameron. Do you suppose we'll be doddering off into the sunset by the end of the summer?" We both laughed and returned to the house in time to see Tim drive down the main street with Tricia sitting close enough that there was room for three more people in the front seat.

I asked about the party plans. "How many people are coming?"

He chuckled, "Twenty if every one gets there. That's one of Tricia's jobs tomorrow morning, to finish the calling. The party's at three o'clock to fit in between dinner and supper for his other customers. I didn't know if he'd have room for us to sit together but he said he certainly did and it would be his pleasure. I think he really likes JW. In fact every one in town was at the game and they all stopped around to see how things were going with his hand."

"Michael" I wailed, "what am I going to wear?"

"I don't know, but you'll think of something, besides, I think Roslin may steal the show. She's the only one of you ladies without a cast. Goodnight Sara."

Sunday was off to a glorious start. A dry front had gone through early in the morning and the sky was brilliant, crisp blue. All the baby birds were peeping and begging and testing their mother's patience. Robins were rushing back and forth with worms for their teenagers and even the usually docile doves were making extra, distracted sounds to each other.

Michael and I decided to slip away long enough to go to early Mass while the others were still asleep. The little church was about three blocks away on a side street, tucked up under a slight rise of ground. As usual in many churches, the early service was the "Baby Mass", and most of the pews held families with stair-step children. I was delighted to see Abe and Kylie Lou a few rows up. When the service was over, we stopped to greet them.

Kylie Lou smiled with pleasure. "We'll see you this afternoon. It was so nice of you to include us. I'm sorry about your injuries."

I touched her hand. "Maybe this was a wake up call to slow down and enjoy life again. Did the fire hurt your place, Abe?"

He shook his head no. "Fire went uphill from your place. Everything's burnt out. It looks mighty bad. I'm not sure you should go up there. The cold air drainage brings the smell down the draw every night. I hear the city lawyer guy decided to move away."

I laughed. "That's marvelous, Abe, did he take his lawsuit with him?"

He shrugged "Haven't heard one way or t'other."

We continued out the door. "We'll see you later."

We returned home by a different route, taking the back alleys and glancing into people's more private spaces. The Campbell house was not in an affluent part of town, but neat and clean. JW's father had continued as a carpenter after the loss of their child, and the family stayed in town. His mind never recovered from the tragedy. I thought about Mrs. Campbell. Surely she would have missed her farm, her beautiful trees, her flowers and garden. We could never know what she went through after their baby girl died.

It was wonderful just to rest for a few hours. No worry about the upcoming party or the arrangements. Michael came out on the porch to tell me about the adventures of the evening before. "It was so neat last night at the ball game, like something straight out of a movie. During the seventh inning stretch, Thad, the beloved catcher, came on the loudspeaker and said he wanted to ask his girlfriend to marry him. JW led Margot down to the field and Thad said, 'Margot Renée Palmer will you marry me?' Then he walked down on the field and gave her his ring. Everyone in the place was whistling and stomping and cheering. They have a lot of good friends in town."

Then I had a stab of worry. "What do you think the Greers will do?"

He shrugged his shoulders. "We'll know more by tonight. The Greers are supposed to be home in time for the party. At least they've been invited."

I decided Michael was right. It was a party for many reasons and many people and I wouldn't fret about my clothes. I hated the baggy tops needed to go over my bulky cast. I went up to begin dressing. There was a box on my bed. Inside, was a lovely silk tunic outfit altered with a neat slit at the shoulder to fit the cast. A soft drape came diagonally from the right down to my waist on the opposite side. The outfit was a luscious soft sea green, the color of the ocean off the beaches of St. Croix. Wrapped in tissue, in the bottom of the box, was a shawl of cream-colored silk, so airy and thin it floated around my shoulders.

Michael came in to help me dress. "Do you like it, Sara? She did well, considering the challenges."

"Oh, Michael, it's so lovely, thank you. I want to look nice for you today. I'm glad you're here. Roslin returned my locket and I'd like to wear it. Would you help me put it on? It was our promise to each other thirty-five years ago and it is even more so now." His tender kiss was a nice beginning to the afternoon.

"Let's make sure the men are about ready. Tim is going out to pick up part of the Forester kids. Tricia said this morning they were as excited as a basket of puppies."

I sighed happily. "I'll go see what Roslin decided to wear. She got some nice things when we shopped in Ohio." Her choice was a lovely cream-colored dress with tiny flowers scattered over it, wonderful puffy sleeves and a bodice with lace trim. She seemed so happy and JW was watching her as though he couldn't believe she was there in flesh and blood and was promised to him.

Michael said to the others, "I think we'll take one car in case someone needs to dash home for something. We'll see you there, kids."

I was the one getting the wiggles now. It had been a long time since I'd been allowed to enjoy a happy party. It was about 2:30 when we got to Gary's. It was my first look at the guest list and it pleased me. I made a few requests on the seating and left the rest to Gary.

We had always referred to the cook at the grill as "that French cook down at Gary's". When we finally learned her name, I realized the glorious, happy party would belong to Roslin. The young chef's name was Yvette Sorley.

People began drifting in about quarter of three, and even though I didn't want to think about the past few weeks' trauma, I was glad to see Dave and Dodie Finch. They were seated with Margot and Thad and next to them; places were saved for the Greers and their new servant, a young man named Lars. I was happy the Greers were able to join us. The Forester's older children were seated with Tim and Tricia while little Susan was my seatmate by request. Michael was on my left with Roslin and JW next to him.

JW got up with some words of welcome before they began serving the meal. He introduced Michael and Roslin, the Finches and the Greer's new servant. He announced the engagement of Thad and Margot. Then he said quietly that we were mourning the tragic death of Michael Cameron's niece, Jenny Cameron. He asked Abe Forester to give the blessing.

Gary and Yvette came out to help the other servers and I was watching Roslin as they entered the room with their platters. I think someone had been kind enough to warn Yvette, but it was a complete joyous surprise for my daughter. She rose from her place as Yvette put the tray down and they embraced, as long lost friends should, with much weeping and hugging. Even Baby Susan clapped her little hands in delight.

I whispered to Michael, "How wonderful a present for us all."

It was a pleasant meal, with conversation flowing to many topics. We left the table after dessert so Gary could get ready for the evening customers. What a nice party. I was thinking about several wedding receptions he could do for us if all went well.

People seemed to be circulating well and there wasn't any one who could claim the party as his own. Michael seemed to be enjoying the people and he spent time with everyone. We made an appointment to go up to Forester's on Monday morning and in the afternoon, to look at some property Renquist thought might replace my burned out farm.

Suddenly, I was so weary I clung to Michael. "I'm so sorry, but I need to say goodbye and get home to rest."

He took one look at my face and said softly, "No goodbyes, we need to get you home, right now." Our heartfelt thanks were given to Gary and Yvette; and we left the others to continue their visiting. I was disappointed but there was no way I could have managed to stay.

I was surprised when he lifted me from the car at JW's and carried me inside. I was trembling and clung to his neck. "Michael, I'm so frightened. What's the matter with me?"

He helped me to undress and slip into my gown and robe. I reached out to him. "Please don't leave me, Michael."

We sat together, his arms sheltering me from my fears. They overwhelmed me and I began to sob, heart-wrenching sobs that wouldn't stop.

He held me close. "Would you allow me to give you something to help?"

"No, I'll probably need it more later on."

He whispered, "Are you in pain?"

"No, except I can't bear to think of losing my beloved family and friends. Michael, hold me. I love you so much, I can't lose you now."

My sobs diminished to little whimpers of misery. "It was a nice party. I'm glad we did it. Roslin will be happy here, raising her babies. She and Margot and Tricia can push their baby carriages down the street to the park and visit in the afternoons. I want part of the ill-gotten gains from the Andretti jewels to go to a fund so my precious girls can stay home with their babies."

I was so exhausted that I fell asleep in his arms.

Monday morning before dawn, Michael came to waken me. He whispered, "We need to get on the road as quickly as we can. You need to have some work done on your arm. I've been trying for days to figure out why you've been so tired. I finally called Rick to look at those X-rays again. That's when he found it. Everything was so torn up it was easy to miss. I'm afraid to have you fly with the injury so we'll make tracks as fast as we dare. I've arranged for JW to cancel those appointments we made for today. Tim and Tricia have promised to keep helping Kylie Lou and Abe. We probably won't be back for a while. JW and Roslin will fly back in time for his Friday surgery. Help me by telling me what goes into your suitcase."

Roslin came to help. "Mama, I trust Daddy to take care of you. We'll be back Thursday. I love you." She was crying and looked so frightened.

"I love you too, Sweetheart. Enjoy your visit with Yvette."

We left town at five o'clock and headed west as fast as we dared. The sun was up but the traffic was just as bad as later in the day. All the truckers wanted to get through Pittsburgh before the commuters took over the highways.

"I'm going into prayer mode, Michael. Let me know any time you need for me to keep you awake. I love you." I slept most of the way, just waking to get out and walk around when Michael needed a break. He looked so worried I felt worse for causing him pain.

We got into St. Louis in the late afternoon and Rick was waiting for us.

"Man, am I glad to see you two. We've been worried sick since you called last night, Mike. I can't believe we all missed it. It was there plain as could be. We finally found it using the cancer scans."

I closed my eyes. I was tired of hospitals. I just wanted to sleep. I must have been out a long time after the surgery. Just as I was drifting between asleep and awake, I thought I heard Jacques calling to me. I went into a full-blown berserk fit and everyone came running to protect my IV's and the equipment. They put me out again and I didn't waken until long past dawn.

This time a crying fit lasted until my whole body was wracked with pain. Michael came in and ordered something else and I was gone again. I lost several days, because JW and Roslin were sitting in my room when I finally wakened drug free. At least I felt sane and after assuring them I would rise to fight again, I went back to sleep.

Next time awake, I began to worry about JW's surgery. How could I help him this time? Michael would have a fit if I tried to be involved. Well, I wouldn't tell him. When the kids came in the next time, I asked about the schedule.

JW grinned, "No you don't, Lady. No help is requested for tomorrow."

I smiled, "It will be a lot harder on me if I have to keep going all day since I don't know when it will be. Come on, we don't have to tell him."

Then, I heard a beloved chuckle. My Michael was sitting so I couldn't see him, but he had heard it all. He chided me. "Be reasonable, Sara. Who knows what weird things might happen with you in your state?"

I pushed the button on my bed to raise myself up. "Michael Cameron, what state do you think I'm in? I want out of here right now. If I don't get some fresh air and some dirt under my fingernails I'm going to throw a real fit."

I could feel the tension in the room dissolve. Everyone knew then, that Sara Harvey was going to be all right. In fact, I felt better than I had since the morning I was shot in Jacque's workroom. "Please Michael, I want to go home."

He was quiet a long time. "JW, what do you think? Will she harm herself more stewing about not helping or staying here where we can keep an eye on her and letting her help?"

"That's not fair, you two." I whined.

JW became the arbitrator. "We need one more round of tests tomorrow morning to be sure your injury is healing. My surgery is at 7 o'clock and shouldn't take more than an hour. Would you be willing to wait just that long to go home? It would make it much easier for us to care for you and get mine done as simply as possible. Michael has a full schedule tomorrow and I don't want to cause him any more hassle than necessary."

I sighed. "I bow to the voice of reason." The men went quietly. I think they were so glad I was going to be all right, they might agree to anything tomorrow morning. Michael went off to evening rounds and JW and Roslin took me for a walk down the hall.

I was a bit tottery, but felt wonderful. "JW, what did they have to do?"

I could tell he was translating into layman's language in his head. "They went back in and repaired the vein. The loss of blood around it was causing most of your symptoms. They cleaned it up and stitched you back together. We wanted to give you some blood but it didn't work out. You'll just need to be careful a little longer."

I had a gut feeling something had gone wrong, but he didn't elaborate. The change in his voice warned me not to ask.

JW's surgery went off without a hitch. I was able to be of some help from a chair at the end of the hall. About eleven o'clock, Michael poked his head in the door. "I'm doing the paperwork to get you out of here. Pack your stuff and we'll be on our way in a few minutes. I have some news for you." He must have had a cancellation of his big afternoon surgery to be able to go home early. I felt grateful we would have a few hours alone. When he came with the wheelchair, Michael had three big envelopes of papers and X-rays stacked on the seat.

My heart fell. "Did you have to bring work home for the weekend?"

His smile was gentle and teasing. "These are the results of all the tests done last week on Dr. Sara Harvey. I wanted to go over them with her before we celebrate."

"Celebrate what?" I whispered.

As he helped me into the car, he answered. "For the time being, she is nearly free of cancer."

I clutched his shoulder. "How can that be, Michael?"

He kissed my cheek. "I don't know, but I have some ideas and a heart full of joy."

I made a request when we returned home. "Please, Michael, pull into the back by the door so that I can walk in by myself. It's been a long journey."

After a short nap and lunch on the patio, we returned to the office so he could explain the most important test results for me. He hung the X-rays from the viewing screen and showed me the differences in the films. My lung and liver lesions were gone. Only the bone ones remained, one in my pelvis and one in my femur. Some-how, precious time was gifted to us, and we were deeply thankful.

We returned to the garden to enjoy the antics of the robin teen-agers trying to perfect their hunting skills. From the nest of the dove family in the big Colorado blue spruce, you could hear the ruckus each time the babies saw their parents coming with delectable treats. They would be out of the nest soon and the parents would be starting another family.

I turned to Michael. "Do you suppose that's God's plan? We're all part of the cycle of love; birds, flowers and humans? That we keep trying; not always right, not always successful, but if we're fortunate he gives us another chance?"

The look of love in Michael's eyes took my breath away. "Mi-chael, are you all right?"

We went into each other's arms as he murmured, "How could He have been so kind and loving to us, Sara? I still can't believe I found you. I'm continually in awe of what you've become. Your mind, with its exquisite logic and classic form, is held together with a childlike sense of wonder. Your soul shimmers and glows, growing more trusting and loving each moment. Your spirit seems ever wait-ing to take flight in a dance of delight. Teach me, Dear One, I want to be with you forever."

I smiled at him. "Michael, how eloquent and lovely. I didn't think anyone but tubercular Nineteenth Century romantic poets talked like that. Of course you may come with me. You're the reason I sur-vived all those terrifying years. I wouldn't think of not sharing my joy with you now."

Our kiss, gentle and filled with promise reminded me of another happy thought. "Did you remember we have an appointment with Father James tonight? Let's think of a gift we would like to give the other. That's not fair really, because I already know what mine will be. Want to?"

He surprised me with the quickness of his answer. "Mine is al-ready written. I'll bring it with me when we go. Let's go now to get Roslin and JW so they can have some quiet time alone."

I went inside to prepare my gift, folded it and placed it in an en-velope with Dave Finch's address, and then into one with Michael's name.

It was a good thing we went early to the hospital because the paperwork to get JW released seemed to take an eternity. Roslin looked weary. I'm sure that the events of the past few days had been very difficult for her. We dropped them off at the house and went to the church office. After we finished the specific tasks for the meeting, I told Father James about our gift exchange.

"What an interesting idea." He said, "Who'll go first?"

We each laid our envelope on the desk. "Why don't you flip a coin for us, Father? Heads I win the choice."

The coin ended up tails. Michael reached for the envelope I'd made for him and opened it to find the other envelope addressed to Dave Finch. As he opened my letter of resignation from the CIA as of June 8, his eyes glittered with tears. "I love you more than life itself. I will protect you and keep you safe, now and forever. Thank you for your gift, Sara."

I whispered, "Amen."

Next it was my turn. I had no idea what the gift might be, but was intrigued by the idea Michael had prepared it even before I'd asked. The official letterhead page contained only two paragraphs. It was his resignation from his Naval Reserve job as of June 8. Now it was my turn to weep. "Thank you Michael, I love you and I trust you with my life."

He whispered, "Amen."

Father James blessed us and we headed for home. I had such a feeling of peace and closure. The little café was busy but we found the last table tucked up next to a flower box. On this pleasant, cool evening every guest was in a festive mood. The robins were doing their final murmurings as they settled babies for the night and nighthawks came to begin their supper of insects attracted to the lights along the street. Flickering candles changed the glasses of wine into shimmering rubies and topazes on the tables. The time was magical.

Roslin and JW were dawdling over a late supper when we returned home. We said our goodnights and Michael helped me upstairs. I would miss our evening bath ritual when my cast was gone. I hoped he might consider it a part of our loving as I did, and we would continue it even when I could perfectly well do my own bath. We settled down together for the night.

CHAPTER TWELVE

Something was very wrong. I hurt all over and I felt as though I'd swallowed a bottle of acid. Where was I? What had happened?

I opened one eye and then the other. The room came into view, at least the legs of the chairs and table and bed. It was daylight and I was huddled in a nest of blankets and pillows on the floor in the corner of my bedroom.

When I crawled out from behind the chair, I saw my beloved Michael, sitting in the big chair by the window, sound asleep. His cheeks were streaked with tears and he was dressed in his Saturday clothes. My injured arm had deep red marks and bruises around the cast, but it didn't feel like anything had been reinjured. When I turned to get up, I saw Roslin, wrapped in a coverlet, sitting with her back to the wall.

She was not asleep. "Mama, are you all right now? We were so worried about you."

I stumbled upright and tried to wrap a blanket around my shoulders. Michael wakened when he heard us. His frantic look told me that something terrifying must have happened.

"Michael, what happened?"

His whispered answer frightened me. "You scared the holy shit out of us last night. I don't know what happened. I do know we would have lost you, if it hadn't been for Roslin."

JW appeared at the bedroom door and helped Roslin to her feet as he said, "I'm glad you understood what was happening. Would you go downstairs, please, and make some warm milk for Sara, I expect it would feel good right now. Just leave it by the door."

Then he made a hand signal to Michael, who left the room in silence. I stood, waiting for an explanation of the mystery. I had no idea what had happened after Michael and I had settled down together for the night.

JW went to the closet, found my robe and helped me into it. His voice was full of compassion as he spoke. "You deserve an explanation. Your throat is sore because you vomited for nearly an hour. Your body is battered and bruised because you struggled so hard when we tried to protect your cast.

"Sara, I'm so sorry. It was devastating to watch you struggle with your personal demons. But Roslin was right. When we turned you loose and she began to talk, she seemed to be able to reach you, though you were light years away in your own private hell."

I reached out to him. "Is there any clue about what caused it?"

He took several long moments to consider his answer. "Each person lives a different and separate life, sometimes with joys and sometimes with deep fears and sorrows. When we meet a new person, many times we can't begin to understand what their life has been like. Because of Roslin's history, she knew immediately what was wrong. Your Michael was an innocent party to what happened last night. There's no way he could have known how certain touches or certain loving ways could trigger the terror that was unleashed. Let's see if your milk is by the door and then we'll talk about what we're going to try to do."

I drank the milk in tiny sips as he continued. "Although you went through a terrifying time last night, I think you were in some ways healed by it and so was Roslin. She talked to us about what we can do to help and it makes sense. You'll have a lot more responsibility for everyone's actions. I hope your sense of humor will rise to the occasion."

His voice was filled with tenderness. "May I touch you?"

He had always asked permission, since the first day on the farm. I nodded yes.

"May I kiss you, to welcome you back to us?" I nodded yes, again.

He turned my outstretched hands upwards and buried his face in them. I could feel the tears on his cheeks as he kissed my palms. "You're going to rise to fight another day, Sara. I salute you."

He slipped out and sent Roslin to help me dress. I decided to wear one of Michael's shirts over my slacks. It would slip over my head and I needed to feel that he was protecting me. I'd be so glad when the cast was off. It made life very awkward and difficult and was a constant reminder of what had happened to tear my world apart. On the way out, I picked up Michael's gift envelope and put it into my pocket.

Roslin and I gathered up some breakfast and sat on the patio enjoying the early morning air. The birds were busy taking their morning baths in between worm-hunting lessons for their teenagers. There was some evidence they were thinking about another round of babies and I thought about my precious daughter who soon would be starting her family too.

Perhaps because of JW's new interest in counseling he took charge of the family meeting later in the morning.

JW asked Roslin to speak first.

"Mama, I believe that you and Daddy are committed to each other, but it's much too soon to get married. This should be a time of courting, to gain one another's trust and love. "Either one of you may decide it won't work, that you can't do it; that thirty-five years apart is too much of a chasm. There's no sin in that. The sin would be in marrying because it seemed to be the thing to do.

"Even though Margot and Thad are going to be married in July and it would have been fun to do it too, Jamie and I decided this morning to wait at least until Christmas. After seeing what you're going through, I decided it was much too soon to ask Jamie to take on the responsibility for me. Jamie has said you and I will be welcome to stay in the house in Campbell's Point, if that's where you decide to live. He needs to be on campus to concentrate on his studies, but he promises to be home most weekends." She smiled at JW. "We have some courting to do too."

Apparently, Michael was to speak later, and JW continued. "For the next few weeks and perhaps months, we need to make sure we ask your permission before we touch you or kiss you. You must do the same, to keep the exercise fresh in all our minds. For a while you need to sleep with the lights on, and when Roslin leaves, you must sleep alone.

"Also, in my opinion, you should refuse all of the offers made to you by the college in Pittsburgh. Right now, your health and welfare should take precedence over a new job you can take on later when you're feeling better and stronger. I think the job offers are too restrictive for you and further; I have serious questions about their motives.

"The other health related issue is exercise. You must get back to strength training even before the cast comes off. Bone strength is very important to your long-range health recovery."

To my surprise, JW asked me to speak before Michael. I began with an apology. "My dear family, I'm so sorry about what happened last night. Thank you for staying with me, and for your promise of support. I'm trying to restore my life to some semblance of normality but instead it seems to be full of both good and bad surprises. I understand the logic behind your requests and I agree to try to do them, with your help."

I turned to Michael. "My Dearest, I know now what it must have been; a French kiss."

I stepped to his chair. "Michael, may I touch you?"

He looked up with surprise, but nodded yes.

Then I knelt by him. "May I kiss you?"

He began to weep as he nodded yes.

I took his face in my hands and kissed him lightly on the cheek. "My Love, please don't abandon me now. I love you so much. Please wait for me."

He rose from the table and went to the doors that looked out over the garden. When he turned back towards us his stricken face was covered with tears.

"Sara, I feel so inadequate. I've become a coward doctor; one who hides behind anesthetic and gowns and masks and who doesn't have to deal with the knock-down-drag-out trauma of real living.

"What you said to me in the hospital about arrogance is true. I hope to God I can somehow make up for those years. Sara, I love you more than life itself. I'll never abandon you. I'll wait for you forever. Even if you decide you don't want me, I'll still be there waiting for you. Sara, may I touch you?"

As I moved to him, he whispered, "May I kiss you?"

Now I was crying too, but I was so happy at the same time I couldn't resist leaning around his broad shoulders to give JW and Roslin a big wink. "OK Michael, put it right here," I pointed to my face and smiled. "We've had enough heavy stuff for today. Let's go find some lunch and then play Scrabble until time for church. We might even fit in a nap, on doctor's orders."

We were glad to end the session. Michael said, "There's one room in the house you haven't seen yet. Let's go downstairs and I'll show you around."

I knew he needed something like it since he was in such good shape and I knew he didn't have time to belong to a club. Down in the basement we found the layout for a very efficient workout area, not nearly as large as Jacques Grayson's but quite adequate for one or two people. There was an open area for floor exercising and along the wall, a treadmill and bench for weights as well as an exercise bike. In a rack against the wall, there were sets of wooden sticks of different lengths, three, four, and six feet long. He was watching me as I stepped to them and picked up the bō.

"Michael, I didn't know you were interested in stick fighting." Usually I didn't use the bō, because it was too long and awkward for my arms and body. I preferred the smaller three-foot hanbō and had put in a lot of time practicing with Dave Finch. It was his favorite weapon of defense especially with a knife added in the other hand.

"We'll get together soon if you like, Sara, and I'll work with you on a left handed variant for the three foot one. It's a little early for lunch. I think I'll stay down here and work out for a while. Anyone is welcome to stay."

The kids decided to go back upstairs and I stayed to loosen up on the treadmill. I had become slothful since the attack and I needed to get back to work. After twenty minutes, I stepped off and stretched out on the floor, propped myself up next to the wall and promptly fell asleep. I wakened to find Michael doing a fascinating floor exercise. His back was towards me and his motion was fluid

135

and elegant. I was trying to analyze the meaning of the movements when his pattern brought him to face me and he realized I was awake. He finished the sequence and stepped to the wall.

His voice was filled with tenderness. "May I touch you, Sara?"

I reached out to him and grinned. "I could use some help. I'm going to be stiff as a board tomorrow. Michael, what a beautiful sequence you were doing. Where did it come from? I've never seen anything like it."

His answer surprised me. "I picked it up during a tour of duty in Finland. It's Russian."

My next query was a surprise to him. "Are you fluent in Russian?"

"Yes, just as you are."

I wondered how he knew about my Russian work. His job with the Navy must have included more than being a doctor to patch up wounded SEALs. I didn't know how long he was on active duty or when he'd gone to St. Louis to practice orthopedics.

I moved away from him. "Michael, can you tell me anything about what you did in the Navy?" I watched as he seemed to struggle with his answer.

"It depends upon a renegotiation of our exchange of gifts. I was sincere when I did it. I thought it would be best for us, but now, I've decided to give back your resignation letter. I can't expect you to give up a job with such meaning for you; one that has kept you surrounded by friends and protectors. It's been an important part of your life. Besides, when I called Dave Finch, he wouldn't accept it. He said you were much too valuable to lose. That's how I knew about the Russian language skills and the other talents you keep so well hidden."

I pulled his resignation letter from my pocket and handed it to him. "I was planning to do this at the meeting this morning but it didn't seem like quite the right time. I wish to do the same for you. It wouldn't be fair or wise for me to make you give up your connection with the Navy SEALs. I expect if I'd figured out to whom it should be sent; they would have refused it too. Is there any rule about marriage with our combination of jobs?"

He grinned, "I hope not, or we'll just have to live in sin."

My mind was already making plans for the rest of the summer. "When does your summer duty start and how long will you be gone?" We moved up the steps and went outside to the bench by the pond. It was quite warm but it felt good after the coolness of the basement.

"I don't have much latitude because of my hospital schedule. They usually give me July 1 to August 15 off as leave of absence because it's military duty and then I don't lose my other holidays. I'd like to finish off JW's case and be sure he's matched up with a physical therapist in Pittsburgh and I hope the timing coincides with your cast removal. You'll need therapy for a few weeks too. Tim has promised to make sure you get where you need to go while I'm gone.

"And, before you and Roslin and JW leave town, I'd like very much for you to get to know my mother as she is now. She's entirely different since my father died. She's blossoming into a very wonderful and happy person. Roslin needs to meet her grandmother and you and JW need to meet your mother-in-law-to-be. Maybe I can pick up some Muni tickets when she can be here."

I was smiling now. "Sounds fun. Do some sleuthing to find out what's going to be playing and we'll make it a grand occasion.

"Michael, do you suppose we might be able to persuade Roslin to teach us some sign language? I'm already beginning to squirm when you have to ask permission to touch me, though I understand why we need to do it. Let's ask her to begin with; 'May I touch you? 'May I kiss you?' and 'I love you more than life itself.'" We were both smiling as we went hand in hand, back inside to the coolness of the library.

Now it *was* time for lunch and the kids had laid out a perfect one. There was carrot-ginger soup, fruit salad and fresh bread and jam. We took our glasses of iced tea to the library and settled down to a game of Scrabble. I was no longer surprised at how well-educated Roslin was in her second language, but I was delighted and intrigued to discover the broad education obvious in JW's game. He delighted in words as much as I did. The four of us were well-matched and the winner was usually determined by who got the best letters and breaks in playing position.

It was about time to get ready for Mass when the phone rang. Michael was on call this weekend and I had a feeling he wouldn't be going with us to church. I was right, and we rearranged our plans to wait until morning. At least it would be cooler for the walk. Michael was gone as soon as he hung up the phone, with no idea when he would be back. JW and Roslin were doing the physical therapy routines for his hand. I settled into Michael's favorite chair by the French doors and fell asleep.

I was still asleep when he returned about nine. The kids took off on a late evening walk and Michael had a bite to eat before he helped me carry my things down to the other bedroom. I whispered to him, "He didn't say we had to give up our bath ritual did he?"

"Let's take a chance and not ask him." After the new ritual of asking permission to touch each other, we shared our evening bath. He went to get me one of his shirts. I loved wearing them; they were like a mantle of protection. He returned and slipped it over my head.

We whispered to each other at the same moment, "May I kiss you", and folded into each other's arms. Our kisses carried a new passion and urgency that both thrilled and frightened me. This night it was Michael who had the control to stop.

One last gentle hug and he helped me settle down in bed. He left the light on, opened the windows, and took his place in the chair by my bed.

"I'll stay until Roslin gets back. Sleep well, Sara."

It was a joy to get through a night without my usual nightmare. I slept so well I didn't hear Roslin come to bed and she was up and away before I wakened. She'd closed the windows so it must be warming up outside even earlier this morning. I could feel the air conditioner cycling the air in the room. I didn't like being closed away from the bird songs. Glancing at the little clock on my night-stand, I realized I'd need to get moving if we were to make it to early church.

Everyone was gathered around the kitchen table reading the Sunday Post Dispatch, each person with a favorite section. Roslin tackled the comics, sometimes with hilarious results. A misunderstood phrase could cause wonderful twisted interpretations of why they were funny. Besides, we had to assure her that many times the funnies were anything but. JW was devouring the entertainment section and had found the Muni schedule for the next few weeks. Michael was mumbling about McGuire and "that Rocker guy."

"Anyone else going to church?" Michael rose from his place and volunteered. He was dressed for it so I knew he was waiting for me. He picked up the shopping list.

"We're going to drive since it's so hot. We'll do the shopping on the way back. There won't be any calls from the hospital because I worked late last night. It's Rick's turn today."

Roslin added a few more items as we headed out the door. The air was so humid I felt like I was smothering. After all those years in the Palouse desert, I remembered with fondness the low humidity we enjoyed in the summers. Sweat was rolling down my back by the time we settled onto our kneelers in the little church and I was thankful for the air conditioning. The early morning worshipers in the St Louis parish were quite different from those at Campbell's Point. There were hardly any children this morning. Many elderly folks replaced them, and several rows of the front pews had been rearranged to make room for wheelchairs. The next rows had special hearing assistance devices and the spaces were all full.

I dreaded getting old. I hated the thought of losing my agility and my mind. I prayed for the grace to accept what would be my lot and even more, to do a better job of living each day and each moment to the hilt.

After Mass, I took Michael's hand. "Let's hurry and get the shopping done so we can get back home to our cool cave." We divided up the tasks and were finished in record time. As I slipped into my side of the car, I leaned over to give Michael a kiss.

"Oops, I forgot. May I kiss you?"

He chuckled as he nodded yes and murmured "The same?"

After several nice ones, I asked him, "How long do you think the request is good for, until sundown or only an hour?" Taking me into his arms, he settled it by claiming "House Rules".

We hurried home and I slipped into my workout clothes for an exercise time before lunch. I was surprised when Michael greeted me in French, and offered me a silk scarf to cover my eyes. After assuring me he would protect my cast, he began a series of moves for the left side and of much greater difficulty than Jacques had taught me.

In the middle of our workout, as he was encouraging me when I did well and chiding me when I seemed to let my mind wander, I wondered if he might have been Jacques' teacher or had shared workouts with him. It was humbling that Michael wanted to work with me now. It was something we could do together and would be good for both of us.

When the session was over, he bowed to me. "You have spunk, Sara Harvey, but you need a lot of work to get back in fighting shape again. I'm especially interested in teaching you the stick maneuvers because when you're working outdoors, you'd be more likely to have access to the double weapons of stick and knife.

"Oh, by the way, that's a most intriguing pair of boots in your closet; the ones with the knives built in. I've never seen anything quite like them. A real craftsman made them for you."

"Craftswoman. Her name's Debbie and she is indeed an artist. They're made for fieldwork but they've come in handy for some other times too."

We did a bit of cool down and then I enjoyed watching Michael do some kata. He was such a big man I was surprised at his agility and grace. He must have seen the admiration and raw passion in my eyes because he finished one set and came close to me, teasing. "I may have to put the scarf back on your eyes, if you're going to look at me that way, Munchkin."

After his cool down, we went upstairs to find Roslin and JW, snuggled together on the couch, sound asleep. I smiled at Michael. "Looks like lunch might be a little late. Let's go try it in the library. I've wanted to see how we fit in your favorite chair."

We pulled the drapes against the now scorching sun and settled in. "What a lovely way to spend Sunday, Dr. Cameron. Do you realize that we're celebrating our four-week anniversary today? It seems like a hundred years instead.

Jeanne Anderegg

"Michael, may I call you Mike, like we used to when we were kids?"

He grinned. "I guess if I can call you Munchkin, and Beloved and Sara, you ought to be able to call me Mike." His eyes changed to a smoky brown and his kisses were gentle and comforting.

Roslin wakened us a little later with a kiss of her own, and said lunch was about ready in the kitchen. It was too hot to eat much and we drank three pitchers of iced tea. JW settled down with a music book and Mike returned to the library to phone his mother and make plans.

Much to our surprise and disappointment, he reported that she said she just couldn't come in the next three weeks. First thing I thought of was a new boyfriend but Mike just laughed. He did a perfect imitation of her voice and body language and passed on the message.

"Darling, I just can't come right now. Our Church Ladies' Society is getting ready for the biggest moneymaker in all history. We're going to have a booth at the First Annual Tourist Trap Bazaar and Dinner in the town square. We've been baking and cooking for weeks and we're days behind schedule. Come down if you can. We'll take your money too. I'll talk to you after it's over. Bye."

I grinned. "Well, that takes care of that. I guess we can try to get down there. It's the same distance each way. Let's wait and see what the weather's like by then. I don't seem to take the heat as well any more. I can remember as a kid, playing baseball in this and loving it. Of course we finished it off with a trip to the local swimming pool to cool off afterwards.

"Do you remember the ice cream cones? We used to see who could get the most scoops on one cone and then we'd all eat off of it. Big trouble came when your flavor was toward the bottom and you were nibbling on your dip."

We were all laughing and decided ice cream sounded wonderful. At the same moment we all said, "What flavor shall we make?" Mike found the old freezer in the garage and made sure it still worked. Then we sent the men off for ice, salt and cream.

Roslin and I started the custard so it could cool, and prepared the strawberries. They smelled so heavenly, so truly summertime that when the men returned, we were dancing around the kitchen laughing and singing Beatles songs. We loaded the can with ice cream mix and the men went out onto the patio to set up the operation. Actually, Mike and Roslin would have to turn the handle since JW and I were still handicapped with our casts.

The Cameron crew brought in the finished ice cream and of course, they got to lick the dasher since they did all the hard work. We repacked the canister, knowing we wouldn't wait long to dip into

140

its delicate sweet pinkness. The aroma of strawberries was overwhelming as we licked the last spoonfuls of extra that dropped into the pan. Roslin and I put the bowls and spoons into the freezer to cool, while we cleaned up the kitchen. Then, we filled our bowls with ice cream and carried them to the library.

Mike sat in his favorite chair and we gathered around him. He spoke in his gentle voice. "Let's be thankful for this day. No matter what may lie ahead, we have each other; our love, our loyalty, and our trust in each other." The ice cream was perfect.

Mike had a full operating schedule for the next few weeks before he left for California. I touched his hand as I asked, "Is there some project we could tackle for you, one to help keep things in order, inside or out? It's rather satisfying to find out how well one can use the non-dominant hand out of necessity. I can't shovel or swing a Pulaski but I can weed and deadhead flowers. I miss my gardening and being outside with the birds."

He rose from his place and tucked my hand under his arm. "Come out and I'll give you a tour of the garden and tell you how I'd planned to develop some of the yard."

The kids decided to take a walk so we went out the library door into the back yard space. I was about to see another side of the talented Dr. Cameron. We walked to the bench by the pool and he opened the book he'd taken from the shelf above his desk. It was a scrapbook full of gardening ideas and pictures. There were examples of stonewall, edgings, fences, garden bed arrangements and flower portraits cut from magazines, and there were sketches he'd made.

I was surprised and delighted. "Mike, I have some of the very same articles clipped and saved in my own scrapbook. Isn't there something enchanting about a French kitchen garden?"

He turned to the design pages with pictures of screened porches and greenhouses. "One of the things I've wanted to do is to design and put up a screened porch that converts into a greenhouse in winter. They had them at the time these houses were designed so it would be possible to keep it integrated with the neighborhood architecture.

"Another thing I'd like to do is put in a kitchen and herb garden like the French have. It would have a combination of vegetables and flowers and herbs with paths and permanent structure. I don't want it to be as regimented as a knot garden but with the size of the space I have, it will need careful design. Here are some sketches I've made. There's only one space right for it. I know now I've been waiting to share the planning and planting with you." We spent a long time talking about the best way to get started.

It had started to cool off. There was a flurry of birds rushing to get their last minute tasks finished before they settled down for the night. The dove was talking with his mate, and an arrogant cardinal was announcing his kingship. I whistled to him. He cocked his head, fluffed his wings and went right on.

I took Mike's hand. "This is my favorite time of the day, when the light turns things to shades of gray and all is reduced to its essence. I always sang a lullaby to my precious daughter, about this time. I still can't believe she's with us now; safe, healthy and so lovely."

The mosquitoes had discovered us and we needed to move back indoors.

"Mike, let's do a short workout and then go to bed early. We can talk about the garden and about our meeting tomorrow night with Father James. What comes up at this one?"

"Money, if I remember right. Surely it will need to be geared differently than for a couple of teenagers with hardly any income, or still in school and supported by their folks."

I was having a bit of a struggle trying to decide how much to tell Mike about my financial situation. My deceased husband, Henri Lambert, had left me with more than enough money and property to be well off for many years. In fact, I was quite wealthy.

When we finished the shortened workout, Mike turned to me. "Sara, we need to talk."

As the evening had progressed, I knew something was troubling him. I couldn't remember him ever hesitating or making a mistake in his workout, but tonight there had been several.

"I know something's wrong, Mike. I can feel your pain. How may I help?"

The moment I spoke the words, a deep sadness brought tears to my eyes. JW spoke those same words to me not too many weeks before and I'd opened my heart to him. Now Mike needed me and I must do the same.

"Would you like to stay here or go up to the library?"

I was surprised when he took me in his arms and whispered, "Let's stay here. Please, I need for you to listen."

He was crying now. I held him as best I could and waited. The basement door was closed and it was deathly quiet except for his anguished sobbing.

"Mike, for God's sake! what's wrong?" I started to rub his back and neck and then to wipe away his tears with the sleeve of my shirt. "Come on; let's walk around a bit, maybe it will help. I think there's some water in the cupboard at the other end of the room."

He was like a child and went with me hand in hand, holding me tight as if he feared I would lose him. We found the water. There was something sacramental about drinking from the same cup and he began to calm down. I put some of the water on a towel and washed the tears from his face and then kissed his eyes and dear face. We settled on the floor in a corner with our backs against the wall so we could see and touch each other.

I whispered, "Now, My Love, start talking."

"After you disappeared, I struggled on without you. During college I added Naval ROTC to my load and when I graduated I started as an officer. My first foreign assignment was in Scandinavia. While we were in Finland we were supposed to get to know the local people and practice our language skills. I met many wonderful people and we're still friends today, but there was one woman to whom I kept returning.

"Her name was Wilhelmina Porter. She was much older than I, and fascinating to a young man because of all the places she knew and things she had experienced. For her part, the relationship was strictly friendship. She was quite lonely. Her husband had died in the war. I was smitten with her elegance and beauty. She was a watercolor artist and loved to paint the lake country and the beautiful forests of dark fir trees and birches at the edge of the sparkling water.

"One glorious summer day we decided to take a picnic lunch and go on a wilderness jaunt so she could paint. We were well dressed to hike, with proper boots and walking staves. We took a wrong turn and found ourselves on a trail that hadn't been groomed yet for hikers. As we turned to go back she stumbled and fell. It was a freak accident and she injured her back. She still needs help with her daily living tasks and uses a wheelchair."

Mike began to cry again. "I paid for all her hospital expenses and when she returned to her village, I took care of her with the help of a neighbor, until I had to go home. I begged her to marry me so she could come home to the States with me and I could care for her. She wouldn't hear of it. She said my whole life lay ahead of me and she would only be a burden.

"She's 75 now, still living in the same small town outside Helsinki. I go to spend time with her several weeks each year. She's very frail but her spirit is indomitable. I told her in a recent letter that I'd found you. Her answer was gracious and loving. She wants to meet you as soon as possible. I think she knows her time is getting short.

"I've cared for her financially all these years and I'll be continuing to care for her until her death. It's a debt of honor and a promise I won't break. I make enough money for my own modest needs and for her care. I'll need to keep working after she dies, at least long enough to save some money for retirement. I have nothing put away except Social Security. All my doctor friends are multi-millionaires and have huge houses and many possessions. All I have is my quiet, plodding, honorable life. Not very exciting, not very special, but I've kept my promise to myself and to her.

"Sara, My Beloved, I have nothing to give you."

I took Mike's hands in mine. "Let's finish this conversation upstairs in the library. I need some fresh air and the last bird songs to cradle my soul and yours. We must get some things settled before we leave each other for the night."

I made some iced tea. We opened the doors to the garden so the soft cooler air could enter the room. We held hands as I tried to begin mending his heart.

"I knew from the moment we met at the farm in Pennsylvania, that there had been a very special feminine spirit watching over you. I honor her for that and I honor you for taking responsibility for her all these years. Please make whatever arrangements are necessary for me to get to Finland. I think you will be going there soon, but I shouldn't come while you're on duty. We'll work it out.

"As to your other concern, you're wrong to say 'you have nothing to give me.' What you've given me already is so precious I weep to ever consider losing you. You have given me our blessed and beautiful Roslin. You have given me your loyalty and love over many long years of waiting. You have given me your willingness to accept me with all my wounds and imperfections. Most of all, you have given me a growing trust in people and their goodness. We've been together for four weeks, Mike. Can you imagine what wonderful things lay ahead?

"And as for money, it is a trivial pursuit. The amount from the Andretti jewel box should take care of many years of retirement, even if we chose to share with Roslin and JW. If the government figures out a way to take the fortune away, we will still manage just fine.

"Mike, why were you crying?"

He reached for me. "Because you're the only person I've ever told about her. I suppose I should feel ashamed that I could believe your reaction would be any different than it was, filled with gentleness and understanding. Thank you."

We went upstairs to prepare for bed. Tonight, I shared the bath ritual with Mike and it was his turn to need it. Somehow, our relationship was so solid and secure I no longer felt the need to cling to him or to have so many reassurances of his love. Tonight, for the first time, I knew he needed me too.

I whispered to him, "Do you want me to stay with you tonight?"

Taking my hands and turning them palms up, he kissed them and murmured, "I'm going to be all right now. Of course I want you, but I can wait, since I've told you my darkest and most difficult secret. Good night, Sara, I'll see you at suppertime. Our appointment is later, at eight o'clock as I remember. It should be cooler by then."

CHAPTER THIRTEEN

A glorious, drenching rainstorm hurtled through town about midnight. The biggest blessing was the drop in temperature. By morning the air was crisp and cool and the sky was an amazing expanse of purest pastel blue. There wasn't a cloud to be seen. The birds were ecstatic; flying crazy dive-bombing patterns and singing their hearts out at the same time. I opened my windows as wide as I could, to let in the air. I heard Mike stirring as he got ready for his day and decided to slip down to fix his breakfast.

I found him in the kitchen singing. I whispered to him, "May I kiss you good morning?"

He turned to me and held out his arms. "Precious Sara, I love you so much it hurts."

I thought of Abe and Kylie Lou, and how loving their marriage must have been all these years. Abe had said the same thing about their love. Our kiss was gentle and comfortable. We fixed breakfast, carried it out to the patio and joined the kids. I thought about a days' worth of work in the house but then voted to work outside in the flowerbeds while the grass and weeds would be easier to pull and the air was cool and filled with birdsongs.

When the men got home at three o'clock, the house was spic and span from Roslin's work inside and I had several bags of weeds ready to go to the curb. It was nice to spend a day in concentrated sweat work even though my cast was a major handicap. We were relaxing in the garden when the phone rang. Mike answered it and I knew something was wrong. When he handed the phone to JW, I knew something was very wrong in Campbell's Point.

JW said in a calm voice, "Hold on, Tim. Slow down and start over. Where is he now? Where are you? Yes, we're on our way. We'll be there on the next possible flight to Pittsburgh. I'll call you back to tell you the flight number. Hang in there, buddy. We love you."

He turned to Roslin. "Will you come too? I know Margot will need you. Thad was working with Tim to help finish up a job. He's been hurt. God almighty! We didn't need this right now. Mike would you give us a ride to the airport?"

We all hurried inside to begin packing for them. We didn't think how long or anything, just clothes to keep them going. In fifteen minutes we were on the road. At least the evening traffic was all go-

ing the other way for a good bit of the trip. We were so close on timing we left them at the curb with our prayers and most of the money
in our pockets.

I was trembling when we drove off the ramp into the night traffic. "We have several hours until our meeting. Could we stop for
some supper? I didn't have any lunch and I feel like a damp cat."

We found a small, family place off the main street and hunkered
down together in a back booth. I looked around at the people. How
many of them were worried about family or friends hurt by the
world? I calmed down and reminded myself we weren't alone, someone cared very much about what happened to us, and we needed the
faith to believe it.

A large bowl of chicken soup and a huge stack of toast brought
me back to the land of the living, and we shared a bowl of ice cream.

"Mike, let's go back now. Could we spend some time in the
chapel before we meet with Father James? I need it tonight."

He nodded assent and we returned to our nurturing neighborhood to clean up and then headed off to the chapel. So much had
happened in just the time since our last meeting. I had trouble getting my thoughts in order. It was a little before seven, and we spent
the time in prayer.

Father James took one look at us and knew we needed a different kind of evening with him. We spent the time talking about our
child and our kin and how important and precious they were to us. I
could speak without hatred about what my parents had done and
how it formed the path I was forced to take. We also spoke about our
loss of Jenny, Mike's beautiful niece. It was the first time he had
spoken of her since her death such a short time ago, and we struggled to gain closure for our disappointment and feeling of loss. Father returned us to the world with acceptance and peace. Joy was
more difficult to find.

We returned to the house and gravitated to our favorite place in
the library, Mike and I settled into his favorite chair as he said, "Do
you realize this is the first time we've been alone in weeks? How
would you like the sleeping to be arranged?"

I sighed. "Let's not think about it yet. Right now I need for you
to hold me. I want to feel the beat of your heart in my breast. I want
to be so close to your body that nothing can harm only one of us. I'm
so frightened. The world is such a confusing and untrustworthy
place. Hold me while I weep for all the sadness in people's hearts."

He stroked my hair and my back as I fell asleep in his arms.
Later, I felt him lift me and carry me to the bedroom Roslin and I
had shared. He left the lights on, opened the windows to the cool
night air, and settled on the other bed.

I wakened to the odor of a perfect yellow rose beside me on the pillow. The early morning dew still glistened on the petals. A note on the kitchen table said he hoped to be home early. Mike had told me his afternoon surgery patient was somewhat reluctant to go through with her surgery and he never ever pushed or rushed his patients. I think he hoped the woman would decide to wait. Mike seemed weary. We both needed rest and quiet and perhaps the next several weeks would gain us some respite.

After spending the morning in soothing domestic chores, I was sitting on the patio in the last bit of shade when I heard the garage door open and then close. The gift of an afternoon was given to us and I was glad. Several reasonably elegant leftovers later, we announced at the same moment that the afternoon should begin with a nap. As we settled in, the phone brought word from Pennsylvania. Thad was battered and broken and his baseball was over for the year. JW said he and Roslin would stay in Campbell's Point until the final evaluation of his surgery the Thursday before Michael left on Maneuvers.

We put the phone on silent record and I snuggled into Mike's lap as best I could. "I'll be so glad when all this structural steel and fiber glass is off my body. How much longer do I have? Is there any chance it could be sooner?"

I watched Mike calculating in his head. "Monday after next we'll go by and have some X-rays taken. Perhaps we can put a smaller, different one on if the bones are healing well. I'd hate to have to start over, Munchkin. Even Rick would have trouble hurting you if he had to reset them, and I know I couldn't do it to you. We'd have to send you to Omaha. That cast is a little high for a chastity belt but it works about the same way, so maybe it's not all bad."

We smiled at the same time and curled up together as close as we could get. After a glorious, restful nap I wakened him with my recurring worry.

"My Dear, how long has it been since your last physical? You seem so weary and you know you're not getting any younger."

He kissed me with more passion than I was ready to handle.

"Mike, be serious. I've heard that doctors are even worse than teenagers about their life and their health. They all think they're invincible, that they will live forever. Answer me."

Mike squirmed a little. "I have to have a full one the first day I arrive at Coronado Island." He sighed, "It's kind of creepy you should be thinking something might not be OK. I haven't been feeling like myself lately. I'll be relieved to have the checkup and find I'm just tired. You and your buddies have turned my stolid world upside down the last few weeks."

I decided not to push any more. We dawdled over supper and then took a walk around the block as the neighborhood was tucking its babes into bed. You could hear mothers calling their children home from play, while the birds settled their nestlings for the night. I felt so at peace I was frightened by it. By bedtime, a nagging sense of dread drove me into his arms.

Mike left for work extra early because of an ethics hearing and I wakened to the smell of his earlier toast and coffee. After struggling with my growing anxiety, I decided to pack my suitcase for a difficult trip. The morning was spent gathering up what I thought I might need, including my sturdy work clothes, business suit and several evening outfits including the apricot dress I'd bought for the concert. I tucked the suitcase, my field pack and work boots into the closet and went into the kitchen to see what I could make for Mike's meals while I was gone. I thought about all his lonely days and wondered again how he had done it all those years. I settled down for a nap but was unable to rest.

When I greeted Mike after work, he was carrying an armload of mail. I liked his system of not having mail delivered to his home, but would have figured out a way to toss the junk mail, instead of bringing it home to fill the garbage can. He dropped it on the kitchen table and reached for me.

His voice was husky and full of passion. "I can't believe you're really here waiting for me when I come home from work. I don't want to play house anymore. I want you, Sara. I don't want to wait any more."

He must have seen the panic and fear in my eyes as I pulled away from him. He didn't touch me. Instead, he whispered, "I'm so sorry. Let me go out and come back in again."

He waited almost ten minutes. Long enough for me to gain control and to think about how he must be feeling. I went to our library sanctuary and waited for him by his favorite chair. When he entered, I turned away toward the French doors, trembling, waiting for him to speak. To my surprise, he came around in front of me and began a simple sequence in sign language, the ones Roslin had taught us. "May I touch you?" "May I kiss you?" He included the last, "I love you more than life itself". I answered silently as my weeping drove me into his arms.

He reached for a light blanket, wrapped me in it and settled with me into the nest of his chair. His gentle scolding was filled with concern. "You need to set the air conditioning above 70 degrees when it's so hot outside. You worked too long in the hot sun, and I expect you skipped lunch if there was an ounce of extra fat on the scales this morning. You know that's not good for you. Why don't you nap for a few minutes and I'll kiss your tears away like we did the morning we were reunited at the farm?

"You miss the farm, don't you? I think we need to find you another place as soon as we can, even if it's here in Missouri."

I sighed and snuggled into his warm chest. "I'm so sorry, Mike."

He took his finger and laid it gently on my lips. "Shh, you have no reason to apologize. Old awkward Mike just said what was in his heart. We'll work it out. Now you rest."

I really was exhausted and, he was right. I'd worked too long in the garden during the heat of the day and I'd skipped lunch. I drifted off to a tiny nap and I could feel his gentle kisses on my face as he whispered loving things. When I wakened, Mike was asleep.

I kissed him awake and we returned to the pile of mail in the kitchen. As he sorted, I laid out salad, fresh bread and fruit.

He tossed an envelope over to me. "Look at this. How would anyone know you're here?"

It was from my drop mail service in Canada. I shivered as I thought about the last mailing I'd received from them, with Nelson's sad note. After I raised the thermostat on the AC I decided to eat supper before I opened it. We cleaned up the kitchen and took our iced tea into the library, along with the bills and my envelope.

Inside it were two letters, one from Dave Finch and one from a law firm in Chicago. Very mixed feelings rose as I read the first one to Mike.

> "Dear Sara, This letter came to the office at school today. You'll notice it's addressed to you in care of me. I have no idea what it's about.
>
> I have news too. Finally, after waiting two years, the shop has finished the special solar-powered instruments we designed for the plots in Idaho. I want you to come and pick them up so that when you do the data gathering later this month, you can install them. We need to get them up as soon as possible to be able to include the new data in this year's professional paper.
>
> Also, I got a call from the police station. They really want the box out of their safe. I checked to find out who did the appraisal and he's probably as honest a merchant as we will be able to find. You need to sign for removal in person. I'd rather you didn't haul it around in the back of your car, so we need to get him involved in the pickup.

I hope all is well with you. Our weather has turned cruelly hot and everyone is huddling around whatever air conditioner they can find. It makes for strange bedfellows. Dodie sends her love. Dave.

P.S. I hear the strawberry ice cream was a big success. D.F."

When I read the last line, my heart sank. The letter contained an imbedded coded message and I would need to work on it before the message would make sense. I picked up the second letter. The return address was for a law firm in the financial district of Chicago. My heart nose-dived again as I opened it and began to read.

"Dear Madam Lambert.

An unusual situation has come to our attention this week. We are involved in the settling of the estates of Anthony Andretti and Ms. Jennifer Cameron. Associated with these, some of the affairs of your late husband, Henri Lambert are now coming to light. You are named in each of these trusts and we need to arrange a meeting with you to begin the procedures for settlement.

We have scheduled an appointment for you to meet with us on Monday the 25th of June at 9:00 a.m. If this is not convenient, please call our office to reschedule.

Sincerely, K. Skorski."

It was the first time I'd been in contact with Kostyan Skorski in many years. He'd married my college roommate, Anna. She and I had kept in touch over the years because of our work, but she never spoke about him or what he was doing. I knew he was a financial planner but not where his office was based. Mike had a strange look on his face, as though he knew more about this letter than he could divulge.

"Oh, Mike. I spent most of last night struggling with unknown fears. When you left this morning I had a powerful feeling I needed to pack my suitcase to leave on some unknown task. I don't want to go and face this with Skorski. And how can I possibly install those instruments for Finch, fifty feet up in the trees with only one operational arm and hand? It's true I'm the only one left in the group who does that kind of climbing, but I'm afraid now."

Mike's comment was very odd and somehow frightening. "There's more to this than appearances. Let me think about it and make some phone calls. Why don't you go out into the garden and wait for me on the bench by the pond?"

I stepped out onto the patio and was met by the heat of the day not yet gone. After walking around the yard, I decided to sit by the pond and splash my feet in the water. The evening birds discussed their new neighbor and agreed to allow me to stay. Everyone, bird and human alike, looked wilted. The birds walked with a weary gait as they pecked listlessly on the ground among the parched shrubbery. Finally, I picked up my sandals and went back to the library door. Mike was sitting with his back to the door and didn't hear me come inside.

He was speaking on the phone in a low tone, with more intensity and anguish than I would have thought possible.

"Jacques, for God's sake, can you come out of that damn woods long enough to help me? I have to go to California the first of July, and Sara won't have anyone to protect her."

I slipped out into the deepening night shadows, trembling with fright. What did he mean? My gut went into waves of knots and I clutched at my body, whacking my knuckles on the bars of my cast. What good could I possibly be, when I wasn't in safe fighting condition? I remembered Jacques telling me it was the only way to be free. You had to be in control of your body and know what it would do for you when you needed it. I was injured, out of condition, not in control. I was terrified.

Now I knew true panic. I'd let time go by in slothful ease when I should have been working to strengthen my left side. I was weeping when Mike came out several minutes later.

He took my hands in his and said, "How much did you hear?"

There was no reason to lie. "Only that you asked Jacques to come out of the woods to help you protect me, and then I went back outside. It's time to stop being in panic mode, Mike. I've trained my whole life for this. I chose to do it of my own free will and now's my moment of truth. We don't have much time. Let's go down to the workout room and start."

I heard his sigh of relief. At least we would do the best we could to be prepared for what he felt would happen. He took my hand and his gentle strength entered my body like an IV of love. When we got downstairs, he brought out a calendar and note pad. "First we need to work backwards to see just how much time we have to get ready. The date we're working around is the 25th of June when you have your appointment with Skorski.

"You must be at the meeting at the proper time, with the information he's expecting and with an appropriate wardrobe. I promise I'll tell you as much as I dare as we go along, but tonight we must start your conditioning.

"You're going to need both a review of your self-defense skills and some more aggressive new ones. The element of surprise may be worth a few seconds and could save your life. The strengthening of your left side is paramount. It will help that you're ambidextrous. Since your injury, you haven't been standing straight and your walk is uneven. We must improve your balance. I have one defense move .you must perfect. It uses a fighting stick and a knife.

"I've been told Finch has had a pair of boots made like yours. This is bad news but we'll work around it. He's so arrogant he'll think you won't know."

Mike was watching me as he spoke about Dave. My expression must have betrayed my puzzlement. I'd worked with Dave since our college days in Paris. We'd done research together for many years, besides my other job for him with the CIA. Somehow I didn't want to know just yet and I didn't ask. Right now there was difficult work to do and Mike would be working full days too.

I remembered the agonizing routine Jacques had put me through not long ago and knew this one wouldn't be any easier. Somehow this situation was beginning to sound even more ominous and I was not in good health or fighting shape. We did simple stretching for a long time and then a few of the night maneuvers. Mike asked me to show him how I would practice during the day and at eleven o'clock we headed for a shortened night's rest.

There was no slacking for Sara now. I tried to bring back the tough determination that had finally driven me to work so hard for Jacques. There was a desire for survival, I guess, and pride and loyalty to an ideal. I didn't know what my challenge might be but I would try to be as ready as I could.

First, I decoded Finch's message. It sounded innocuous enough; in fact I didn't quite understand what he wanted. It was something about the timing of a trip to Brazil that he was making with Jacques. I carried the phone and a timer down to the workroom and spent most of the day; ten minutes rest each hour and a short nap between workouts. Mike called about one o'clock to say he'd be home to get me for X-rays in a few minutes. I was on the doorstep when he got there.

It had been only a few weeks, but I was more than ready for the freedom. I couldn't believe my good fortune when Mike came back with the films and said Rick was ready to turn me loose. He showed me the pictures, including the rods they'd left in. I felt like a bionic woman.

"How shall we celebrate, My Dear?"

153

I didn't even hesitate. "With strengthening exercises for the right arm, Mike. I want to be a real surprise, a nasty surprise."

Thus began my new education. I had a feeling I was being given some of the training SEALs learn; neat, efficient and very deadly. We worked especially hard on my balance and coordination and used the night self-defense training as a reward for a good practice.

Most of my time alone would be spent working on strengthening my legs since they were so important to my first task. My right arm and shoulder came along slowly as I struggled not to favor or protect them. I began to trust my body again and then it was time for some of the new material. I had always liked the hanbō because I could substitute a piece of wood from the forest with the same results. I practiced pulling the knife from my boot while using the stick and found it easier with each practice. It was late and we decided to call it a night.

Mike stepped to my side. "I'm pleased with your progress, Sara. I want you to do mostly strength-training and balance tomorrow. When I get home we'll talk about the schedule and when you need to leave. I finally got hold of Cade this morning. He'll be here by tomorrow night."

"Cade?"

Mike chuckled. "My brother will be a good match for you. Maybe he can keep you in line."

As we went up the steps, Mike's hands slipped around my waist. He stopped me and turned me around so we were face to face. I realized how big a man he was, or perhaps how small I was. I shivered as his hands moved up to my face.

"Sara, would you sleep with me tonight?" His kiss was gentle but the passion in his eyes was very real. "Please, Sara. Deal with your God tomorrow, but let me make love to you tonight."

There was no hesitation. "Yes, Michael, I will share your bed tonight."

After our bath ritual was complete, he turned me and loosened my robe. He folded me into his arms as he whispered, "Come My Beloved. Let us send our souls to sing with the angels, and our spirits to dance with the stars."

CHAPTER FOURTEEN

When I got up to fix Mike's breakfast, he reached out to hold me in his arms. "Thank you, Sara. Your joyous abandon was a sweet surprise."

I took his dear face in my hands. "And your passion was pure delight. I love you, Michael. Thank you for waiting for me.

"What time did you say Cade would be here? What does he look like?"

Mike's laugh was mixed with a funny snort. "God only knows! He marches to a different drummer and I love him dearly. That I would trust him with you should give you some clue about how much. He doesn't look much like me at all. He's a bit lighter and taller, his eyes are black and his hair is red."

As he turned to leave, I had a wonderful, funny thought. "Mike, remember those two little urchins always hanging out at the hospital ER door? I'll bet one of them pipes up with a smart remark this morning, something like, 'Look at old Cameron, he must've laid his lady last night.' And you'll answer, 'you betcha' kid'." We were both laughing as he climbed into the car to leave.

It was early yet and the air was still cool as I took my breakfast out onto the patio. I decided how to structure the day's practice sessions and then relaxed to the cooing calls of the doves and the jaunty strident sounds of our resident blue jays. It was going to be very hot again today and I stepped out into the yard to water the tomato plants and the flowers. I added some water to the pond and then went inside to tidy up the kitchen. I remembered our meeting with Father James this evening and hoped we could have supper at our favorite place afterwards. From what Mike said, one didn't make solid plans around brother Cade's comings and goings.

I'd always felt so safe in Mike's house, but this morning I went around and carefully locked all the windows and doors. I dropped the long bar into the space at the bottom of the library door and drew the curtains. It was still quite cool in the basement workroom as I began my practice with an hour of balance and coordination moves. Then I decided to make some circles and straight lines on the floor to use for practice. I needed to find something to make a small difference in feel or texture that wouldn't be too hard to fasten down or take back up. What I needed was some garden twine or yarn. I returned to the library and slipped into the "Mother's Apartment" where I found both, along with some sturdy tape. The project took an hour but I was pleased with the results. I took the silk scarf from my waist and tied it around my eyes.

It was quiet downstairs and concentration filled my body. Even the flow of air made by my own movements became part of my awareness. I'd just finished practicing on the straight lines and their crossings and was beginning the first circle, when a slight draft of air drifted across my left side. At the same moment, I heard the refrigerator upstairs click on. I felt an almost imperceptible motion followed by total silence as the door to the basement closed.

I had uninvited company. I hoped he hadn't been far enough down the stairs to see my slight hesitation as I decided what to do. It was Mr. Vaughan listening in, who spoke now. "OK, don't panic. You're probably safer if you let him think you don't know he's here. If he's intent on killing you and has a weapon you have two strikes against you already. It's time now to make Mike proud of you. Play it out to the end. You're warmed-up and ready if he tries to attack. Keep your scarf on and your guard up Sweetheart."

It was the longest message my old buddy had ever sent but it made sense. I calmed down and my pulse slowed toward normal. I switched to my French mindset and began to do the moves around the inner circle. I imagined Jacques by my side, encouraging me and protecting me from harm. I reached a cross point, turned, and went down the path to enter the outside ring. I'd be closer to the stranger, and perhaps could get some clue to his whereabouts. I switched from coordination to strength-training and slowed down my pace even more, making an extra effort to be absolutely silent.

This person was a real pro. I felt no motion, heard no sounds of breathing, and there was no scent of him in the room. In a small way, I was relieved. At least he wasn't some slimy thug hired to murder me; one who smelled of garlic, cigars and sweaty clothes in need of washing.

The shrill ringing of the timer shattered the silence. I turned it off and walked the circle to find a cross-path to the center. I felt as though I'd entered the center of the Chartres labyrinth and would somehow be safe. The compass directions were marked out on the floor with yarn and I positioned myself to face away from the stairs. I dropped to my knees and began to pray.

Why I chose to do the prayers in Russian, I'll never know. I was weeping when the timer rang again to begin the next practice.

My visitor was in no hurry to make his presence known. I rose to my feet and began the series of Mike's Russian kata. We had devised a new series to be done in the dark and I left the blindfold on. I brought him into my presence as I remembered his fluid motions and supple strength. The series took a whole hour. I loved them because they were his, but also because they were so beautiful as well as very deadly. At the end of each sequence done slowly, I speeded up the motions to fighting pace and did ten. At the end I did the whole series without a break, ending on the far side of the outer circle.

The timer rang again and I began to return to the center to rest. As I approached the inner ring, I sensed the stranger's presence. The strength of it was amazing. I hesitated, trying to decide what to do.

A low whistle followed his gasp. "Mike's right. You're amazing. I've never known anyone as sensitive or as courageous as you've been this morning."

I was exhausted. Sweat rolled down my back and my clothes were soaking wet. I wanted to run and hide from this stranger, without knowing who he was. My hands were trembling as I tried to undo the sweat-soaked knot in my scarf. He stepped forward and helped me.

My first look at Cade Cameron took in his jet-black eyes and his wonderful red hair, trimmed in a jaunty butch cut. Then I was greeted by his quirky smile. It seemed to be waiting to break into laughter if anyone looked as if they needed it. No question about this man. He fit Mike's description of his brother all right, a bit taller and leaner, and in top fighting condition.

He must have seen the quick assessment and the admiration in my eyes because his smile turned to laughter. "Ma'am, first order of business is what name you wish to be called."

"My name has caused nothing but trouble since this whole mess began, Cade. I'd like to chuck them all and get a new one like Iris or Phoebe or even Robyn. I don't feel like any of the others belong to me any more."

He took my hand as we went toward the stairs. "Well, let's use Sara Harvey then. Right now, our first order of business is lunch. Mike said you tended to skip meals on some misguided notion of vanity. You listen to me, Sweetheart, right now you're going to be working so hard you're going to need a lot more calories than you've been taking in. We need to take a survey of the kitchen cupboards and the freezer and make some shopping lists. You need meat and carbs along with a lot of veggies and fruit. And, you need to take better breaks between workouts. I want you to lay off the weeping."

I turned away from him toward the counter. "How did you know that?"

He shrugged his shoulders. "I was watching while you prayed. Your scarf filled up and turned dark pretty fast. Why ever were you praying in Russian, for cat's sake?"

"I don't know. Sometimes I can't explain what I'm moved to do. I get hooked up in a train of consciousness I didn't ask for and usually suffer the consequences. I was thinking about the anguish of the Russian peasants over centuries, their fear and hopelessness in the face of brute power and starvation.

"I was terrified earlier during my practice, when I felt the change in the air pressure as the basement door opened and I realized there was someone trespassing in my sanctuary. By the way, how did you get in?"

He was apologetic. "I came in the front door while you were on the patio. I went to an upstairs bedroom and took a little nap while I waited for you to go downstairs and get started. I'm sorry I frightened you. I saw you hesitate as I came down the stairs, so I suspected you knew I was here."

I sighed. "Cade, not only did I feel the door open, but I also heard the refrigerator come on before you closed the door. If Mr. Vaughan hadn't warned me, I probably would have pulled off my blindfold and given it all away. He's saved my hide several times in the last few weeks. I'll tell you about him later.

"So, did you already check out the refrigerator? Mike and I have a meeting tonight and we usually go out to supper afterwards so there isn't much in there. We go shopping on Saturday, if you want to add to the list. For now, how about a big salad full of shrimp and eggs and some fresh bread?"

We worked on the salad in companionable silence and since it was too hot to be nice outside, we took our lunch into the library.

"Let's go into your mother's special room. It should be nice and cool yet and there's a table in there where we can look out into the garden. Mike wants to build a screened porch over the patio so we can enjoy it more. We can sit out there when it rains and we need mosquito protection most of the summer.

"This is a comfortable house and I think we'll stay here, though he's still open to moving to Pittsburgh if I really want to. There are things coming up that may change our minds one way or the other.

"Where's your home, Cade?" My change of topic caught him in an unguarded moment and I watched his face struggle with several emotions, none of them happy.

I laid my hand on his. "Please forgive my rudeness. It was just social chatter. I didn't intend to cause you pain."

His eyes had turned a steely hard black and his answer was curt. "I have no home. I'm a nomad, traveling all over the world, from job to job, making money but not having any one to share it with. My wife Susanna died five years ago and I'm still grieving, I guess." He quickly changed the topic. "Come on, you need a short nap and then we'll get back to work. When does Mike get home?"

158

"About three thirty and he's on call this weekend so we won't be away from the house much. Our meeting tonight is with Father James."

We carried the dishes back into the kitchen and Cade cleaned up while I rested for a few minutes stretched out on the floor in the library. As I drifted off to sleep, I felt a new sense of hope and peace. All I could do about my situation was to be prepared and to hope my training would protect me when I needed it.

It was early afternoon on a sunny day. Why then was I wakened from my nap by a gut-wrenching, screaming nightmare? Cade was there but he didn't touch me. Instead, he watched to make sure I didn't hurt myself. Otherwise, he sat in silence, waiting. I turned away from him as I lay on the floor, sobbing. A whirlwind of emotions swelled and exploded in my body, fear, grief, and anger.

After a few minutes, I felt a pillow drop down by my head. I crawled to it and buried my face, stifling the sobs. After a few minutes the sobs turned to whimpers, as I began to tremble and shake. I was ice-cold and terrified of what was happening. He dropped a blanket on me next, and stepped back out of the way. I rolled up in it and curled up into a tight ball. I began to cry again, a strange gentle weeping that was somehow healing. I felt as though all the anguish and despair of the whole world had passed through my body, and for some reason I had been allowed to survive.

Cade knelt down by me. "I'm going to make you some tea. Sugar and milk?" I nodded a grateful yes and started to uncoil from my blanket as he went off to the kitchen. I stepped to the window and looked out at the garden. It seemed to be waiting for the coolness of evening to revive the limp and thirsty flowers. Other worries had taken precedence over their care the last few days.

Cade was carrying two mugs of steaming tea when he returned. "I don't know if I'd want to sleep in your bed if you have dreams like that, Sara."

I reached for my mug. "I afraid Mike won't want to either."

There it was, simple and pure, from my mouth and my heart. There were no more tears. We finished our tea and returned to the workroom to continue practice. Mike and his brother must have worked out together at some time or other. There were close similarities in the ways they did the sequences. We were in the middle of a stick sequence when I felt the basement door open.

Mike came downstairs to greet his brother. "Well, I see you got here OK. What adventure did I call you away from this time?"

Cade bowed to me, stepped from the ring and shrugged his shoulders. "I was estimating a contract for a big Mall complex in Norway. My partner can finish the rest. We're so swamped now anyway I don't care whether we get this one or not. I'm running about a

159

month behind and that costs big bucks if you're under contract to finish at a specific time."

Mike moved to the edge of the practice circles. "What are these, Sara? Looks like a good idea, especially for the night tactics. Would you excuse us for a few minutes? Cade and I need to catch up on the situation here. Why don't you switch to some careful stretching and cool-down and you can call it a day?" As they went up the stairs, I wondered what Cade would tell his brother about our time together so far? While the men were working in the library, I decided to fix supper so we could be together for a meal.

I had an increasing feeling of unease, almost dread, as the evening approached. When I figured out what it was about, I was both relieved and frightened. At least there was something I could do about it. I went upstairs to get the things I would need.

Our meal was a pleasant family affair. The men did most of the talking; reminiscing about earlier escapades and adventures of their boyhood. I vaguely remembered Cade Cameron as the big brother who'd left home and was whispered to be the black sheep of the clan. His business must be successful, if he had an office in Europe and he worked all over the world.

I asked him, "What do you do for a living, Cade?"

He grinned. "I'm a plumber and Mike's a carpenter. We just work on different houses. I probably make more than he does."

I glanced at my watch and nodded to Mike that we needed to leave. As he left the room, I stepped to Cade's side and gave him the car keys. "In a few minutes, please be ready."

He showed no emotion. He really was a pro and I would need him even more, now that I knew what I was going to do.

It was getting late; still muggy and too hot for comfort, but I insisted on walking, pleading the need to get out in the daylight for a bit after the day in the basement. As much as I appreciated the basement workroom, it did give me claustrophobia not to have windows or fresh air. I carried a small soft-sided briefcase bag with the things I needed for the weekend.

Father James was waiting on the steps. I expect he enjoyed a chance to get away from his desk after a long day too. I turned to Mike. "Michael, would you please give me a few moments alone with Father before we begin?"

I didn't touch him or look into his eyes. I was already weeping as Father and I went inside. As he closed the door of the study, I dropped to my knees and whispered, "Father, it has been six months since my last confession. Now I come with contrite heart and misery to confess my sins before God and before you."

When I finished and received absolution, Father James said, "I have a feeling you've already decided your penance. I'll help if you feel you must do it, but I pray it's not a mistake."

I rose to my feet and handed him the paper with the phone numbers. "Would you please call and ask permission for me to spend the weekend at the convent and then call Mike's brother Cade to come and take me there. I don't want to see Michael until Monday afternoon when he returns from work. I plan to spend my time in prayer for the girls in the birthing rooms and for those about to lose their precious babies. Pray for me, Father I have need of it. Not only did I sin but I led Michael to sin. God have mercy on us both."

There was a back exit from the study into the sanctuary. I slipped in and changed my clothes. I was kneeling in the back of the church when Cade came for me. I was the only person there, but he still gasped when he stepped inside the door and saw me. He lifted me to my feet and we left by the front door. I didn't turn to look back. I couldn't have seen anything through my tears anyway. My sandals and long black clothes made me feel as if I were returning to the Middle Ages. I was terrified of what lay ahead; but it had to be done. I heard Michael's anguished voice call out my name as we drove away.

CHAPTER FIFTEEN Cade continues

When I got back from the convent, Mike was pacing and talking to himself out in the back garden. I studied him from the kitchen window, judging whether I could defend myself if he decided to beat me to a bloody pulp. He had fifty pounds on me, but I figured his two major heart attacks in the last few years had stolen the stamina and strength he once had. In an instant I decided my strategy. I'd stay out of his way as long as I could. He was my brother and I loved him too much to fight him unless my survival was at stake.

I began to clean up the kitchen. When the lights flipped on, Mike headed in the back door. I slipped the knives into their drawer holder by the stove and edged my way around the kitchen island to keep something solid between us.

I felt like I'd been kicked in the gut when I realized Mike was crying. He was like a hurt child, talking with his hands, wiping his tears and his dripping nose off on the sleeve of his shirt.

The hurt child was frantic. "I give up. I don't understand. I've tried for weeks. She's crazy! What am I supposed to do?"

At this he turned to me as if he'd just noticed me. "Cade, I've tried so hard. I just don't understand. One minute she's eager to love me, and the next instant she's off to a convent because she's somehow sinned against God. What am I going to do? I've lost her, haven't I?" At this, he crumpled onto a stool.

Poor brother, learning about women this late in life must be disorienting. Even though I was tempted to laugh, I stayed serious. "Now Mike. I don't think so. She's been under a lot of pressure. Maybe she needed the weekend to rest."

Mike sat bolt upright. "Rest! Do you know where she's gone? Into the fiery furnace of hell! That convent is like the one she endured in France when she was fifteen years old. What good can come from going through that again?"

I waited a few long moments before I replied. "Maybe she wants to bear some of the pain of those frightened girls; in exchange for the gifts she's been given. She's an extraordinary woman. I for one, hope she'll find some semblance of peace from her sacrifice."

Mike sat, thinking the idea out to its conclusion. "I hope you're right, brother, I don't want to lose her now."

As I put my arm around his shoulders, I hoped he and Sara would be able to work it out. I wasn't ready for another relationship yet, but I was so drawn to Sara's soul and spirit, I knew this assignment could be the toughest one of my whole life.

We returned to the library as Mike filled me in on what would be coming up. As we talked and as I remembered my thoughts while I'd read her files, I couldn't believe the people in the working group hadn't realized who the true traitor was, and more important, why.

"We'll have the weekend to work on this, Mike. Let's call it a day. I haven't slept in 48 hours and there's a seven-hour time change besides. Where's the most convenient place for me to sleep? No comfort required. I'm so tired I could sleep on a bed of knives."

He set me up in the downstairs room with the twin beds. In the few minutes it took me to shower and collapse into bed, Mike appeared at the doorway in his pajamas.

"Cade, can we sleep like we used to when we were kids? I need you, big brother, even if you still snore like a freight train. My life is so full of terrors right now. I feel like a frightened kid with a room full of monsters, all of them waiting to kill me. They just hang around and haunt me in the middle of the night and I hope no one can hear me whimper."

I reached out my arms "Come on, nothing's as scary with two of us. I already have some ideas about what to do. We'll tackle it tomorrow, together."

A couple of hours later I wakened in my strange bed; trying for an instant to remember where I was. It happened a lot since Susanna died and I had no home, nor a bed with her sweet presence to share. I reached over and turned on the light. Mike was lying on his back, rigid; his fists clenched white by his sides. Tears trickled down his cheeks.

I got up and went to sit on his bed. "That's it, Mike. I know something else is bothering you. It's time to 'fess up. Neither of us is sleeping anyway. Come on, let's go make some hot chocolate and you'd better start talking."

We went into the kitchen, made cocoa and carried it to the library. I waited for him to begin.

He was struggling to speak. "I'm scheduled for surgery Tuesday afternoon. The surgeon is coming over from Germany or it would have already happened. When they did my preliminary checkup for Coronado yesterday, they found a new cerebral aneurysm just waiting to explode. They told me my chances of successful surgery are only about 10%, my chances of coming out with brain damage or worse is about 20%. Subtract that from 100% and you know what my chances of dying are. I can be philosophical about my own life; it's Sara I'm frantic about."

163

"You haven't told her, have you, Mike? And now, she won't be home until Monday. How can I help?"

Mike struggled with his thoughts. "I wish I knew. I want to provide for her. Not financially, she's very wealthy, but I have the feeling she won't handle this well. She's just come off a traumatic life with Lambert and then all the stuff with Andretti and Jenny. And now, apparently, there's this Finch thing. Is she never to find peace?

"Our courtship hasn't been easy because of what those people did to her, but she's so brave and honorable and loyal to her own beliefs. I can't bear to think about losing her now, and losing my beautiful Roslin. Did you know Sara and I have a daughter? She's thirty-four now. That's a story for another time."

He reached out and clutched my hand. "Cade, there may not be another time. I'm sorry we haven't had more chance to be part of each other's life, and now I'm going to die."

There it was. He'd said it, and he was inconsolable. I sat and held him in my arms, rocking back and forth like I had when he was little and he'd broken the neighbor's window with his home run smash.

"OK Mike. Do you want me to take charge?"

"God, yes! I feel like I can't even make a decision about which shoe to put on first."

I grabbed a pad and pencil. "Are you on call this weekend?"

He nodded yes. "Saturday, 7 to 7 but Rick said he'd cover for me if I needed it. He's the only person who knows. I told him because he's my best friend on staff and he's become a close friend of Sara's since we've been through so much together these past few weeks."

"Are they expecting you to work next week?"

"No, I told them I needed time off for personal reasons. They're getting a little impatient with my performance but I can't help that now. I've worked my last day for them anyway."

I made a calendar and filled in the time slots. "What time is the surgery?"

"The surgeon is supposed to get in Monday evening from Frankfurt and the surgery is at two o'clock Tuesday afternoon at another hospital where he's been given temporary privileges. He's coming because he's a long time friend from Navy days and he's the world expert on this surgery. He invented it."

"Sounds like the wagons are circling, Mike. We'll do the best we can to get you into the 10% category. That's all we can do. Sara will be back at nine o'clock Monday morning. By then, I want you to have made all the decisions on her behalf, made all the phone calls and plans you wish for her care, and made lists of names and phone numbers of those you want to have notified of your progress. Then, you must call your lawyer even though it's a weekend. You need to update your will and select a durable power of attorney for health care.

"We'll spend all weekend going through your papers and financial affairs, clearing out your desk and cleaning up your computer. It will give you something else to do besides worry.

"Most important of all, when Sara walks through the door Monday morning, you're going to tell her everything. By then you'll be able to apologize in a reasonable manner, and tell her what you would like to arrange for her. Give her some credit, Mike. You may be surprised at her response and you'll have given her a gift if you let her help.

"It's two in the morning. Let's get some sleep now and I'll set my alarm for 8 o'clock. If you wake up sooner, wake me up too so we can get started. I love you little brother, we'll do the best we can with a bad situation."

I poked my nose out the door to check the weather and was greeted by cool Canadian air. The front they'd promised for the weekend had arrived early and we went through the house, opening it up to the new day. Two Cameron brothers were sawing logs when the birds wakened to greet the blessed cool morning, and still were, when the alarm went off at eight o'clock.

Our work was efficient and careful during the morning. Mike admitted I might find a few strange entries but just to ask. Well, I looked up a bit later, and I had a bunch of questions alright.

"What's the deal with the checks deposited to a bank in Switzerland every month? The balance hasn't changed in all these years? Are you buying gold to hide somewhere?"

Mike answered. "I don't have time to lie. They were for Wilhelmina."

"Good God! Brother. Have you had a mistress all these years? Have you been paying blackmail or something? Who the hell is Wilhelmina?"

"I'll tell you later. We need to keep working now or we won't get done in time." He finished the lists and put the people in the order he wanted them to be called. It was odd. Why had he put his mother on the bottom of the list?

He handed me a slip of paper with some numbers. "Would you please go up to the bedroom at the back of the house and open the safe behind the dresser mirror. Take a box with you to carry stuff down in. It's been a long time since I've been in there. I don't remember what's there. I need to make some phone calls now."

I could take a hint. He wanted some privacy and I would give it to him for a while. Mike was still on the phone when I returned so I went to the kitchen to see about lunch. Sara said there wouldn't be much around since Saturday was shopping day, and she was right. I checked the cupboards for something so we'd have to go out only once. My comfort food has always been tomato soup and toasted cheese sandwiches and I did find the stuff for those. I laid things out on the counter ready to put together, and returned to the library.

The look of relief on Mike's face was heartening. He'd been able to contact the guy he called the Duke, a close friend from his Navy years. I dropped the box of things from the safe onto the middle of his desk. He picked up a photograph from the top of the pile. It was a picture of our family at the beach during a summer outing. I wasn't in it because I was gone by then. Mike and the Becky of his high school days were clowning in the front row, like all teenagers do. I could see Mom scowling in the background and my little runt brother Zachary on his hands and knees in the sand. I figured my father took the picture because he wasn't in it. I was surprised at how little changed Sara was. She was easy to recognize.

Mike was crying as he looked at me and said, "I want to make sure my mother doesn't get this box of things. They're for Sara. It has my Navy medals and pictures she'll understand. It's full of stuff little boys treasure, like foreign coins and rocks and turtle shells. If only things could have been different in our lives. Don't give it to her right away; wait until she can treasure it herself, alone, because it was mine.

"This is a lot worse than running into a concrete abutment and getting it over with fast. That's a cop-out because you're done with it and people left behind have to do all the grieving later."

I took his hand. "Come on, let's have some lunch. I'll carry the box out to my car and lock it up in the trunk. We'll do it for the things you don't want to have pilfered while strangers and people you don't love are in your space."

We were starting lunch when the lawyer returned Mike's call. He made an appointment for early Sunday morning. We were to go to his place so we would have witnesses on hand for the changes he wanted to make.

Then Mike explained to me about Wilhelmina. "And yes, Sara knows. Her response was more understanding and loving than I could have hoped for."

"How are you going to continue to provide for Wilhelmina, if something happens to you?"

"The house in Finland is in both of our names. If I die first, it belongs to her. The house here belongs to me also. I want to make sure mother doesn't get it back. It should be sold to help support Wilhelmina. It should be enough. Wilhelmina is very frail now and wishes release from the bondage of her body. I'd hoped Sara and I could go to see her in August. I'd even bought the tickets."

The look on Mike's face frightened me. It was almost as though he were saying goodbye to everything and everyone; touching, hearing, feeling, seeing, all the things he wouldn't have anymore and all the people he would lose.

"Come on, we need to get back to work. Then, let's get cleaned up and walk to church. I'd like to meet Father James and worship in your church. You know, there may be a problem about the service since no one but you and Sara are Catholic. Your mother will have a fit."

He shrugged it off, "So be it."

By the end of the afternoon, Mike had written the letters he planned to give to Sara, his daughter Roslin, Wilhelmina, the Duke, Jacques Grayson, and to me. With each task done, he was more serene but also more otherworldly. I, for one, was glad to get out in the warm afternoon and work up a sweat walking to church. After what I'd gone through with Susanna's last illness and watching her go, I didn't know whether this was harder or not; and it wasn't over.

Mike promised to clue me in about what to do during the service, and then he sank to his knees in prayer. It seemed like a very natural thing to be doing right then and I joined him on the kneeler. I was glad he wasn't crying. I was the one crying. He gave me his handkerchief, and took my hand in his. The sense of peace and serenity in his touch soothed me but frightened me too. I hoped he wasn't going to stop trying to survive. It would make things mighty tough for the rest of us. After the service, we stopped to greet Father James.

Father said, "Remember, you can call any time, day or night, you two. Give Sara my regards when she gets home Monday."

We decided to go home by another route and Mike took me to their favorite restaurant for supper. It was a good idea, since our cupboard was bare. As we waited for our meal, I asked Mike, "Are we doing what you had hoped to accomplish? More important, are you OK?"

He started in as though he hadn't heard me. "When we get home, I want you to go through the house and pick out what you might like to have, pictures, furniture, books. There are some things I want you to put away for Roslin, like the little statue of the water sprite in the pond.

"I want to have the locks changed on the house tomorrow, even though it's Sunday. When I was going through the desk early this morning, I found an envelope with copies of some old papers. I don't know where they came from. I found one that proves that my mother was the signed witness for the transfer of Rebecca Jane Campbell by her own parents, to Henri Lambert. I can guess how Lambert tricked them into giving her up. My folks must have told him about her father's gambling addiction. Lambert gambled him into financial ruin. My own mother was the one who essentially sold Becky into slavery.

"The Duke will be here tomorrow morning in time to go with us to the lawyer's. We're going to need him this week to protect Sara and Roslin from what's going to happen. Since we're not married yet, my mother will certainly contest any arrangements I wish to make, even claim I wasn't of sound mind. You may need to keep Sara away until the service. I think Jacques Grayson is coming in on Wednesday to help you too."

He was really scaring me now, talking like he was going to die. "OK, what if you make it and everything's fine?"

He laughed. "Then, I'll have all my precious family and friends together and we'll have a big party while I recuperate from the surgery." His voice dropped to a whisper, "My chances stink and you know it, Cade."

We agreed to talk about something else, but it hung over us like the blackish-green cloud formation of a Missouri tornado; spinning us out of control into blind terror.

We were both pretty tired but there was something I wanted Mike to do for me and there might not be another time after tonight. When we got home I asked him, "Tell me about the Russian sequences you and Sara have been doing. Would you teach a few of them to me now?"

He agreed and we went down to the workroom. While we were loosening up, I said, "It's spooky being around Sara. She has some interesting powers and she isn't asking for them. She had a nightmare yesterday while she was taking a short nap between practice sessions. She almost acts like my best buddy in Vietnam who had Post Traumatic Stress Disorder. What happened to her, Mike?"

When Mike finished telling me Sara's story, we were both crying. I asked, "Do you think she'll make it?

"I don't know, but I was willing to help her try. Come on, we'll do the first sequence and then we need to get some rest. I'll be glad to get the legal part over, and I'll be glad to put you in the Duke's hands. He's a wise, competent and gentle man. If you choose not to keep Sara, I hope he will look after her."

There he'd said it, in plain talk. He was giving me the responsibility for the care and love of his most prized and beloved woman. I was terrified.

Mike was a patient and competent teacher. I treasured the time we spent together, working on the thing he loved most, teaching.

Sunday morning began too early but we needed to get the lawyer part over so we could return to work in the house. When the doorbell rang, Mike and I were ready to go. As we opened the door, I gasped in surprise. The man standing on the doorstep was someone I knew well, but in my circle his name wasn't the Duke. It was the Fox. Man! It was a small world.

It didn't take long to make the wording changes in the will and the durable power of attorney for health care. We were surprised, dismayed and then resigned, as Mike told us he hoped he wouldn't have to go through the surgery on Tuesday because it would devastate his friend if he died under his knife. He chose DNR for his chart. I didn't understand why, but we had to help him do as he wished. We agreed to make me the responsible party rather than Sara, to save her from any criticism by our mother.

As we left the lawyer's house, the Duke said, "We need to get every sign of Madam Lambert's presence in the house removed and she must find another place to stay. I plan to stay with you and Michael until the immediate crisis is over. Johnson has arranged for a private plane to fly me back to Boise on Saturday night. If the worst happens, Mike, I'll honor your request and take Sara with me to the ranch."

We made a stop at the grocery store. I shopped for simple food and tucked a dozen yellow sweetheart roses into the cart. I dreaded to think about tomorrow, but at least we were doing the best we could.

Mike was so weary we took him home and settled him in the library in his favorite chair. The mental exhaustion of the many decisions and explanations he needed to make would have wearied even a healthy person. As I sat with Mike, I gained more and more respect for the skill and professionalism of the Duke. I suspected he'd done this same job for some important and highly placed people in our country. As I followed his train of thought and realized what he was devising, I was glad he was Mike's friend and not his enemy.

The Duke called for a break from the work while he made some phone calls. Mike got up and folded the blanket from beside his chair as he said, "Cade, would you go find an empty box in the closet? There are some things I'd like to lay aside for Sara before we forget or someone removes them. This is just the first sweep. She'll do one when she comes back and then, the Duke will do the last one, since that's one of his jobs.

"He's right. We must erase any clues she's been here. I'm sure when she understands what is being done; she'll do a better job of the garden and porch than I could, since the plants were her pride and joy." He smiled in remembrance. "I think she gave many of them names and talked to them when she was in the garden."

We began in the basement workout room. He took the pair of hanbōs from the rack, a small pottery cup and long silk scarves from the cupboard. We found the box of things from the workroom at Jacques Grayson's and I carried it to my car. The folded blanket from beside his library chair was used to wrap up his scrapbook of gardening ideas and sketches before it went into the box.

From her bathroom, Mike took a white bathrobe, a new bar of lavender soap and a soft clean cloth like the one hanging on her rack and put them into the box. In his own bedroom, he folded some of his favorite shirts, and wrapped them with his favorite sweater. It was as though he were going through his day, remembering the things she enjoyed or loved. When we finished, he needed to rest. I was very worried about the way he looked. He went into the bedroom, crumpled onto his bed and promptly fell sleep.

It was almost lunchtime but I hated to waken him. The house was so quiet that the ringing of the phone a few minutes later was jarring.

It was Sara. "Cade, come right now and get me. Michael's in trouble and he needs me."

I sighed in relief. "You betcha' Sweetheart. I'm on my way out the door." I leaned over to Mike and whispered, "Hang on Mike, Sara's coming as quick as I can get her. Don't you dare check out without saying 'goodbye'?" I was fighting tears as I dashed down the steps to the car.

The Duke was sitting with him when we returned. He gave the health care directive to Sara to read. She nodded assent.

"I trust you, Kostyan."

Mike reached for her and whispered, "Please forgive me, Sara. I should've known you couldn't be sheltered from the truth. Sing me away, My Beloved."

Sara was distraught as she turned to us. "His soul is like a tiny plane trembling to go, gaining speed and making those tiny bounces before it takes off, soaring into eternity. Yes, Michael, Dear Heart, I'll sing you away to the angels, and your spirit shall dance with the stars."

She raised him up and put her arms around him and began to sing a lullaby in French that broke my heart. She was weeping. Her tears fell onto his face and ran down his cheeks.

She leaned down and kissed him on the lips. "Goodbye Dearest One, Godspeed."

As she lowered him onto the pillow, she whispered, "His soul and spirit are gone. We have died together of a broken heart."

His look of serenity brought no consolation to those of us left behind. The Celtic lament she sang next was terrifying, full of anguish and sorrow. When she finished, she rose from her knees,

170

crossed herself and then Mike. She unfastened his locket and hung it with her own. The two lockets gleamed in the early afternoon sunlight shining into the silent room.

She and the Duke left to begin the phone calls. Father James was there within the hour. Mike had requested a Navy burial at sea so the service at the church would be for the consolation of family and friends. Johnson made arrangements for the trip to Coronado Island with his remains for a Saturday service. Within the hour, Sara had finished packing all her belongings and had made her trip through the house to check for signs of her presence.

Then, she took a large garbage can, lined it with a bag and began to destroy the evidence of her sweet presence in the garden. Within moments, the place was as barren as a desert. I watched as she pulled up all the petunias and marigolds and zinnias, the asters, cosmos and cleome. She emptied all the baskets of geraniums and Impatiens hanging from the front porch ceiling and all the flower urns on the patio. Then she pulled up the tomatoes, the other vegetables and herbs she had planted with such loving care.

A hush fell over the garden, as though the birds had gone into mourning for the death of beauty.

Sara carried the bags to the back of the lot for the trash. Then she lifted the lovely yellow water lily from the pond and put it into a small bucket for Roslin to take back to Pennsylvania. She put her flowered gardening gloves, clogs and hand tools into a box and walked away to the car, not looking back. Her eyes were brimming with tears.

The locksmith was just pulling up as Sara and the Duke prepared to leave. She reached out to me. "Cade, I'm so sorry for your loss. Thank you for all you did to help him and for being his big brother. He loved you very much."

I handed her the bouquet of tiny yellow sweetheart roses. As they went down the street to settle her at the Inn, I wondered what Mike was doing now.

CHAPTER SIXTEEN Sara continues

The Duke and I went down the street and away from Michael's home. I was numb with grief and exhaustion as I sat rigid in the seat beside him, not speaking. I realized I wasn't doing a very good job of breathing either. Small lines of tears drained down my face.

The Duke reached into his pocket and gave me his handkerchief. "Madam Lambert, I'm so sorry you have lost Michael Cameron. He was a good and faithful friend for many years. He asked me to do some very specific things on your behalf. Some of them are complicated and aren't important right now.

"I'm taking you to the Courtyard Marriott and you are to stay there until the service on Wednesday. I expect Jacques Grayson to be in town this evening and you are to stay in your room until he gets here. I have reserved four rooms on the second floor for your group. Your daughter and Dr. Campbell will be in Tuesday night.

"I'll give you and Jacques further instructions, but when the will has been read, you must stay as close to him as you can, until Mrs. Cameron has been removed. She is in for a series of unpleasant surprises.

"By the middle of the afternoon, we should be finished. I've arranged to have the moving people at the house to begin loading things as people make their choices. It's simpler to have one mover go several places than to have many small loads picked up by different people. I should have all the legal paper work done so we can leave for the ranch in time to arrive on Wednesday night.

"Mike made one specific request and I must ask you to agree to it, even though right now you may not wish to. You are to be a guest at my ranch for six weeks. You may find yourself a working one. We've lost one of our helpers and Johnson is gone much of the time to Boise to be with his wife. We need someone to help with the care of the pups. I hope you will take this with good grace and won't refuse; because if you do, I'll have to take you by force."

I was clutching the bouquet of roses Cade had given me as we left. I lifted it to my nose and breathed in the haunting sweet odor. I was so exhausted I couldn't resist. I hadn't eaten since Friday and knew I was in no condition to make decisions on my own behalf. I glanced down at the bouquet and saw something wrapped around the stems of the roses. It looked like a roll of paper money tied with ribbon and a large bow. How odd.

I hid it in my lap as I answered. "I will do as you wish. I don't have enough information to make an intelligent decision, so I'll have to trust you."

I turned to look at him. "I was surprised to see you at Michael's. You've been living two very different lives. Kostyan, the Paris Fox and Anna's husband is also the Duke. I had no idea you were one of Michael's closest friends."

When we reached the Marriott, he went in with me. My room was beautiful. A balcony looked out over the courtyard where tables were scattered among the greenery. Guests were settling in for a late afternoon of conversation.

From somewhere deep inside, I conjured up the persona of the "Ice Queen". Perhaps it was because he'd called me Madam Lambert. I smiled at him. "What a lovely place. Would you have time to join me for supper? I haven't eaten since Friday and I'm not sure I'm willing to wait for Jacques, since he may have eaten on the plane. Please say yes. Surely you could use a small respite after the weekend's happenings. Let's have it brought up to us."

He hesitated for a moment before he agreed to stay. If we were to be together for six weeks in the woods, I needed to begin the task of learning to know him as he was now.

The Duke was back at Michael's when Jacques checked in with me later in the evening. I was sound asleep after the traumatic weekend happenings and Jacques had trouble waking me. I finally wakened enough to get up and unlock the door adjoining our rooms. I had no idea what they were protecting me from but they were serious about it.

As I slid the last latch, he opened the door and took me in his arms. "Sara, I'm sorry about Michael. I think he chose not to tell you because he wanted to have as many precious days and hours with you as he could, without worrying you. You knew anyway, didn't you?"

"I knew something was wrong. I'm sorry he wasn't willing to try the surgery. Something terrible must have been bothering him, to choose death so easily. Right now, I don't want to know. It's time to grieve and to hope I was not the cause of his decision."

I kissed him on the cheek. "We have two precious days together. What shall we do with our time? There's someone coming from Lord and Taylor's tomorrow morning, to bring some black dresses and work clothing for me to try on. I need work clothes in my wardrobe since I'm not to be a guest at the ranch. I'm going to be put to work. It was part of Michael's plan; to keep my mind off what's happened. I have no idea where the place is, do you?"

I looked up, surprised at Jacques' gesture. He'd put his finger to his lips and reached up to the doorjamb. He pointed to a tiny black square inset into the frame. Was it another game of gotcha? Who had put it there? And why?

Jacques began to search the rest of my room. He motioned to me to keep talking. Generalities were in order and I kept up the chatter until he finished. He found several others and then went into his own room and found none. They must be interested in me.

I took a sheet of thin paper from my notepad and wrote,

I'm scared, Jacques. I hope it's just the Duke being extra careful. But why would he do it? Do you know anything about him? Do you trust him?

He turned it over and answered.

I need to think about it. I don't know why he did it or even whether it was his doing. All I know about him is that Cameron trusted him. I don't know yet if I do, it may be too soon to tell.

We took the paper sheet and flushed it down the toilet. After a few words about tomorrow's plans we said good night.

The last thing I did before going to bed was to retrieve the yellow roses from their plastic bag deep in the bucket of ice. I untied the bow hiding the roll of bills and gasped in amazement as I spread them out on the table. One hundred, hundred dollar bills, lay in front of me. Whatever did Cade mean, to give me so much money? Did he want me to have enough to escape while I still had a chance? Or enough to bribe my way out of most anything. As I drifted into restless sleep, I wondered where Michael was now, and prayed for his eternal peace.

I was slow to waken from my exhausted night's sleep. My mind said my world had been blown to bits. I felt as if I'd stepped on a landmine and not been killed; bloody, torn to shreds and waiting to die. Michael was gone and I had no idea what would happen now.

The clock was ready to ring eight and I needed to get moving. I put on my favorite forest green silk tunic and pants, figuring they would be easier to get in and out of later. I took another piece of thin paper from my purse and wrote a note to hand to the woman before we began the morning's shopping. I might be taking a chance if she were part of the surveillance but if she were that covert I was in big trouble anyway. The note said simply,

Please be very careful what you say and reveal.
The room is bugged.

Jacques called to say breakfast was ready. He was an observant man and remembered how much I loved fruit. Breakfast began with a generous bowl of strawberries, blueberries, raspberries and melon. Next there were lovely, fluffy scrambled eggs with toast and Danish pastries and a plate of bacon. Jacques said he'd decided not to mention the bugs to the Duke just yet. He needed to get a better feel for what was going on and what kind of a person he was. Even I knew nothing about him in this time and place.

The shopper was there promptly at ten o'clock. I've never been treated to such luxury, even in the years with Lambert. The first thing she did was offer condolences. I handed her the slip of paper with my note and she nodded as though it were not unusual.

She had assumed I needed everything. I didn't know if the Duke chose the dresses, but all three of them were perfect in style and size. The financial arrangements had been made and I was to do what pleased me. I wanted two of the black dresses. One was quite severe and the other was a softer design with long chiffon sleeves and gathered skirt.

Then she brought out wonderful, luxurious work clothes. I didn't know designers made clothes like these. They were so well crafted and the cloth was so practical I decided to splurge on enough outfits to make a generous week without laundry. She had even brought a real barn coat trimmed in leather. The shoes fit perfectly, but the work boots made my heart sing. They were designed and made by someone as talented as my friend Debbie.

Just as we finished, the hairdresser came to work. The shopper's assistant remained with me until the hairdresser was finished. I put on the undergarments, black dress and shoes, and we looked at the full effect.

She handed me a black veil. "This is for you, if you feel it is needed and appropriate. It's also very handy for a disguise in an emergency." She gave me a slight hug and left the room. The person waiting outside the door came in to help carry the extra clothing out.

What a morning it had been. I knocked on Jacques' door and slipped in to model my new dress. His first comment, from his eyes, said perfect. "It's good you chose a skirt with some flare. You may need to move quickly in it."

Then he told me about his morning. "Apparently, the Duke is a master of many disguises. I've been on the phone while you were doing your job. The Duke is legitimate, extremely competent and we need to follow his orders without complaint or questions. We are to stay here this afternoon because he'll be over to talk to us a little later. Need some lunch?"

My smile was a bit wan. "I'm exhausted. I think I'll try to get a nap instead. May I leave the door open to your room? Sometimes I don't realize how much I need the out-of-doors until it's taken away; and I feel trapped now. See you in a little bit."

A gentle knock on the inside door wakened me about three o'clock. It was the Duke and he was all business. "Madam, we need to talk now. It's time you knew more about what's going on."

I swung my feet down to the floor, put my finger to my lips and pointed above his head. "Let's go into the other room to talk. I'll bring another chair." After I pointed out the other three bugs, we went to Jacques' room and closed the door.

I chose not to sit down. "What do you know about those, Fox?"

I was watching his face when I used his name from school days. After an instant of surprise, he smiled. "You are a formidable woman, Madam. I'm glad you're on our side."

Jacques looked puzzled but kept his own counsel.

"Fox, answer me. Are those yours or is someone else interested in our business here? Why are they only in my room? We found none in here."

"They are not mine or ours. I wish you'd told me sooner, but we can't do anything about it now. Was anything indiscrete said during the visit from the shopping advisor?"

"No, because I warned her. She seemed to understand exactly what I meant; though I was taking a chance she might be working for someone else."

He rose from his chair. "Please have a seat, Madam. I need to be as succinct as possible. First, in none of this are you to think we're not grieving for our friend and your lover. His death has been a terrible blow. Commander Cameron was beginning a joyous time in his life because of you, and it was cut short most cruelly.

"Second, you must be informed now, that you are under the protection of several different government agencies. If it gets much more expensive we may need a bill in Congress added to the Defense budget."

This didn't sound like a game of gotcha. I whispered, "Whatever for?"

"The Russians have wanted to learn more about your empathic skills for years. They couldn't figure out how to get to you while you were so well protected by Lambert. Since his death, you were protected for a year by his insisting you remain in mourning. Then when you were on your own; the Russians decided to try to kidnap you. Two agents attended Dr. Campbell's surgery in St. Louis. They would have gotten you except that Grayson knew something wasn't right about the day and protected you. Madam, I can keep you safe another six weeks at the ranch and then I don't know what we'll do."

My mind was whirling. I couldn't believe my good fortune.

"My dear Fox, why didn't someone tell me sooner? I could have saved you a lot of both worry and money. I am first and foremost a scientist. For many years I've wanted to do research on my empathic skills. No one in the United States would touch the project, for fear of their academic reputations.

"A few years ago, after the big breakup in Russia, I sat down and wrote up a full research project complete with experimental design, required statistical analyses and all the parameters to be used. I even had a list of scientists, believers and non-believers, doctors and biophysicists, Russians, and Europeans, whom I would have accepted as research partners. The proposal, written in Russian, French and English is in a folder with my things in Pittsburgh.

"Fox, do you think we might be able to make a deal of some sort? There's a source of funds to help with logistics and equipment. I'll give the project two months of my time. If we can get the people organized, each of them would need only a week or so, working in pairs. They could consider it a vacation.

"I do have some requests; first, that it be done on neutral ground in Switzerland, second, that Dr. Grayson is present for the first two weeks to make sure everything is run according to the guidelines, and third, that I may stop if my health deteriorates."

I said softly, "Fox, I want to be home by Christmas."

In moments he'd worked it through in his mind. "Madam, I think it might work now. Ten years ago it could not have. With your permission I'll begin making contacts. Perhaps with a tentative promise from them, you and Grayson could go to the Missouri Botanic Gardens and spend tomorrow like normal tourists. Time is short to catch people on Capitol Hill yet today. If you'll excuse me, I'll get started.

"Please be content to remain here until I return. Mr. Cameron and I will join you for dinner at eight this evening. My compliments, Madam." The Duke bowed over my hand with a diplomatic kiss, and was gone before I could reply.

Glancing at Jacques, I murmured, "What have I gotten myself into now? I may end up going out in a blaze of glory. What we need now is a deck of cards. Why don't you go see if the gift shop might have anything as common as a cribbage board and some cards? I'd really like a couple of cans of Dr. Pepper. What's your favorite?"

He grinned with relief. "Always has been Mountain Dew 'cause it has the most caffeine. I'll be back in a few minutes. Don't open the door to anyone, OK? This isn't set up yet and it will take a while to get the word out." He grabbed the ice bucket and took off.

Was this a clue to the fearful happenings of the months and years past? Then I wondered how Andretti fit in. My thoughts went back to the morning at Jacques' when Andretti was murdered. It still made no sense to me and Dave still wouldn't allow me to see the tapes.

When Jacques returned from his successful run we poured our drinks and opened the cribbage board; but I wasn't ready to play. I asked him, "Have you seen the tapes Jenny took from your place? Where are they now? I want to know what happened that morning."

He didn't answer right away. Maybe he was deciding how much he could tell me. "Dave Finch wouldn't let us see the tapes from the control room. It was only because I had some others from the work-room, that Michael, JW and I were able to piece together what may have happened. Dave didn't know about them and your Mr. Vaughan saved my hide. Mike and JW decided it wasn't in your best interest to know. I disagreed with them but was out-voted."

I didn't ask the obvious question. Instead I asked, "Why did you disagree with them?"

"Because I thought you needed to know right then what the possible implications were, instead of having information that could put you at even greater risk. They felt it would be too hard on you, because of your longtime, working relationship with Finch."

"Will you tell me now?"

"Yes, but God forgive me if I'm doing the wrong thing." He stood up from his chair and stepped to the balcony door as he began.

"The time printed on the tape was nine o'clock. It showed Angela checking the workroom, so she was there that morning. About ten minutes later, Dave came into the workroom, stayed a few moments and left through the door into the kitchen. He was carrying a pack-age.

"Shortly after, Andretti stepped in to look around. I think you were probably in your room writing notes."

I gasped at this news. "Why was Dave at your place that morn-ing?"

"We don't know. We also don't know why Andretti was there or how he got in. We also don't know whether he was looking for Finch or for you. I believe the latter, because he was too good an agent to be caught by surprise. In the tape, his eyes were closed when Jenny fired the first shot. It hit you instead of Andretti. Andretti turned around with you in his arms, shielding you.

"Then the tape showed Finch for an instant in the doorway. We heard him tell Jenny to shoot again. He ducked behind the door and after Andretti was down, Jenny ran.

"The most damning and graphic thing was Finch entering the workroom. He bent over Andretti's body and checked to see if he were still alive. Apparently he was. Dave pulled a knife and slit his throat."

"The traitor in our midst, the murderer and liar, was Finch. He set up the murder attempts on you and ordered your farm burned. His professional jealousy of your scientific talent festered for years.

"He lied to us about Andretti's trying to kill you. It was his doing, and he ordered the killing of Nelson. Andretti was a highly-skilled Italian agent sent to this country to keep track of Lambert's jewel smuggling.

"Andretti maintained his association with Lambert on a personal as well as professional level, because he was trying to protect you as best he could. Andretti loved you very much all those years, Sara."

"He'd figured out the blackmail scheme Finch was working on your husband and Dave somehow found out Andretti suspected him. That's why the Idaho Rendezvous was set up, and Finch was diabolical enough to plan for you to be the assassin. His motive was pure and simple jealousy, of Andretti, and of your talent as a scientist.

"Then, Finch essentially destroyed Jenny by lying to her about who had killed Andretti. She believed she'd killed him and would be charged with murder. She chose to commit suicide in Bermuda instead.

"Sara, I don't know whether Jenny knew anything about what Dave Finch was doing. In the last few days before the attack, she must have figured out some of it, if she chose to warn you about the bomb. You would have been next to be killed that morning, but Dave couldn't find you. He hadn't seen you behind Andretti as you talked in front of the picture.

"After Andretti was dead, he continued searching for you; Jenny destroyed the control room panel and got away. Dave continued to go through your things looking for the letters and tapes, but Jenny had taken them. He must have given up when the phone rang and he knew someone would be coming to check on you. He escaped just before we got there."

Dave's treachery terrified me. At least Jacques believed Jenny was innocent. I too couldn't believe she would have done it if she'd known the truth.

"Was there some connection between Jenny and Andretti before this?"

Jacques turned to face me. "Yes, and Dave knew it.

"The only reason I know is because Dave bragged about it to me when he was drunk one night. It's the story of a young woman student in Paris language school and her crush on her language teacher, Andretti. A story of a one-night stand, a child named Tony Cameron, with you in the triangle, though neither you nor Jenny knew it. Andretti supported them generously but wouldn't marry Jenny. He waited all those years for you to be free so he could propose marriage to you."

I whispered, "That's what Jenny meant when she confronted Andretti in the workroom. But even as angry as she was, I don't think that she wanted to kill either of us. She was following Dave's orders; but missed her mark twice even though she was an expert markswoman."

We sat down at the table, each with our own thoughts. "Do you realize how many innocent people have died because of this affair?"

"Dave blackmailed Lambert for years. He took a cut of the jewels. When Lambert died, the source of foot soldier students disappeared and the jewel contacts were harder to make. The scheme was going bankrupt. I suppose the trip to Brazil is his last. He could live for years on the profit from those jewels."

"Now I've been assigned to go after Dave Finch. I've never killed anyone in cold blood. I've killed in self-defense and in war but never something as sordid as this and never in such a foreign and unforgiving environment."

I picked up the deck of cards and began to shuffle. Jacques stopped me for a moment. "Do you still have Lambert's letter; the one that came by drop mail from Spokane?"

I wondered what he might be getting at. "Yes, why?"

"I want you to make some copies and then send the original to the Forensics people in the government section dealing with Finch's case. I have a feeling they'll find the letter was forged by Dave to strengthen his deception about Andretti. Nothing in the letter is true and I don't believe that your husband wrote it. There's one really sharp lady in Forensics who specializes in this area. She can take word usage and phrases and make comparisons. It would help if you could send some other examples of Lambert's writing too, and some of Dave's if you can bear to do it. Perhaps the College would have something they could use.

"If I don't come back, Sara, you will need this information to protect yourself. Finch won't stop until he has destroyed you."

We settled in for several rounds of cribbage until Cade and the Duke arrived for supper. The meal was delivered at eight o'clock, wheeled in on a table with a white cloth. Closing my eyes, I listened to the preparations, the clinking of silver and glasses. The aromas wafting about made my mouth water. There were lovely flowers but I went next door to get my yellow roses and placed them on the table too. I nodded an acknowledgement and thank you to Cade.

We were finishing dessert, a cloud of chocolate mousse. I reached into my lap for the folded piece of paper I'd picked up from the floor just inside my room door as I went for the roses. I handed it to the Duke with a smile. "You work fast, my friend. I'm glad that you're on *my* side."

The handwritten note said,

Madam, Thank you. Thank you. My partner and I will actually get a night off. I'm off to my son's soccer game and Al is going to the Cardinals game. Good Luck to you. It's been fun. Tom and Al."

"Theirs or ours?"

He smiled. "Theirs. It's already morning in Russia. I need to make some phone calls before I go to bed. I'll be at Mike's place all day in case you need me. Madam, please enjoy your trek to the Gardens tomorrow. Here are some papers for you in case any problems arise."

He poised over my hand. I was expecting a diplomatic kiss. Instead he asked with a quizzical smile, "Why did you and Grayson decide to trust me?"

"I asked Cade about you."

"Good idea, Madam. Trust is built on knowledge." He and Cade took off and Jacques and I made plans for breakfast. It had been a long and difficult day but I'd survived. I wondered how many days or weeks or years it would be before I could live my life with trust and love again. I spent a long time thinking about Jacques' story of the treachery of Dave Finch. I tried to understand what had driven him to such evil and no explanation would come. I prayed for Michael's soul and the safe completion of Jacques's assignment.

CHAPTER SEVENTEEN

Jacques rapped on my door when breakfast was laid out on the table in front of the balcony. As we settled in to enjoy it, he began with the day's news. He'd been to see the Duke already and they met Priscilla Cameron·when she came by to take possession of the house. She didn't·take the news at all kindly when the Duke told her the house had been sold.

Jacque said, "I hope there won't be trouble at the reading of the will, but she was mumbling something about her lawyer as she left us on the porch."

"Any other news?"

Jacques sounded puzzled. "Yes. The Duke got a phone call that really upset him. Cade will have to fill us in, but I think some woman in Finland died Sunday morning early, a few hours before Mike did, and it's going to make some big work before Wednesday to add some new information to the will. The Duke said a strange thing to Cade, something about wondering if Mike had known. Then he whispered, 'Lord have mercy on us now'."

I shivered and rose from my place. "What shall we do first?"

"Your choice."

"You know what I'd really like to do? Let's go to the Botanic Gardens this morning while the roses are still in their prime and then visit the Japanese gardens. Next, Jacques, could we go to the zoo? I haven't been there for years. The kids are as fun to watch as the animals."

The parking lot for the Botanical Gardens was fairly full. Every one came to see the roses this time in the summer. I had heard that people arranged to have their weddings in the rose garden in June because it was so beautiful. I loved the ramblers and climbers growing yards of garlands of red, pink, white or yellow flowers, but my favorite roses of all were the Peace tea roses and their genetic offspring. The colors were exquisite swirls of pink, rose and yellow.

It was too warm to enjoy the greenhouses but we stopped by the gift shop to find Christmas gifts for Roslin. We strolled through the Japanese garden, and then headed for the zoo.

The visitors there were entirely different, mostly families, or single parents with their children. We were headed across a wide path to the bird area when I stumbled and Jacques reached out to steady me. As I looked up to thank him, I heard a mother whisper loudly to her young teenage child. "Look at that nigger touching that white woman. What will they do next?"

I could feel Jacques stiffen and become still. Then, a most amazing thing happened. The little girl stopped and said very plainly, "No Mama, he's not a black person. He's an American Indian. I've seen pictures on television of them. See his beautiful moccasins? Each tribe has its own pattern. There was a program about them too, with a map of the different tribes and where they lived. Let's see, his moccasins belong to a Northeastern forest tribe. Am I right, Sir?"

Jacques knelt down to look into her face. "Thank you, young lady. Yes, you are correct. I am honored that you cared enough to learn about us. Perhaps your generation, with you as their leader, may begin to ease some of our pain."

She held out her little hand. "I am honored to meet you, Sir. What is your name?"

Jacques was fighting tears. "My name is Jacques Grayfeather."

He stood again and bowed to her. Then he turned away. The mother grabbed her child's hand and jerked her away, scolding her about speaking with strangers. The little girl turned back and blew us a kiss.

Both Jacques and I were in need of some privacy. We stepped off the path and found a bench. After a few moments, we decided to return to our rooms to get some rest before the evening. The reservations were for eight o'clock, for the six of us, at Bristol's. The kids would be in from Pittsburgh soon, and I wanted to see Roslin before the evening started.

"Jacques, my friend, it has been a good day. I'm glad we came, even though we'll need to come back another time to see the wombats and the wallabies. Sometime, I would like to hear about the loss of your name. Someone else who has suffered it too, would understand how devastating it was." I thought about how my own name was taken from me in Paris so long ago.

The trip back was shared in thoughtful silence. A note at the desk was from the children. Jacques took me to Roslin's room and went off to rest. He would be on his way to Brazil this time tomorrow and I knew he was becoming more concerned as the time grew nearer.

When JW opened the door, I was thankful we could begin our family grieving. For two days I had put aside remembrance of Sunday's events. Now I would have to relate them, perhaps several times, to those who weren't present during Michael's dying.

JW stepped aside so my daughter and I could be together first. Her eyes were red and splotchy from crying. "Mama, how could this happen now? Everything was so perfect for you and Daddy; your love was growing so beautifully. Why did this happen? It isn't fair."

I took Roslin into my arms, cradling her head on my shoulder. JW was standing beside her as I looked into his eyes rather than hers. "My Dearest, I don't know why God allowed this to happen but I know we must do the best we can to keep living our lives as Michael would have wanted us to. We don't know what's in store for us now, but I'm glad he had the joy of knowing you and that you are safe in the care of your precious Jamie."

I couldn't cry now. I would be nurturing everyone else and taking their pain into my heart until tomorrow afternoon when we left for the ranch. My grieving would come later when I was alone and abandoned to my misery.

I continued to fill them in on the plans. "The Duke has arranged the evening so you'll have a chance to begin to know him and to know Michael's brother, Cade. They are the ones who will be in charge of my safety for the next six weeks. There are two very serious situations coming at me at once. One has been partially resolved but the other is becoming more ominous each day.

"I wanted to come home with you to Campbell's Point tomorrow, but it would be much too dangerous. I must trust Michael's judgment and the skill of these two men, one of whom I have just met, and I have to do the job for which I have been trained. I'm terrified but it must be done."

Roslin looked so frightened. I whispered, "It wouldn't help to resign now, Dearest. Sometimes you just have to play the game until the clock runs out."

I reached out to JW. His face was tense and pale. "You're in such pain, JW. I feel it in my deepest heart. What's going on? I feel as though it's been too long since we've heard about how your hand is doing. Is that what's wrong?"

I moved to sit on the couch by the balcony door. "Come, you two, and tell me about it."

Roslin was crying. "We felt so bad when things weren't going right. We didn't want to tell Daddy. Several of the bone grafts didn't take; they just disintegrated. The nerves growing back have turned into a nightmare. Jamie's in such pain he hasn't slept for days.

We've been to the Curtis Center and they're willing to try one more surgery. Then if that doesn't work, an artificial hand. We have an appointment set up for this Friday for the surgery."

I searched JW's face to see how he was taking the whole business. "I'm so sorry. We wanted so much for it to work, to be perfect. Perhaps we were just too much ahead of our time. What do you want to do, JW?"

"I don't know."

"I'll pray for you and all my beloved family. I'll pray while I am feeding puppies and cleaning pens." I rose again and stepped to the balcony door. "We may not have another time alone together, to talk about Michael. I thought you would want to know about his death. We were dismayed by his health care directives but honored his requests. He died in my arms, at peace with his God.

"The Duke is anticipating trouble from Michael's mother when the will is read, and he has made plans for what we will do. We won't be sitting with the immediate family at the service but I'm going to wear black anyway. I don't know if there will be a receiving line or whether we will be included. Mrs. Cameron says she refuses to attend Mass so we may be able to share the service and reception with Michael's brother, Cade, before she arrives for the reading of the will.

"I think the Duke and Cade will be here at 7:15 to pick us up for dinner. It's a pleasant restaurant, and I would guess he's chosen a secluded place so we'll have some privacy. I'm sorry we must meet under such sad circumstances but I'm glad you came. JW, would you walk me next door to my room, please? I need to rest now."

There was time for a healing nap. As I dressed for the evening, I thought about what Michael would have enjoyed having me wear. It would be a long time before I could wear the beautiful apricot dress without weeping for my loss. I chose my dove gray tunic and pants. I could close my eyes and remember happier times in Campbell's Point when I walked the path to the Greers' Secret Garden to spend the evening at supper.

What would happen to all my great plans for the Hospice? I had no energy now to think about the broken promises to my new friends and to myself. Where would I find the will to try again, or even to supervise someone else who might want to help?

I was in tears and didn't hear Jacques as he came to me from his room. He opened his arms and I went to him. When my crying slowed, he led me to the bathroom, sat me down and began to wash my face with cold water, gently kissing each place as he finished. He spoke to me in French. "Dear Heart, you must be brave and patient. Do as you are told and be careful. I promise to return as soon as my mission is completed. Fill your heart with hope for me, Sara; hope that it is I who return and not Finch.

"Now, we have only a few minutes before we must be ready for the evening. I think our man named Duke will have some interesting revelations before the night is over."

I was interested in the seating arrangement at dinner. The Duke must have assumed Roslin would be more comfortable with French-speaking dinner partners because he placed her with Jacques on one side and Cade on the other. JW was on one side of me and the Duke had chosen the other. Then I realized it was probably for safety's sake too. There was no wine at the table. These men were professionals and they didn't drink; it was too dangerous.

After we made our choices for dinner, the Duke said, "I would like for us to have a pleasant evening without complications. The rest of the instructions can be given tomorrow morning before the service. While we're waiting for our dinner to arrive, there are two things I would like to take care of.

"Dr. Campbell, I have a portfolio I wish to give you, in repayment of a debt of honor. Please accept it with my sincere apologies for what she did to you. At the time, I could not stop her, but I have retrieved it almost in its entirety during these last few months. She's dead and I am free to return it to you. I wish to do so now. If you will trust me, I will continue to manage it for you. The Mafia bribe is paid so this is yours to do with as you wish."

All of us were puzzled since he spoke no names. Then I suddenly remembered. The Duke was Mrs. Campbell's financial manager too. When he handed the portfolio to JW, Roslin helped him place it on the table. The pages contained the summary of JW's holdings; each thing his wife had stolen or sold and how the Duke had replaced it with financial paper. The oriental rugs were there, his piano and the house on the lake, the property he owned and the things related to his practice. As he turned to the last page with the summary, a gasp escaped and he closed the folder. His voice trembled. "I had no idea about the extent of her betrayal. Thank you for your honesty, Mr. Skorski. I accept your offer to continue to manage things for me for the time being."

Next the Duke turned to me. "Madam Lambert, Michael Cameron asked me to give this to you on the evening before his service. It was given to him by his grandfather and has been in the Cameron clan for many generations."

The box he handed me was quite heavy for its size and I put it on the table before I opened it. The wooden box was decorated with carved Celtic designs. Inside, on a cushion of pale garnet silk was a silver necklace with a large garnet cabochon. The links were incised with patterns of spirals and knots and a small cabochon of moonstone was in the center of each link. Somehow, I was not drawn so much to its beauty as to its power. As I reached to take it out of the box, Cade stepped to my side and took the necklace from the case. As he helped me put it on he said softly, "It is worthy of your beauty, Sara Harvey."

A huge storm came into the area about dawn, with driving rain, hail and tremendous claps of thunder. I couldn't really enjoy the fullness of it from inside the courtyard. I wept in misery as I whispered, "Michael, come share the storm, come wrap me in your blanket and let me fall asleep in your arms."

I turned away from the window and decided to go ahead and dress in my uniform for the day. Somehow the black underwear and stockings seemed even more mournful than the black dress. I folded the veil and put it into my purse. I wouldn't wear it unless the Duke felt I should.

In the time before eight o'clock, I tried to quiet my fears and give my grief over to God. I settled back into my relationship with Michael as it had been for all those lonely years. I prayed for him to be with me and with those I loved, to protect them from danger and to bring them home safely again. Somehow, I felt better and was in a state of relative calm and peace when Jacques came to get me. All the bags had been loaded and I steeled myself for the day.

Roslin was wearing a simple black dress, perfect for her position in the family group. The men looked so different in their mourning clothes, especially Cade. He would be in the receiving line if they decided to put one together. I hoped Mrs. Cameron would not come until we had shared time with the people who cared about and loved Michael.

Cade had looked so weary last evening at the dinner I asked about it now. "What did you do yesterday while the Duke was doing paperwork?"

"I made a round trip to Pittsburgh to Finch's home to pick up all your professional papers and possessions you left in Pittsburgh. Dave has already gone to Brazil, but Dodie helped us find the things. The portfolio with the proposal was there, just as you described it. The Duke said he made important contacts last night. He thinks the project will work.

"Sara, I brought Dodie Finch back with me and left her in a safe house here in St. Louis. I thought you would want to know."

I whispered, "Thank you."

When we entered the church, we were surprised at how many people were already seated. It was to be a very simple and short Mass for the Dead and I settled onto my kneeler to pray. Cade and the Duke were in the front of the church. Roslin, Jacques and JW were seated toward the back with me.

Father James made sure the non-Catholics would be comfortable and would understand the service. Actually, many of Mike's friends and associates from work were also Roman Catholic and participated in the full Mass.

The gentle and loving celebration of Michael's life continued as we joined together to greet one another. The Duke decided to set up a short reception line. Cade Cameron first, as the closest relative, I was next, as Michael's fiancée, then Roslin and JW. We were pleased

187

Jeanne Anderegg

to have the time to greet people before Mrs. Cameron arrived on the scene, just before eleven o'clock. True to her word, she refused to enter the church.

She was in the rectory when we came, seated on one side of the table in full mourning clothes including a long black veil and black gloves. Cade went to sit with his mother. How odd. She didn't speak to him. Didn't she recognize her own son? I wondered if the story about his being disowned were true.

The five of us sat in a row opposite them. Instead of making Roslin more frightened than ever, the Duke just told her to do as he asked at the time. He seated us away from the table and I knew what he planned.

Although the Duke wrote the will at Michael's request, the Cameron family lawyer was there in an official capacity. I couldn't tell yet whose side he might be on. As he began, Priscilla Cameron shifted in her seat and I saw the Duke, Jacques and Cade all watching her hands. They were good at their job, no question about it and I tried to settle down to listen. No one but the Duke and the lawyer knew what was to happen.

In the beginning paragraph, Michael said he wished to redress former wrongs, to give gifts to those whom he loved and to repay treachery. We couldn't see Mrs. Cameron's eyes behind her veil but she couldn't see out very well either. How interesting this might be.

The lawyer began to read. "My dearest brother, Cade Cameron. First, I wish to return to you your rightful place as the firstborn son of Robert and Priscilla Cameron, along with the titles and honor so accorded to the son in that position. I return to you all the Cameron lands, houses and buildings, to be used as you wish. I also wish you to have first choice of any and all possessions and furnishings in my St. Louis home.

"My dearest daughter, Roslin Marie Parmentier. First, I wish to acknowledge you as my beloved child. Although we knew each other a very short time, I cherish each of those moments and I wish you much happiness in the future. I gift to you the account described below with all my love and affection. It is a gift from my friend Wilhelmina Coras Porter, late of Kotka, Finland. I wish you to be the second to chose those of my possessions that would give you pleasure.

"My dearest and beloved Sara Harvey, my fiancée and soon to have been my wife. First I acknowledge you as the mother of my child, Roslin, and say that you were the love of my life. I gift to you the proceeds from the sale of my property in St. Louis as well as all the remaining funds in the trust, to use at your discretion for your care and for the development of the project closest to your heart. May God's Peace be with you.

"My mother, Priscilla Cameron. First, I acknowledge you bore me as your second son. For this I honor you. However, because of your treachery in the plot causing Rebecca Jane Campbell to be sold to Henri Lambert, causing her to lose her birthright, her name, and to lose her child to adoption; I leave you nothing except my pity. And with great difficulty, I offer you my forgiveness. Only God can judge what you have done and I pray for his mercy upon your soul."

Our stunned silence was shattered with her shrill shrieks. The door burst open as a policewoman headed for Mrs. Cameron. Jacques grabbed me from the chair and we rolled onto the floor. The Duke got Roslin into his arms and ended up on top of her, shielding her. JW rolled under the table on the end.

We could hear Priscilla Cameron as she swore she would kill us all. Cade had her wrist in a locked grip as she waved a tiny pistol in the air. The police officer disarmed her and took her away. The Duke had guessed right this time.

As we started to come out from under the table, Jacques held me a moment and kissed me goodbye. "I must go now, or I'll miss my plane to Manaus. Pray for me, Dear Heart. I'm going to need it." He helped me up and vanished in the turmoil.

The Duke found me moments later, trembling in a corner. His touch was gentle. "We will all pray for his safe return, Madam. Now, we must get everyone to the house as quickly as we can, I don't want to rush the procedure but we need to be finished by two o'clock. You are a brave comrade, Sara Harvey. Hang with us for another few hours and then we'll collapse together and let Johnson fly."

I had already thanked Father James for the service and probably would not return to St Louis again. I thought of our evenings with his kind counseling and knew I would miss his gentle guidance and caring. I took a few moments to change into travel clothes and then stepped outside into the muggy heat of the St. Louis summer day. I felt myself ready to shatter into a million shards of exhaustion and grief.

It was Cade who took my elbow and led me to the waiting car. "Only a few more hours, Sara." He whispered, "Hang in there, Sweetheart. Then, you can sit with puppies in your lap and sing songs and hear the birds in the pine trees and the water in the stream. There's some good trout fishing for the patient."

The Duke was showing a little strain but he also showed infinite patience. As people made their choices, the pieces were carried out and arranged in groups for loading. The truck arrived and by the time we were finished, the truck was loaded to go.

We were ready to leave. Roslin flew into my arms and wouldn't let go. The morning's events had terrified her. I didn't have a great deal of reassurance for her but said again that I was going to the safest place I could.

We took JW and Roslin to the public boarding area of the airport and then made our way to the private plane hangers. Because Johnson and Cade had loaded everything they could the night before, we were ready to leave at the appointed time. Johnson and the Duke sat in front and Cade and I in the back.

As we began to taxi, I whispered, "Take me home, Cade."

"And where's home?"

"I'm a nomad too, My Friend. We'll just have to do the best we can."

ISBN 141208344-3

9 781412 083447